Swallow

Swallow

a novel by

THEANNA BISCHOFF

NeWest Press

Copyright © Theanna Bischoff 2012

Library and Archives Canada Cataloguing in Publication
Bischoff, Theanna, 1984–
Swallow / Theanna Bischoff.
ISBN 978-1-927063-19-4
1. Title.
PS8603.183S93 2012   c813'.6   C2012-902344-2

Editor for the Board: Nicole Markotić
Cover and interior design: Natalie Olsen, Kisscut Design
Cover photography: (portrait) gedankenstrichfabrik/Photocase
(fly) irin-k/Shutterstock.com
Author photo: Katie Hyde

NeWest Press acknowledges the financial support of the Alberta Multimedia Development Fund and the Edmonton Arts Council for our publishing program. We further acknowledge the financial support of the Government of Canada through the Canada Book Fund (CBF) for our publishing activities. We acknowledge the support of the Canada Council for the Arts which last year invested $24.3 million in writing and publishing throughout Canada.

#201, 8540–109 Street
Edmonton, Alberta T6G 1E6
780.432.9427
NEWEST PRESS   www.newestpress.com

No bison were harmed in the making of this book.
printed and bound in Canada   1 2 3 4 5 13 12

For two sisters
For Elena, my sister of dolls and bunk beds and matching dresses
And for Nicole, my sister of sushi and step class and stats assignments
I am better for you both

There was an old lady who swallowed a fly
I don't know why she swallowed a fly
Perhaps she'll die

There was a Chinook the day my sister died.

The unexpected warm winds drifted across from the mountains, trailing the scent of spring. Having grown up in Toronto, I had not yet grown accustomed to these bursts of warmth in the middle of winter. In Calgary, I had to plug my car in overnight and the motor still coughed phlegm from its frozen lungs in the morning — from October until nearly May. That morning, I'd opened the windows in my classroom and let the warmth breeze its way inside, taunting me, taunting the kids, making us wonder how long the reprieve would last.

During recess supervision duty, I took off my parka and hung it over the fat base of a tire swing circling slowly in the wind. The snow banks huddled together to keep from melting, massive solid chunks of ice, dissolving from the outside in. The kids shrieked with bewildered joy, unsure of what to do with themselves, with their mittens and toques. When the sun cast its smirking face downwards, the snow glared back, fierce enough that I had to shield my eyes. High-gloss white.

& I remember smudges from Carly's infancy. My father spent his days — and often nights — at the University of Toronto School of Business.

"You want to take ballet?" My mom yelled. "Then maybe your dad should get a job and stop spending all our money on text-books!"

The floor directly above our apartment housed a slimy pool. Our apartment always smelled dizzy, like chlorine. I remember trying to see over the canopy of Carly's stroller, driving a treacherous path down Bloor Street. I remember having to push the Jolly Jumper, hung in the entry between the living room and the kitchen, out of the way in the mornings, blurry with sleep and hungry for Cheerios. Stupid baby stuff in my way.

I remember naps in piles of laundry, emptied onto the living room carpet, still warm from the dryer. Mom told us to be careful of the bits of metal hiding in the clothes: the buttons and clasps, the hooks of her bras. We could get scalded; a bare knee, a thigh, the underside of a foot.

I held Carly safe on top of me, her scrawny six-year-old sister's stomach — away from both the warmth and the burn.

Sometimes Carly blurs into my other memories. On my first day of kindergarten, before Carly was even alive. Yet there she is, in my mother's arms, wearing a cloth diaper and waving goodbye, her new trick. Or, decades later, when I moved to Calgary and she stayed behind in Toronto. My synapses fire, a recollection of tasting salsa during a Calgary street festival, Carly joking, "That's nacho cheese, that's mine!"

Even now. I get out of the shower, naked and cold, and reach for a towel, only to remember I left them folded in the laundry basket in the living room. Then, she's there, in the fog.

"It's okay, Darcy; I'll grab one for you."

The moisture prickles on my skin.

    & My sister embodied primary colours, like magic markers — not *blonde*, but yellow-haired. Yellow-haired, true blue-eyed. She wore red lipstick in the daytime, like a '50s pin-up girl. When I moved from Toronto to Calgary to get my teaching degree, she sent me sequin sweaters and T-shirts in rainbow hues, leprechaun greens and valentine pinks, bubble wrapped. In high school she wrote her lecture notes in purple pen that got smudged on her knuckles. She carved purple reminders into her wrists in inky swirls: *pay visa!!! call d.* She had permanent ink marked onto her ankle to celebrate graduation: a tattoo of a fuchsia balloon.

    & My first year student teaching, the staff took the kids to the Calgary Zoo on a field trip. As a child in Toronto, field trips involved riding the subway; our chaperones counted our heads to make sure they hadn't lost any of us and tried to find places where we could sit. They doubled us up, two bums per seat, and hoarded the skinniest of us on their laps.

In the dark tunnel of the subway existed a fantasy population, like trolls that lived underground, whooshing back and forth between Etobicoke and Scarborough, North York and Front Street; people with stained coats, from whom garbled words burst like hiccups and farts. These people clipped their fingernails, slept with their heads tucked onto the strangers beside them, and laughed so loudly and unabashedly they shook along with the rumble of the train on its tracks.

As a child, on the subway, when strangers dominated all available seats, I would put my hand out to hold onto a post, the metal smooth and cool to the touch. But, rare times, the metal felt warm, the heat left by someone's hand, someone who'd held the pole only moments before me.

Teachers took us to the Royal Ontario Museum for yearly field trips, ignoring the fact that almost all of us had already visited the ROM, and more than once. Afterwards, they let us eat in Queen's Park, picnic style, and warned us not to climb the giant statue of King Edward VII and his feisty stallion, yanking down those of us who still tried.

The zoo was Calgary's field-trip equivalent of the ROM. The children, paired with buddies, clamored for seats at the back of the yellow school bus we took to get there, despite the fact that the C-train actually stopped right near the zoo's entrance.

"Every year, I swear," my supervisor muttered, her eyes darting from child to child, keeping track. That September, she'd announced she was going vegan. "You have a zoo in Toronto, right?"

"Yeah."

"It's sick. Caged animals on display."

"My grandpa worked for an animal shelter when I was a kid," I offered.

"Good for him." She picked at her nailpolish. "It's sad. The kids don't even really pay attention to the animals. They only like the dinosaur statues."

"Dinosaur statues?"

"I know, it's ridiculous. Prehistoric Park. Haven't you seen the giant Brontosaurus head when you drive down Memorial? HAYLEY BETH! Bum on your seat!"

"No."

"There's a Brontosaurus, and a raptor. . .thing. There's supposedly an Albertosaurus, too, which sounds made up, but it's not. Tell you what, I'll take your picture with the Albertosaurus. Make you a true Calgarian."

Rain began to speckle the asphalt. Kids dangled their fingers out the windows to catch the drops.

"Arms stay inside the bus!" my supervisor warned.

We sat in the cafeteria, waiting out the storm, the kids still paired-up with their buddies, eating rubbery, dinosaur-shaped chicken nuggets. We followed them with wet-naps, wiping their grimy hands. The rain made the cafeteria smell dank, of animals and manure. The tabletops looked slimy — grease, perhaps, or condensation. The kids poked each other, fought over who got to sit next to who.

I let Tia McConaughey-Morales sit beside me. According to her Ontario Student Record, Tia had been Tia Morales, until her parents divorced midway through her first grade year. Back then, Tia had also been communicative. When she acquired the McConaughey, she stopped talking.

Tia picked up a French fry and held it out towards me, an offering. Since Tia started second grade, I had tried unsuccessfully to get her to talk, enticing her by singing songs from *Dora the Explorer*, handing her warm Hershey's Kisses from my winter coat pocket. She'd flashed me dimpled smiles and waves and carefully printed rows of alphabet letters and spelling words. She mouthed all the songs in Music class. But the volume stayed on mute.

Tia tugged on my coat, then tapped her nose with two fingers — the code we'd developed to signal that she needed to go to the bathroom. The other code was two arms straight up in the air, fingers waving. This signaled emergency; I'd never seen her do it. School protocol dictated that I should ask her to use words when she gave signals or pantomimed what she wanted. She squirmed in her chair, her black hair woven into two stubby braids, one resting on each shoulder.

"Okay, Tia," I said. "Let's go."

I stood in front of the stall, waiting. Spills from the taps lay in puddles across the countertops. Damp paper towels bulged from the garbage opening. Tia slipped out of the stall, smiling. She bent down then, reaching for something on the bathroom floor; a small, plastic monkey — a Capuchin with its arms outstretched, a gift store trinket left behind.

"What's that?" I asked. "What'd you find?"

She paused, held the monkey out, her mouth open.

I felt hot. "Tia," I said, "What'd you find? Tell me? Use your words. Be a big girl, okay?"

Her mouth hung open for another second. Her fingers closed around the monkey.

& Stefany Beale, a nine-year-old girl from my neighbourhood, only two years younger than me, went missing. Before this, it was my responsibility to walk Carly the six blocks from school to our apartment and watch her until Mom came home after work. Born at the beginning of September, Carly turned five just before starting kindergarten, younger than a good half of the kids in her class.

Our mother cleaned other people's houses, often taking Carly with her. After Carly turned four, our mother put her in daycare and picked up a job as a waitress at a nearby diner where she could work the breakfast shift. When school started in the fall, Mom dropped Carly off at daycare in the morning, and a bus dropped her off at school in the afternoon. At three o'clock, I had to wrangle Carly home, annoyed by her incessant need to stop and pet dogs, stomp in puddles, crunch leaves, and kick the same rock all the way home. I once kicked one of her beloved rocks away from her and into a gutter. She shocked me by sobbing and wailing for the remaining five-block walk, repeating, "You hate me, you hate me." She pushed me away in the apartment, soothing herself in a way I thought she'd outgrown, simultaneously sucking her thumb and the ringed tail of her ragged raccoon. That damned raccoon! So dirty from being handled all day, dragged around the germy daycare. Shoved in her backpack all afternoon, it smelled like the lunch mom packed her that day, peanut butter, or pickles, or Cheez Whiz.

The missing girl, Stefany, did not attend my school, but the public school closest to it. She was also being raised by a single mother. We had the same middle name: Erin. Stefany had an older sister, Kristen, two years older, the same age as me. I heard these details on the news, which Mom left on while she microwaved dinner. I often checked and then double-checked the locks before finally being able to fall into a twitchy, agitated sleep.

During that first week after Stefany went missing, Mom took Carly and me to the basement to do laundry with her, rather than leaving me upstairs to try to make sure Carly didn't wreck the TV or sneak jujubes out of the pantry. Another tenant, an old man, took his clothes out of the dryer and smiled at us. I looked away, towards the cat he'd brought down to the basement with him, draped lazily on top of one of the dryers while he folded his monochromatic clothes into perfect squares like the ones on display at the mall.

Carly blurted, "Can I pet him?" She always needed to touch things. The cat turned its languid ears in her direction but did not lift its head.

The man introduced himself as Elliot Papisczaw, and said he worked at a no-kill animal shelter that relied on families to foster cats while they waited to be adopted. He had three other cats in his two-bedroom apartment, all named after Toronto subway stations. Wellesley had joined him in the basement to sort laundry. Carly, who still talked like a baby, called the cat

Willy. Luckily, fat and docile Willy had no problems letting her maul and prod him.

After dropping by Elliot's apartment a few times to visit "the cats," knocking shyly with Carly riding on her shoulders, Mom asked Elliot if perhaps he would be willing to walk us home from school and keep an eye on us while she worked, "Just for a couple hours a day. And I would pay you, of course." How quickly she had found a way to unload the two of us.

I liked the way Elliot's cats followed him around, they way they hung comfortably over his shoulder or butted their bony skulls against his bony legs. He told Mom he would think about it, but I knew he would say no. Cats did not make perpetual noise the way Carly did. A couple of days after Mom asked, I entered the elevator at the same time that as Elliot exited. He carried a grocery bag that smelled like warm bread.

"Hello!" He moved his bag to the other arm. "Coming home from school?"

"Mm hmm." I pretended to dig in my backpack for something so as not to look at him. On the ride up, I listened to the distorted sounds of the people who lived on each floor coming and going.

Back in the apartment, Carly lay sprawled in front of the TV watching *Sesame Street* and eating a plate of peanut-butter crackers.

"Eat at the table," I told her. "Do you want to get spanked for getting crumbs all over the carpet?"

She opened her mouth wide, revealing a mash of chewed food.

I found Mom in her bedroom doing up the buttons on her work blouse. She scowled when I entered. "You're supposed to knock."

"You're going to work?"

"Sandra asked me to cover her shift."

I scratched an itch at the back of my neck. "I'm not babysitting.

I have three pages of division due tomorrow. With remainders." Mom had worked only one night shift since starting at the diner, and that night Carly made me sleep in her bed with her, saying she heard scratchy fingers at the window. That was before some creep snatched Stefany Beale right off the street. They hadn't caught him yet. The creep probably went in windows, too, snatched little girls right out of their beds.

"That old man from downstairs is coming over. Elliot. He's going to be picking you girls up after school sometimes."

Papi, we began calling him, because Carly's childish tongue could not pronounce his last name. He never had children of his own. Tall and gangly, all elbows and knees, he folded himself into the space between my upper bunk and Carly's lower and read her Shel Silverstein's *The Giving Tree* over and over.

"Again, Papi!" Carly squealed, each time he closed the hard cover. "Again!"

"But as the boy grew older he began to want more from the tree, and the tree gave and gave."

We filled the time making exotic desserts, folded pastries that grew stiff and crusty in the oven, dusted with icing sugar, which Carly called Elephant Ears. Carly loved when Papi held her upside down and let her walk across the ceiling, Papi's height making this possible. His skinny arms were surprisingly strong.

And the tree was happy.

 Still, my thoughts skipped like a scratched record. Stefany Beale, Stefany Beale. What did it feel like, getting kidnapped? Aubrey Sato, my seat partner in class, and partner in the three-legged-recess-races, told me, "If anyone tries to kidnap me I'm gonna scratch their face." She showed me how to slip a key between my middle and ring fingers when walking around by myself. "It's easier for grown-ups," she explained. "They have a whole bunch of keys." Car keys, office keys, keys to their gym lockers and storage sheds — "They could really do damage."

I had two keys, because I lived in an apartment. Double the weaponry. This gave me a slight advantage over Aubrey. Except that I lost my keys. Weekly, it seemed, Papi and I stopped at the corner store to have a new set cut before Mom noticed. Papi bought Carly ice cream bars, even in the winter, and she sat on the counter licking chocolate, listening as Papi told stories about his wife Tatiana, who, at only twenty-five, died of a blood clot in her brain during an afternoon nap. Papi kept only one picture of Tatiana in his apartment, beside his bed, and I tried to catch glimpses of it the few times we went into Papi's room. In the black-and-white photo, Tati's dark hair lay meticulously curled and pinned back away from her forehead. When I tried to re-member what she looked like, her features swirled together with those of Stefany Beale. I couldn't tell what colour her eyes were. Maybe green, like Stefany's.

Papi pointed out Moscow on the globe in his apartment, the birthplace of Tati's mother. Carly spun the globe around with two palms to see how fast it could go, while Papi spun me stories of Tati's mother, a rich little girl in Russia who received a doll for every one of her birthdays. Matryoshka dolls, Papi called them. Nesting dolls. Lined up on his shelf, they looked like bowling pins. Tati's mother had given them to Tati to keep, so Tati could pass them down to her daughter some day: the daughter they didn't have. Aubrey received a similar set of nesting dolls from her grandparents in Japan, but whoever had crafted Aubrey's dolls painted smiles instead of the serious expressions worn by Tati's Matryoshkas. Aubrey's parents hid tooth fairy money inside Aubrey's dolls. At the core of Tati's ladies, I found a tiny baby, painted in the same style as each one that had come before it. No Russian secrets for me.

Carly preferred the dolls to stay up on the counter, uneasy under their rows and rows of eyes. Sometimes she held her breath and darted by them, the way my mother held her breath while driving by cemeteries.

& Carly and I did not look alike. I could see myself in our mother, in her thin frame and dark features, eyes almost black, knotted hair the colour of coffee beans. She consumed coffee incessantly, as though sucking in this darkness, and smelled of it, its bitterness. We had the same flat chest and snarled hair, not really curly or wavy or straight, but the kind you had to untangle. I was her paler version, slightly washed out, my hair and eyes a little lighter, the way a shirt goes through the wash and its colour bleeds out into the water. I blamed my father's traits, but could not remember what he looked like. I thought often that he must look like Carly, infinitely brighter. I could not figure out how my mother had given birth to something so vivid.

& Patrick telling me he loved me was like pouring aspartame in my coffee — never quite sweet enough. I told this to Carly right after he left me, after she finally convinced me to take a bath, to wash the smell of me off myself. I could see her blurry silhouette behind the shower curtain. I knew she couldn't afford the amount of money she'd spent on a last-minute plane ticket from Toronto to Calgary in the middle of a snowstorm. When I'd asked her about it, she'd said, "That's what credit cards are for. Buy now, pay later!"

"He always said, *You are loved,* or, *You're the love of my life,*" I told her, sliding slippery soap down the length of my arm. "Or he'd sign his cards, *Love Patrick.* But never *I love you.* And it's not like *I* didn't say it. I said it all the time."

She slid the curtain back.

"Car — !" I swiveled around in the tub to face the wall. The water sloshed up and over the rim at her.

"What? We share fifty percent of our DNA. Su bosom é mi bosom." She took my matty hair in both hands, squeezed it in her fists. Water ran through her fingers. "I think you're kinda crazy because you haven't slept in forever. But I agree with you." She raked out one long snarled curl, her warm fingers against my scalp.

"About what?"

"That you deserve sugar."

& Our mother had three kinds of days: work days, phone days, and bed days.

Work days meant Papi entertained Carly while I did my homework. Once, for a school contest, I had to make a bridge out of popsicle sticks, the goal being to bear as much weight as possible. Our teacher had shown us last year's model, balancing her little five-kilogram weights one at a time into a bucket suspended from the bottom.

"I'll eat them all!" Carly volunteered, sucking on a cherry-flavoured popsicle, her lips already lipstick red.

"Last year's winner held thirty-five kilos," I told Papi. My own popsicle made my lips numb. "I think that's more than Carly weighs. We're going to need a lot of sticks."

"Actually — " He sketched something on a napkin. "It's not the number of sticks that makes it able to bear weight. It's the design. The weight distribution. The balance."

Carly nudged up beside him. "Let me see!" She placed a sticky hand on my arm. "My next popsicle is going to be. . .grape."

It took us forty-eight sticks. Papi hung a bucket from the bottom, kept adding various fruits from his fridge. I kept expecting our bridge to break. Apple, orange, grapefruit. . . How much pressure could something so delicate bear?

My mother's shifts often ended before we got home from school. I could judge it — bed day or phone day — just by stepping off the elevator onto our floor.

"I don't want a fucking long distance package! . . . I want to talk to your supervisor. This is fucking ridiculous!"

I ran into our next-door neighbour, Alexa, a biology student at the U of T, while taking out the garbage during one of my mother's rants. Alexa chewed on her lower lip. "Everything okay in there? What's your mom so mad about?"

"Telemarketers," I said. "They call when she's sleeping. She hates when they wake her up."

Alexa leaned against her apartment doorframe. "She sleeps during the day?"

Mom hated telemarketers the most, because *they* called *her*. But sometimes *she* made the calls, harassing the credit card company or Toronto Hydro, trying to get out of paying interest on late bills. After my dad left, she sold the car. We didn't have cable, and neither did Papi, whose TV turned on with a knob. Papi preferred CBC Radio, anyway. But he did manage to rig up a VCR, and rented Carly a series of black-and-white Shirley Temple videos. She loved *A Little Princess* and *The Wizard of Oz*, though the flying monkeys gave her nightmares. I had to watch *Family Matters* at Aubrey's.

Alexa looked between me and our front door, as though trying to decide whether to say something to my mom about the noise. Mom's screaming was probably interrupting her studying.

"Why is there an extra two-dollar fee on my savings account this month? You just add fines and hope your customers don't realize it? You think you can just rob people? You're all swindlers!" Mom screamed, through the door.

On phone days, I put on music for Carly and tried to learn long division over the dual noise.

When it's dark, you're home and fed,
Curl up snug in your water bed.
Moon is shining and the stars are out,
Good night, little whale, good night!

But phone days meant that our mother was at least awake, moving around, doing something. On the phone, she cleaned the fridge, rubbed angry circles into the countertops, stood out on the balcony beating the crap out of the rugs. On the phone, she struggled with the can opener and emptied Chef Boyardee into microwavable bowls; ceramic for her and me, pink plastic with a picture of the Teenage Mutant Ninja Turtles for Carly. I could stomach the burnt innards of an emptied can. At least we had food.

On sleeping days, listening to the quiet of the hallway getting off the elevator, I took Carly's hand and squeezed. "Time to play the whisper game."

Quiet as a mouse?
Quieter than a mouse. Quiet as a turtle. Quiet as a beetle. Quiet as a tiny crumb on a beetle's nose.

&T Carly met Ryan the summer just before she turned seventeen. Ryan lived with his grandparents in a bedroom in their basement with walls covered in carpet in a room next door to the washer and dryer. He would turn them on at night when he couldn't sleep — white noise like mothers make, turning on the vacuum cleaner to lull their screaming babies calm. His drug-addicted mother lost custody right around the time he started kindergarten.

He told Carly these things, and then she'd spill them to me, over the phone, drunk on the tragedy of Ryan's life.

"Does he want me to know this?" I asked her. Carly held in personal information like a colander holding in water.

She brushed it off, unfazed. "I think I love him, Darce. I *know* I love him. I *know* that I *know*." She laughed. "You know?"

For their third date, Ryan took Carly to a restaurant in Little Portugal, near Ossington. Carly had always said that Ossington, one of Papi's cats, a scrappy, carrot-coloured marmalade whose dishevelled fur always looked wet, and who was missing his left front leg, was her "most favouritest." Papi called him "Handi-cat," because he couldn't resist a pun. Carly called him "Oz."

The restaurant, on the second story of a small walk-up, could have easily been mistaken for an apartment, because of the lack of a sign out front. Carly said it had pink curtains and a giant plastic figure of the Virgin Mary in the window.

"How does something like that stay in business?" I asked, my phone warm against my cheek, while I waited for Patrick to get back home.

"Word of mouth? I dunno. Okay, so, the weird thing — "

Patrick's key made a scraping sound in the lock. He fumbled with the Styrofoam containers of Indian food in bags hanging from his wrists as he came in the door.

I'd answered Carly's call before he left to go get dinner. Noticing the phone still in my hand, Patrick rolled his eyes and then made a rolling motion with one of his wrists. Hurry it up. My grey tabby, Kipling, danced out into the kitchen and hovered below the bags of food, following Patrick as he carried them to the counter, her nostrils tantalized by the smell of warm butter chicken.

Carly continued talking, unaware. "So she had like, these tarot cards, kinda — "

I tried to catch up, logically, to not betray my distractibility, to let Carly float happily along with the illusion that she was the centre of my attention. She and Patrick both held the belief that

Carly was, in fact, the centre of my attention, although Patrick, ladling curried meat onto naan, did not seem quite as happy about that fact as Carly. He gestured at me to get off the phone, one wrist working in a circular motion, then a slice at his throat. A frustrated mime.

The restaurant Carly blathered on about, she explained, was owned and operated by a Portuguese couple, a self-proclaimed psychic and her husband.

"They don't take your order. They kinda just *know* what you want. They like, sit you down, and the wife tells your fortune and the husband brings the food."

I resisted asking her again how such an establishment could possibly stay in business. She told me that they brought Ryan spaghetti —

"Spaghetti isn't Portuguese," I interjected.

"Is too. And it doesn't have to be Portuguese, it just has to be what your aura says you want."

"Your aura?"

"And guess what they brought me?"

"Actually, Car, can I call you back later? Patrick just brought dinner home." Patrick had eaten at the office three nights in a row.

"Chocolate cake! For dinner! Isn't that kinda crazy? I mean, how accurate is that? It had like, a gooey puddingy inside."

"How accurate is it that a girl would like chocolate?"

"You're kind of a killjoy."

"Okay, Carly, listen, I have to go eat dinner."

"You haven't heard my fortune."

"Tell me tomorrow, okay?"

Years later, after she left me, I realized that we'd both forgotten the conversation, never followed up. Patrick ate quietly, then said he'd rather work on an assignment than watch the movie we'd planned, a subtitled film Patrick had seen reviewed in *The*

Globe and Mail. One I had no interest in watching alone. I did the dishes, scooped granulated poop out of Kipling's litter box, bickered with Patrick over whose turn it was to empty the litter box, poured a bath that was too hot, then too cold, then too full, argued with Patrick over my hair making the pillow wet, and forgot about my baby sister, the aftertaste of chocolate clouds still on her tongue.

& For a few weeks in sixth grade, a bout with strep throat forced me home from school and into hibernation on Papi's couch, half in and half out of a NyQuil sleep, lulled by the drone of talk shows. That week, the cats gravitated towards me the way they gravitated towards the long radiator that ran down the length of one whole wall of the apartment as a source of heat. Between shallow fever naps, I woke to one of them squatted on my chest, paws tucked underneath her body, eyes shut into slits. I couldn't tell if the vibration inside my chest cavity was coming from her or from me.

Papi's furniture had curves and edges, grooves and contours carved into the wood, each piece of furniture a slightly different shade of brown. Drawers had to be yanked, not just pulled open, which had an upside: it kept Carly from exploring Papi's belongings. Papi poured us juice in round glass tumblers, the kind someone would drink brandy from, though he claimed not to like the taste of alcohol. He kept little porcelain bowls of mixed nuts on the kitchen table, as though his company might want to have a snack, but I never saw any other visitors at his apartment, nor did he talk about having any. He kept a pair of threadbare, navy blue slippers by the door, and had a glass breakfront behind which he kept Tati's china place settings, a copy of their marriage certificate, a hanging row of dusty wine glasses, and a wooden replica of a boat with a white and blue gingham sail.

When I could breathe successfully through both nostrils, and when Papi went to pick Carly up from school, I took down all of Tati's Matryoshka dolls and lined them up on the coffee table beside my gnarled Kleenexes. I couldn't tell what had Carly so spooked. One at a time, I took them apart, watching their concentric bodies grow smaller and smaller. The core of each held a tiny baby, its swaddling clothes painted on. Most of the babies had their eyes closed.

The dolls' severed heads stared at me blankly with heavy lidded eyes, pink circle cheeks, and rosebud mouths. Out of boredom, I switched their babies before reassembling them and lining them all up, shortest to tallest, back on the shelf. They smiled nervously at me, pregnant with each other's illegitimate children.

 On days that Papi couldn't look after us after school, as long as the temperature didn't go below zero, Carly and I played with Aubrey in the park. Aubrey, who had the privilege of being an only child, begged her parents for a pet, so they let her watch her aunt Asa's dog Chewy for a week. After three days, she stopped bringing Chewy, a scrappy little Shih Tzu who peed on the foot of her bed and howled to be let out at six AM, to the park with us.

"He just chases his ball, over and over and over," Aubrey said. "He brings it back, I throw it. He brings it back, I throw it. He can't even do tricks!"

Like Carly. For a while, playing with her amused me, when she first learned to walk and talk. I taught her new words, then laughed when she messed them up. She loved "ton ton" soup and "pis-ghetti." She called her belly-button "bubble gum." When she sneezed, she announced, "Bless you me." On her fourth birthday, one of our neighbours came over and stood at the front door taking off her jacket when Carly, trying to be polite, announced,

"We have hookers in the closet."

But she also threw ferocious temper tantrums. Her nose always ran. She liked to pinch. She stole my favourite doll and coloured "makeup" on its face with permanent marker. She always wanted to sleep in my bed, squishing in beside me and saying, "You're my *best* sister."

I didn't want to have to keep an eye on Carly while Mom ran to Dominion to get groceries or cleaned the kitchen. I imagined Aubrey's mom and dad tucking me into bed, pulling her daisy floral bedspread up to my chin. "You're our special girl," they'd say.

That summer, Aubrey's mother had taken Aubrey to a place on Yonge Street and let her get her nails done however she wanted them. Aubrey chose a different colour for every finger, ticked them off for me, one at a time: red, orange, yellow, green, blue, indigo, violet, brown, black, white. The white looked like White-Out, but I didn't tell her that. For her twelfth birthday, her parents let her get her ears pierced. When I asked, my mother said we didn't have money for frivolous things like earrings. Then she asked me to take the garbage out and push it down the chute. She always packed the bags way too full.

At the front door, I yelled, "I'm going to the park with Aubrey." My jean jacket barely fit, squeezing me tight around the shoulders. I doubted Mom would buy me a new one until school started, if then.

I had the door already open when she yelled back, "Take your sister or you can't go!"

Aubrey lived close to us in a duplex with three storeys and a small balcony off her parents' bedroom. Aubrey's mom worked during the day at a nearby florist. My mom still worked shifts at the diner. We ate cold leftover fries for dinner twice a week.

"My mom almost never lets me eat fries," Aubrey said, when I complained. "She says they have too much salt."

At the park, she wrote her name in Japanese in the dirt with a giant stick. "Does your mom get good tips?"

I shrugged. "I dunno."

Carly, nearby, twirled and sang the gibberish words to a song I didn't recognize. She held a fistful of dandelions. At least the weeds kept her occupied.

"My mom has to work at the flower shop," Aubrey continued, "because my dad said it was too hard being a one-income family. And my dad is a workaholic. You don't even have a dad."

"I do too."

Aubrey's name looked pretty, even in soil.

"Do mine," I said.

Carly kept singing. Mom had said to keep an eye on her. I'd just keep an ear on her.

Aubrey ignored me. "You don't have a dad, you have a sperm donor. The word dad means somebody who raises you."

"Who says?"

"I do." She scuffed her name out with the tip of her sneaker, started again. "Waitresses don't get paid very much. How can she afford to take care of you guys?"

"I don't know, but she does."

"Maybe she's a stripper."

I frowned. "She is *not* a stripper. Stop making stuff up."

Aubrey dropped the stick. "Hey, Carly, does your mom like to dance?"

Carly immediately perked up, dropping the fuzzy yellow blossoms. "I *love* to dance!" She began twirling on the spot.

"You're a bitch," I said. I'd never sworn before, but Aubrey did, often teasing me for being a goody-two-shoes. I pushed my shoulders back, lifted my chin.

Aubrey rolled her eyes. "Whatever."

"I'm not playing with you anymore." It sounded babyish, and

I turned my back to her so she wouldn't see me blush. I started walking away from her across the park, away from Carly, too. Aubrey could take care of Carly for once. Served her right.

I could see something small and pink-looking at the bottom of one of the nearby trees. I approached. A newborn bird! Pink and scrawny, its veins pulsed, visible through its skin. Its eyes bulged. I squatted down beside it. It opened and closed its mouth, soundlessly.

"What's that?" Carly came up behind me, looked over my shoulder.

"A baby bird." It looked like a wet little rat. It shuddered.

"How come he's not flying?"

"Because he probably fell from up in the tree. He's very sick."

Carly's mouth opened into a little O. "He's sick?"

"He fell a long way and hurt himself."

"Wake up, birdie," Carly said, and reached out.

I grabbed her hand. "Don't touch him, he has germs."

"I need to fix him." She struggled against me. "He's sick. Fix him, Dossy."

"I can't fix him. We better just leave him alone."

Aubrey came over to see what was going on. "What's that?"

Carly writhed. "Fix him, Dossy! You have to fix him."

The baby bird twitched.

Aubrey leaned in. "I think it's going to die."

Carly's eyes widened. "DIE?"

I shoved Aubrey with my elbow. "It's not going to die, Car. Let's just leave it alone so it can rest and get better. You want to go to the swings?"

Aubrey shook her head. "It's totally going to die. We have to put it out of its misery. Look — it's suffering."

"Fix him!" Carly begged.

I had no idea when the baby bird had fallen, or how long it had lain there, broken, in the dirt. Its thin skin stretched translucent over its bones. Its eyes bulged. The sun seemed to be slowly baking it from the outside in. Blood welled up under its skin that hadn't quite broken through to the surface, red-black like the cherries we'd eaten earlier in the day that had stained my fingers. What did it feel like to die? Did the bird know already? How soon before it would turn to nothing?

"Put it out of its misery," Aubrey urged.

Carly snuffled.

I clenched my jaw. "*YOU* put it out of its misery."

Aubrey squirmed. "It's suffering! Look at it!"

"Fix him! Fix him!" Carly blubbered. I could hear my sister wailing, almost as though the baby bird was her heart, outside her body, struggling to beat. Carly hated anything in pain. She collected fallen leaves from the side of the road and tried to nurse them back to health. A few weeks prior, she'd gotten a good hard spanking from our mother for using an entire box of Band-Aids to patch up her beloved Raccoon, who'd taken a tumble from the top bunk, from my bed, where I'd forbidden Carly from playing.

Aubrey and Carly would not shut up.

It's suffering! It's suffering!

Squatted beside the bird, I tried to tune them out, curling into myself like an egg, elbows on my knees, hands up over my ears. I squeezed my eyes shut.

Aubrey thought she was so tough. Yeah, right. When I opened my eyes, she had her hands over her face.

"It's *suffering!*" Her voice had taken on a repetitive, whining quality. "It's *suffering!*"

"Aubrey!" I grabbed her wrists. "Take Carly over there. Carly, go with Aubrey so I can fix the bird."

Aubrey took a few steps backwards. "You're not going to fix it, it's *dying!*"

"Shut up!" I screamed. "Just take her."

Aubrey took Carly by the wrist and dragged her away from the tree. I looked down at the bird. It didn't move. Maybe it had already died. I bent in towards it, and, as I did, it twitched again, a little spasm shuddering through its body.

I stood back up. Then, quickly, so that I couldn't change my mind, brought my foot down hard on the spot where the baby bird lay, felt its body crunch under my sneaker. Even though my hands covered my ears, I heard it scream. The bird, or maybe Carly.

I stood there, my sneaker crushing the fragile, broken body of the bird. Now it *had* to be dead. I took my foot away, knelt down beside the tree and began scooping up dirt, dumping it over the bird without looking at it.

There — just a mound of dirt. I let my breath out, all at once. I slid my shoe along the grass — again, again. It didn't feel clean. My hands were black with cherry dye and soil. I brushed them off on my jeans. Still, the bits under my fingernails would not go away.

& During my relationship with Patrick, I relished shopping for Valentine's Day cards. Buying Valentine's cards — me, the late bloomer, who, when we lived together, still woke up surprised to be in *our* bed, in *our* apartment. Patrick often headed out in the mornings before me, leaving just the faint laundry detergent gingerbread scent of him, and his imprint in the sheets. After we split up, I woke and expected him to be there, then had to remember. Just as I'd gotten used to him, he'd gone.

So, I was at the drug store shopping for a Valentine's Day card for Carly. Five weeks before, I'd left her, alone in Toronto, in the apartment she'd shared with Ryan until he'd broken up with her and moved out. I'd spent my entire Christmas vacation in Toronto with her, my holidays on the hand-me-down futon I'd given her when I moved to Calgary. We shared the same lifeless furniture and, apparently, the same susceptibility to rejection. Just over a year earlier, I'd packed my own belongings and moved out of Patrick's apartment.

When I told Carly I needed to pack for my return flight, she begged me to stay another week. It cost me over two hundred dollars to change the flight, and I dreaded arriving home to the prep work I thought I'd have a whole week to complete. I flew a red-eye, arriving with just enough time to take a cab back to my apartment, shower, change, and drive to work, bleary at the prospect of seven sleepless hours with twenty-nine sixth-graders. The edges of my sloppy bun still wet from the shower hung frozen at the back of my neck.

In the drug store, I opened a card that played music, a series of single notes, like bells. One year for Halloween, Carly found a card that, when opened, played a witch's cackle over and over. This she taped open to the back wall of my closet, behind my clothes, so that when I came home, I could not find the location of the laugh. I tore apart my room, the sound eventually mingling with Carly's own laughter.

I'd be lying if I said I didn't fantasize about Patrick showing up at my apartment, at my gym, in the staff room. He would see me first, unaware, otherwise occupied, my hair falling in my eyes. Doing something charming, perhaps a little childish — a rim of latte foam on my upper lip, or humming along to my headphones, or reading *The Chronicles of Narnia* to my sixth-graders and doing the voices. He would tell me he'd made a big mistake. That he missed me.

Sometimes, I used my membership card at the grocery store, which was under Patrick's name, and paid in cash, just to hear the clerk say, "Have a good afternoon, Mrs. Linam."

But I couldn't speak these words aloud — especially not to Carly. *I* was the big sister.

  Over the weeks I spent in Toronto, Carly seemed to get smaller and more childlike, if that was even possible. Waking up beside her felt oddly familiar, the way she, a year earlier, woke up beside me, her pyjamas askew, a smile stretching the big globe cheeks she disdained so much. She'd played Michael Jackson and tried to get me to dance to "Thriller." She hadn't even been born when *Thriller* hit the shelves. But her zombie impression and off-key solo made me laugh. She baked double chocolate cookies but forgot to take them out of the oven. That they burned a little on the bottom reminded me of our haphazard, blackened childhood dinners. Felt like home.

But I didn't know how to be upbeat and silly for her. Practical, I could do: ordering food, vacuuming up accumulated dust, keeping her busy. I let her sleep in the mornings, creeping out of bed and brewing coffee, her apartment dim, the early December sky grey and thick. On the third day, still clumsy with sleep, I stepped on one of the Christmas bulbs she had snaked around the apartment floor's perimeter. It shattered under my foot. I sat on the edge of the tub and picked bits of coloured glass out of my heel. Still, she slept.

On New Year's Eve, I picked through the remnants of food in her fridge and ordered sushi. Carly, wandering aimlessly around the kitchen, gave up and crawled back into bed before the delivery man arrived. We ate, propped up with pillows, but she remained listless, could barely get her mouth around the maki. She dismembered the pieces, peeling salmon and tuna away from rice, poking avocado and cucumber out of the bellies of rolls with her chopsticks. I couldn't tell how much she'd eaten. She fell asleep before the countdown. I read *The Globe and Mail* in bed with her, the newsprint smudging my fingers. Patrick loved *The Globe and Mail*. With a few minutes left until midnight, I climbed out of bed, took one of Carly's throw blankets and stepped out onto the balcony. A fine sheen of fresh snow frosted the wire net that kept pigeons from landing. I stood outside in the cold, waiting for the moment to pass, before going back inside.

As soon as I sat on the bed, Carly jerked up, as though shoved — eyes round, pupils dilated. She coughed and heaved, as though she had too much air in her chest. A panic attack, maybe. A bad dream.

"It's okay, it's okay," I said. On my knees, I pulled the blanket around her. She flinched at my touch, or maybe my cold fingers. I could feel her heart through her back, jackrabbit fast. "Take deep breaths." I breathed loudly in and out, like a labour coach, until her breathing started to slow.

"Fuck 2007," she said.

Her voice sounded like Mom's.

      Carly's early childhood coincided with the children's television frenzy starring Barney, an anthropomorphized purple dinosaur who never let a show go by without singing his nauseating love anthem. The opening notes to the song frequently made me, then bordering on teenagehood, cover my ears.

I love you
You love me
We're a happy family

"Mom, how come you never say 'I love you'?" Carly asked one day. She was maybe six at the time, sweet and sensitive like a nectarine, her feelings always getting bruised. Our mother busied herself cleaning the windows, rubbing the same streak-free spots over and over.

Carly said, more emphatically, "Mom, how come you never?"

Another shot of Windex. "Because." Our mother often sanitized single sections of the apartment — scrubbing grime from the inside of the oven, vacuuming dust from the folds of the curtains. Single tasks exhausted her, leaving portions of the apartment spic and span and others cluttered and chaotic.

"But *why?*"

"Because!" Mom snapped. "Because moms love their kids. They don't need to say it. It's just something you know, like how the sky is blue. I shouldn't have to tell you." She yanked the curtains closed.

The room Carly and I shared frequently mirrored the rest of the apartment, Carly's half littered with her "peoples," half-dressed baby dolls and hand-me-down Barbies, their hair combed so much that it stood almost vertically from their heads, like Trolls. She lined them up in rows, the babies disproportionately monstrous compared to the Barbies. There were never quite enough doll clothes to go around. Carly's Barbies were either bra-burning feminists who didn't care about whether their hair looked decent, or topless whores who overdid it with the hairspray. I kept all my toys and barrettes in Tupperware bins, quick and easy to clean up and stow away.

Even our beds angled out of alignment. The top bunk ran lengthwise against our bedroom's rear wall, but the bottom bunk pointed horizontally out, perpendicular. I'd had to sleep on the bottom bunk for several years, with the top unoccupied, until I became old enough to advance to the top, with Carly taking over the space on the bottom. Carly begged to switch.

"No switching!" Mom snapped at Carly. "The last thing I need is for you to roll out of bed and crack your head open!" Mom had seen the bed advertised in the building lobby and offered twenty-five bucks for it when Carly aged out of her crib. The ladder had foot holes cut to the contours of basic shapes: square, triangle, circle, diamond. Way too babyish.

"Dossy?" Carly asked, that night, from the bottom bunk.

"Yeah?"

"Is the sky *always* blue?"

It took a moment before I figured it out. The sky, seen in parallel stripes through our plastic blinds, was purple black, the colour of a bruise. I thought of sunsets, of snowstorms. Of Mom, furiously scrubbing.

"Dossy?" It came out all chewed up, the way she'd said my name as a baby, her thumb deeply rooted, obscuring her voice. I could tell this from the top bunk.

"Yes," I said, "the sky's *always* blue."

&   Papi had one niece, Frances, the daughter of Tati's younger sister. Frances, in her forties, had never married or had children. Maybe, I thought, Papi and his relatives had been cursed to live lonely, solitary lives. Though Frances often sent small cards or packages in the mail on special occasions, we never actually met her. She lived in Sudbury and did not like to drive. Her lack of physical presence had Carly convinced she wasn't real.

"Then who do you think sends these things?" I asked, dangling a small bundle of chocolate Kisses wrapped in patterned tissue paper in her face. Frances had tied the package with shiny green ribbon, curled the way my teacher had taught me using the open blade of a sharp pair of scissors. I could never get mine into the nice ringlets that adorned Frances's packages.

"Do you think she's kinda like. . .a ghost?" Carly had torn into her package, and had one of the chocolates already dissolving on her tongue.

I rolled my eyes. "She's not a ghost."

"How do you know?" She reached for another sweet and unwrapped its foil package.

"There're no such things as ghosts. And if ghosts *did* exist, they wouldn't mail chocolate." I rolled the package around in my palm, thinking I would save it and pack it in my lunch for the next day.

Carly had chocolate on her upper lip and had started dismantling the foil of her third piece of candy. "I think she is."

"All right," I said, "enjoy the haunted chocolate you just ate."

When she started to cry, Mom abandoned the sloppy sandwiches she was assembling. "Why did you do that? Do you think I want to spend my whole night convincing her she's not going to die in her sleep? Why do you have to be a little bitch?"

"You always take her side," I said. "It's not my fault she's such a whiny brat."

& On my last day in Toronto over Christmas break, it became more imperative to get Carly to perk up. I suggested shopping, which had always cheered her up in the past. Carly loved sparkly earrings and sewed colourful patches onto the butt pockets of her jeans even when there were no rips. She owned a rainbow of vintage purses, a few impulsively purchased from high-end boutiques, others from yard sales.

She raked her fingers through her hair. "I look like shit, Darce."

She did, too. Deep dark moons under her eyes. A scabby nose.

"I'll do your makeup," I offered.

She shrugged. She had a small rip under one of the armpits of her nightgown, where the seam had started to unravel.

I painted her eyelids silver-purple, making the blue of her irises stand out. Stage makeup.

At the grocery store, I stocked the cart with frozen dinners and canned soups and chocolate-covered granola bars: food that required little effort. I bought her a pair of oversized circular wooden earrings, painted yellow, their insides carved out into delicate scrolls. Big and fragile at the same time. On the subway home, I insisted she put them in. Her fingers fumbled with her earlobes, a little shaky.

Back at the apartment, Carly went to take a shower, and I stocked the groceries into her pantry. Photos of her and Ryan still decorated the fridge, stuck in place with her series of childish magnets: Winnie the Pooh; the loopy M shape of Virgo, her zodiac sign; bright, block letters, the kind we'd had as children. Happy Carly and Happy Ryan watched me unpack two tins of powdered French Vanilla coffee. I turned on my laptop, listening to the drum of the water through the bathroom walls. I ordered the first two seasons of *Full House* on DVD, to be delivered after I'd left. Maybe it would make her feel some sisterly love in my absence.

The apartment phone rang. I closed Carly's laptop and reached for it. I heard her shut the taps off.

"Hello?" I said.

An automated voice announced Carly's overdue DVD rentals.

Carly asked, somewhat hushed, "Is that Ryan?"

She had left the shower without washing her face or rinsing off. Her hair clung to her head, greasy with conditioner. Her makeup looked garish.

"It's the video store," I said.

"Fucking video store." She pulled her towel tighter around herself. "Leave me alone."

& Carly was the kind of child who slid down stairs head first on her stomach, her wrists raw with rug burn. In the house my mother rented with her new husband, we had stairs for the first time, apart from the cement stairwells of our apartment buildings, cold through our sock feet when the elevators broke down and our arms ached balancing the laundry baskets as we marched up from the basement.

I worried that she would crack her wrists slamming them into the floor when she hit the bottom step — Carly learned through trial and error, trial and error and error and error. I had a few scars, but Carly was a veritable map of injury: marks from scratching chicken pox; from dropping glass; from falling off jungle gyms, from touching a hot stove.

She often cut her hair short on a whim and then woefully mourned its loss, purchasing lengthening shampoos and intensely rubbing her scalp (while in the shower, while watching television, sometimes annoyingly at the dinner table) to stimulate follicle growth. She would blow her allowance on an expensive sweater, only to spill mayonnaise all down its front, or rip the neck trying to hastily pull it over her head without having undone all the buttons. She fractured her elbow learning how to rollerblade. Six weeks later, having just been given the all clear from her doctor, she merrily knotted the laces on her hand-me-down blades and gave me a thumbs-up. Within half an hour, she'd broken her wrist.

Twice in high school she slept through her alarm and through a final exam. I began phoning her before tests to ensure she would wake up on time.

I, on the other hand, only needed to screw up once, shame and guilt emblazoned on my cheeks and in the crevices of my brain.

&I often wondered whether anything significant would happen to me that very day, years into the future. If, perhaps, a lazy, August 25th would someday be my wedding day. If on January 31st I might give birth to my firstborn son. One September 1st, I lay inverted on my bed, head where my feet should be, listening to the blurry noise of Carly playing in the bathtub, and wondered if, in five years, it would be the day I would move out on my own. When I sat up, all the blood rushed to my head.

February 15th, 2005, exactly two years before Carly died, Patrick and I celebrated Valentine's Day together, a day late, because he had a paper due by five that night and insisted that he needed the entire week prior to prepare. On the fourteenth, I brought him Earl Grey green tea and started rubbing his neck at the computer while he worked, hoping he'd take a break.

"What kind of professor gives an assignment over Valentine's Day?" I teased. "I bet he's divorced."

Patrick wriggled away from my touch. "Darcy, stop. You know, the whole world doesn't revolve around you."

On February 15th, we made basil and seafood pasta together, quietly, the bubbling water threatening to spill. Patrick reached past me for the dial and turned the heat down, brushing my arm. On the way back, he lingered for just a moment, gave me a slight smile.

We went to a yoga class later that night, an activity neither of us had tried, but which Patrick read helped alleviate stress. My stomach felt full from all the carbohydrates. The room temperature inched higher from the sweat and exertion of our contorted bodies. Patrick kept his eyes shut beside me. I hung upside down in a bridge position, my wrists burning, listening to the instructor's voice telling me to pull my tailbone in and breathe slow, deep breaths. My head hanging between my arms, I could see out through the window onto the street, a Coors Light billboard, crusted with snow. How romantic.

At home, we took a simultaneous shower and made unsteady love up against the slippery tiled wall. I pulled myself closer in towards his hips for balance. He stepped backwards, pushing me towards the spray.

Afterwards, Patrick said, "I'm going to do the dishes."

He traced his path in wet footprints leading away from me.

& Back in Calgary, after leaving Carly to fend for herself in Ryan's absence, I dreamed of her vomiting her insides, retching her esophagus, her mangled intestines. She coughed her heart into her hands.

Wet. Wet on my hands, my face — I awoke, hot and fumbling in the dark. My hands felt sticky; I fumbled for the lamp. Blood, almost black, on my hands, my pyjamas, my mattress.

I put my hand to my face, tasted salt. A bloody nose. I sat up, pinched my nostrils shut, coughed blood from my mouth, from what felt like my lungs. Kipling pounced up beside me on the bed, her meows curling up at the ends, like questions. *Are you okay? What's wrong?* I pushed her away with my elbow. I'd had less than three hours' sleep in the last two days, and a class field trip only four and a half hours away. My suitcase lay in the middle of the floor, not yet unpacked, clothes and makeup strewn about. I hadn't washed my sheets, and had fallen asleep on my bare futon mattress, covered only with a thin quilt.

I stumbled through the clutter to the bathroom, tripping on Kipling as I went, her wide pupils glossy in the dark.

That winter, the air hung dry and stale, the lifeless brown grass smashed flat under the snow. I could blame my puffy, bloodshot eyes on allergies, but then, allergies in January? I blinked, unaccustomed to the dark, and fumbled for the shower knob, held a washcloth to my nose, waited for the water to warm up.

The water pooled at my feet, ribboned with blood and tears, swirling towards the drain.

I lay in bed, unable to sleep, for an hour, then phoned Aubrey. I knew that she would be lacing her sneakers for her ritual morning run through downtown Toronto, through construction zones, breathing in the dust, the fumes, the icy smog irritating her scrawny asthmatic lungs. Slow suicide. She liked the bustle of street vendors setting up their stands, two-t-shirts-for-two-dollars. She ran even when the temperatures dipped below minus-twenty.

"You okay?" she asked, and Kipling leapt up onto my chest, kneading at my ribcage. "I'm just about to leave. I have an early group meeting this morning." Aubrey's in-progress master's degree in International Relations meant only a few more years before she left to travel the globe. The Calgary-Toronto distance had diluted our communication. Additional distance would only exacerbate the problem.

"Don't go running, talk to me instead." I meant it casually, but it came out needy, beseeching.

"What's wrong?"

"Nosebleed."

"Don't tilt your head back."

I sighed. "It's stopped. There's blood all over my bed, though."

"That sucks. Just throw your sheets in the wash while you're at work."

"I didn't have sheets on it. I've barely unpacked. It's pathetic. There's blood all over the mattress. I don't know how to get it out."

Aubrey sounded annoyed. "Eh, cut your losses. It's a futon, right? Futon mattresses are, like, seventy bucks or something."

"Yeah, and since teaching is so lucrative. . .maybe I'll try to scrub it out later. I think I have baking soda in the fridge. I can prop it up in the bathtub."

"Not worth it." I heard the door of her apartment open.

"I'm worried about Carly," I blurted.

"You're always worried about Carly."

"I know, but it's *Carly*. I don't like her being alone."

"She's not alone. She has friends. And I'm here. Do you want me to check in on her?"

Just what I wanted her to say. "Yeah. I would appreciate that, thanks."

"Okay, gotta go. I'll call her on my lunch break, okay?"

"Yeah, okay. Thanks."

"Hey by the way — "

"What?"

"My lungs are in the clear. The sky is really blue this morning."

   The week before Carly died, I ventured out in minus-twenty-seven degrees to a birthday party at one of Calgary's cowboy-themed nightclubs for one of the student teachers at my school. While I was getting ready, the power went out. I did my makeup by the light of a flashlight held under my chin, as though telling ghost stories by the campfire. I'd started my period that morning, the cramps nudging in on a dream in which I stood on a stool in Papi's kitchen folding onions into perogies. I fumbled for Tylenol in the medicine cabinet.

I arrived early, before any of the other guests. The thumping bass shook the floor and spread up through my feet. I perched on a stool and sucked listlessly at a Pepsi, watching the door.

When my refill had been reduced to melting ice and still no one had shown up, I went to the doorway and peered out. A long line had formed, patrons huddling on the spot, shifting from one high heel to the other to stay warm. I spotted the birthday girl about three quarters of the way to the back of the line, but couldn't get her attention.

I went back to my perch and pulled out my phone to send Carly a text message, but couldn't get any reception. I picked aimlessly at a scab on the knuckle of my right thumb. It didn't make sense — the empty dance floor, the people outside getting frostbite.

Across the bar, a couple, their bodies close and flirty, stepped back a few paces and into a patch of light from one of the hanging fixtures above the bar. The shape and lines of the male's back looked exactly like Patrick's. I held my breath. The strident bass vibrated the speakers; I couldn't feel my heart beating. He turned then, his cheekbones and chin and hairline not at all the same.

Patrick would never go to a cowboy bar.

And Christ! We'd broken up over a year ago!

I went out the back exit and crossed the parking lot.

In my apartment, the power had come back on, blazing the bulbs of my overhead lights and lamps. My alarm clock flashed at me, perpetually 12:00. I hadn't closed the closet door properly. Kipling had climbed the ledges and knocked all the contents to the floor, pill bottles and shampoos. In what had probably been ecstatic feline glee, she'd shredded my last three rolls of toilet paper. She rubbed up against my leg, purring without shame. She still had some white flakes static stuck to her fur.

The cramps twisted my insides again, the Tylenol wearing off. My insides felt bruised. I restacked the bottles on the shelf, shoved the major bits of toilet paper into a garbage bag, and climbed into bed still in my jeans and tank top and hormones. Before turning my phone off, I typed to Carly: *Quite possibly worst day in a long time.*

 While my sister was dying I was conjugating French verbs. Conjugating.

French.

Verbs.

I'd taught the kids an inane song, to the tune of "The Ants Go Marching," to practice the past tense. Passé composé. While they sang, I sucked at the rim of my dwindling black coffee. The song seemed to run its nails down the chalkboard, but my French consisted only of a few nouns and phrases I remembered from my own elementary school education. This necessitated following the curriculum manual — songs and all.

"J'ai, tu as, il a, elle a, nous avons, vous avez." I could barely concentrate over the singing.

Leila Brewer raised her hand, mid-chorus. "Ms. Nolan, I have to leave to go to my dentist appointment."

I nodded. My coffee tasted gritty.

"Répétez!"

I wondered if the song would actually serve the purpose of helping them remember the verbs, or whether they would simply be haunted by it, years later, whenever they thought back to sixth grade.

    & Shopping for Valentine's Day cards when Carly called, I took my place at the checkout, my arms full with her card and other toiletries, shampoo bottles and tampons.

"Darce — he called."

Our recent conversations hadn't centered on any other *he*. Still, I said, "Ryan?"

The clerk scanned my items. I scrambled for my debit card.

"Yeah," Carly said.

"You don't sound happy."

"Well, *because,* yesterday, everything was fine, we were talking, and I mentioned maybe we should get together sometime and have coffee, or something, because you know we haven't seen each other since he moved out, and he was sort of like, maybe, and he asked how the apartment was, but he called it *our* apartment. Like, *our* apartment, you know? I kinda felt like — "

"Car, hold on, hold on." I put the phone down on the counter and punched in my PIN. When I picked it up again, she hadn't stopped talking.

" — he doesn't even think it's possible! Like, how can you love someone *so* much and then just. . .not?"

I chose my words. "I don't think it's that he doesn't love you — "

45

"If he loves me, why did he leave? Why does he want to talk one day and then think it's a bad idea the next day? Patrick didn't do that, right?"

"Well, with Patrick, things were — I mean, *I* stopped talking to *him* after he broke up with me, right? I'm the one who didn't answer *his* calls."

"I wish you could just make him come back. Talk to him or something, I dunno. I just wish it would all stop, you know! All of it."

I crumpled the receipt in my fist. I had at least two hours of lesson planning that I'd wanted to finish in time to make it to a monthly dessert date set up by my former university classmates. I'd missed the last two. "I know, Hun. Do you want to have a sister's date tonight? We could watch the same TV show and talk about it during the commercials. Whatever show you want."

"Yeah. No. I think. . .I think maybe I'll just. . .sleep."

"How about I call you in the morning? You can tell me all the details."

"Talking doesn't fix anything."

"I'm calling you anyway."

She sighed, long and deep. "Bye, Darce."

Outside, I put my bags down on the step and watched the cars circle around the icy parking lot. The cold seeped through my jeans.

He answered on the third ring.

"Hello?"

"Hi, Ryan."

"Hey, Darcy." He paused, possibly trying to gauge my level of anger, wondering if I wanted to, perhaps, knee him in his unmentionables on my sister's behalf, or some equally sadistic equivalent. "Is everything okay?"

"Ryan," I said, "I need you to listen to me, okay?"

"Okay. . ."

"I need you to stop talking to her. It's hurting her too much. You don't want this for her, this back and forth. You have to just stop calling her, stop answering her phone calls, her emails, even if she keeps trying and keeps trying. Do you want her back?"

"I. . .It's more complicated than that. Like, this whole thing is so messed up. I didn't mean for. . .I miss her. A lot."

"Do you want her back?" I repeated.

In the silence, I thought he'd hung up.

Finally, "I can't right now."

"Then you have to let her go. Okay? You're killing her." My fingers had gone white, numb around the phone.

Ryan's response was quiet. "Okay."

I exhaled fog into the surrounding air.

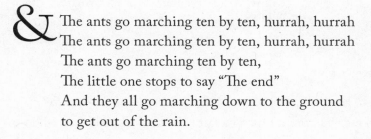 The ants go marching ten by ten, hurrah, hurrah
The ants go marching ten by ten, hurrah, hurrah
The ants go marching ten by ten,
The little one stops to say "The end"
And they all go marching down to the ground
to get out of the rain.

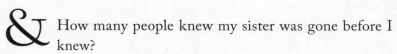 How many people knew my sister was gone before I knew?

This is what the medical examiner told me, afterwards.

Moments before jumping, she'd spread her jean jacket on the platform floor. In the frenzied aftermath, the first policeman on the scene picked up her coat and found her wallet in the front pocket. I imagine the horror of the passengers, having barely registered my yellow-haired chubby-cheeked baby sister pacing along the rim of the subway platform. One witness said she'd seen Carly pacing, but no one else corroborated this, probably too absorbed in their bleary morning Starbucks dreams, waiting for the rush of the train along its tracks.

She had no cash in her wallet; just her student ID and Aubrey's phone number on the back of a Tim Hortons receipt, which meant she'd planned it ahead of time, wanted me to know in the gentlest way possible, as though any way could possibly be gentle.

The police got my contact information from Aubrey, who insisted I had to hear it from someone in person. My cell phone was lost at the bottom of my purse. When I didn't answer, they'd tried the phone number for St. Sebastian, dug through the paperwork I'd filled out back when I'd taken the job. To contact in-case-of-emergency: Patrick Linam.

11:34 AM, minutes after recess. Carly had texted me at 7:03 Calgary time, during my second snooze. I'd mistaken the vibration of my phone for my alarm, reached over and turned it face down without reading her message, which I discovered during recess:

always blur

I wrote her back, *Sorry missed ur msg this morning — what?*

In my classroom, I heard a faint buzzing. The kids settled into their desks, a mess of giggles and pencils and energy leftover from recess. The radiator, maybe. It sounded like a fly. A February fly? I clapped my hands twice, then three times, our classroom code to get settled and pay attention. The class clapped back, out of synch. The buzzing stopped. And at the door, the principal, with Patrick to his right, knocked.

There was an old lady who swallowed a spider
that wiggled and jiggled and tickled inside her
she swallowed the spider to catch the fly
I don't know why she swallowed a fly
Perhaps she'll die

& You wake up, and your sister is dead.

The blankets are twisted around you, clammy, and your sister is dead, and *he* is beside you but not beside you, away in the bed, pillows between your bodies.

Your sister is dead.

When *he* left you, you stood naked in front of the mirror for a long time, until you barely recognized yourself. Across the bed, you barely recognize *him,* the disjointed puzzle parts of him you can see. A freckled arm whose constellations you once had memorized, a foot broken free from the covers.

And it comes to you, then, the flash of her ankle, her bony foot. Pink ink. A balloon, the string dangling around her heel.

Oh god.

He stirs.

& One weekend after I'd moved to Calgary, I flew back to Toronto for the holiday. Carly and I went to see a chick flick. I hadn't seen a romantic comedy since moving to Calgary, since Patrick insisted on only watching movies that stimulated him mentally. Carly discussed chick flicks with seriousness, as though debating one of Shakespeare's plays. "Do you think it's realistic that the main character would *actually* sleep with her sister's boyfriend?"

She'd started taking fine arts classes at a community college, chipping away at her program part-time while working. She kept asking to borrow money so she could buy gesso or India ink. I chipped in when I could afford it, thrilled she'd squeaked out a high school diploma, that she'd actually been accepted to a college — any college, even if I couldn't imagine how she'd actually find meaningful employment given the courses she'd enrolled in.

Her career goals changed daily. That morning, she mused aloud about the possibility of being a tattoo artist, but then wondered whether she could handle all the needles. She had to take an English class and begged me to write her papers for her so that she could at least pass. I'd edited all her high school papers, too — tried to teach her how to properly use commas, how to avoid sentence fragments, how to write an opening statement, a concluding paragraph.

"This is boring," she'd say, when I tried to tutor her. "Can't you just write it for me? You stole all the good genes. You get to be the smart one. You get to be the skinny one. So you owe me." But, during her first college course, she'd received an A-plus on an art project, a collage of a raven on which she'd dyed seagull and pigeon feathers black and glued them one at a time into a ferocious, three-dimensional wing that stood two inches off the page. The first A she'd ever gotten. She hadn't seemed that into art when she'd taken it in high school. Who knew? My baby sister — full of secrets.

She'd forgotten to tell me what she'd really wanted to tell me until we'd taken our seats in the theatre, animated popcorn and pretzels telling us to turn our cell phones off. When a large Junior Mint with eyes said, "Shhhhhh!" Carly whispered, almost an afterthought, that one of Ryan's ex-girlfriends had phoned him. She didn't even really know if you could call it ex-girlfriend, since they'd only been fifteen. Babies, really. I didn't remind her that she'd met Ryan as a teenager, too.

"So — " Carly stopped and put a handful of popcorn in her mouth, wiped her hands on her jeans. The grease made the denim darker. "And so I was like, what is she calling for? And he was like, beats me." But Carly looked calm as she spoke, jealousy not one of the ingredients. "I just thought it was weird. He didn't call her back."

The lights from the movie screen flashed across her face, all greens and golds. She had gained weight since I'd been gone, I realized. I missed her then, suddenly, despite the fact that she sat right beside me, her arm on the armrest touching mine.

The weight looked healthy on her. Cheery. Sitting beside me whole and peaceful, some part of me didn't even recognize her.

&   Near the end of my English degree, I started applying to university Education programs, and Papi surprised me by commenting that he'd enjoyed his own career as a teacher. Hadn't he always worked at the shelter?

I'd been feeding the cats while he went on a brief trip to Niagara Falls over a long weekend, and he insisted on paying me. He counted out soft bills from his wallet. Papi paid for everything in cash.

"You were a teacher?" I asked. "Since when?"

"I stopped after I turned forty. Tatiana loved animals. She was in the process of applying to veterinary school when she died. We had a bird, an ugly little Cockatiel. Nymph, she called him. . .the scientific name was Nymphicus Hollandicus."

I folded the money and tucked it into my back pocket. "Carly loves birds."

"Tati did too," he countered. "But I preferred more traditional pets."

He always had four cats in the apartment, though the four he had at that time were less familiar to me than those he'd had when he babysat for Carly and I. He no longer had any of the original howling quartet from when we lived in the same building. Ossington — Carly's beloved Oz — had died the previous year of diabetes, so happy and fat he'd taken to dragging his bum around when he needed to move closer to his food dish. For two days after he died, Carly tried to get out of going to school, bemoaning the fact that her stomach hurt, insisting I take her to the doctor, hypothesizing that she, too, was a diabetic.

I'd chastised her, "Diabetes doesn't make your stomach hurt."

"Does too!"

Our stepfather, who Carly and I had taken to calling "Dick" (short for his actual name, Richard, and, behind his back, of course), told her if he caught her skipping school he'd make sure she had a stomachache.

One of Papi's new cats was Oz II, short for Osgoode. In addition to being a subway station, Osgoode happened to be the name of one of Toronto's law schools, from which Patrick had been rejected. Of the four he'd applied to, he'd been accepted by only one — the University of Calgary. He had yet to accept their offer. I'd applied and been accepted to the teaching program in Calgary, my school applications mapping onto his. I didn't want to leave Toronto, but I didn't want a long distance relationship, either. Patrick was deciding my future more than his own. When I'd arrived at Papi's, Oz 11 lay sprawled across the kitchen counter beside a discarded whisker. He yawned, exposing a dark birthmark on the roof of his mouth.

"So what'd you teach?" I asked.

"Well, a variety of things. But my favourite course was Theatre Arts."

"You? No way." Papi reminded me often of British guards who hold their position and never flinch, even when troublesome tourists try to incite them to break stance: calm, even tempered. Carly's childhood tantrums had never bothered him. To soothe her, he sang nursery rhymes, even past the age when she should have outgrown them. She especially liked "There Was an Old Lady Who Swallowed a Fly," likely because of the sheer number of animals in it. She'd drawn the old lady with all the animals squished inside her massive abdomen. Fly, spider, cat, dog. . .

Even Papi's voice sounded calm, monotone. Like Carly, he could barely carry a tune.

He scratched Oz 11's chin. "I've always enjoyed the theatre." Oz purred audibly. "You don't have to be dramatic in your personal life to be a good thespian."

I tried to picture it, but couldn't. "So what made you stop? When Tatiana died?"

"No," he said. "Actually, it was a great job to have while I was grieving. When you're acting, you can pretend to be someone else. I enjoyed that escape, and I enjoyed teaching my students about it as well." He looked over at his smallest cat, Dufferin, who I'd had to wrangle earlier to deliver drops into her infected left eye. "Did Duffy take her drops okay?" He scooped up the white feline with one hand, pulling her to his neck.

"Yes."

"Anyway, after a while, I wanted to do something more meaningful for Tati. So I quit and went to work at the shelter."

"That's quite a career change." I folded the money in half, and then in half again. "You know who I always thought would be a good actress?"

"Your sister?"

"How'd you guess?"

"Carly has a tendency towards melodrama. But I don't think she's very capable of portraying an emotion she doesn't feel. She's always reminded me of that old adage, wearing your heart on your sleeve."

Carly did not wear her heart on her sleeve so much as smear her heart all over your face.

 When we moved in together in Calgary, Patrick decided we had to spend at least two evenings a week apart in order to maintain a healthy independence. Patrick's rules left me feeling nauseated; I already knew with Patrick that rules changed. Our relationship came with a guidebook to which I was never exactly privy, full of caveats and stipulations.

"Time apart is what's best for us." He said this looking not at me, but into the mirror while examining his eyebrows. He straightened a flaw I couldn't see. "For us individually, *and* as a couple."

He had a point, but he'd bonded quickly to his fellow law students, and I had yet to form very many friendships with the other students in my program. Most were born-and-bred Calgarians, with lots of friends already. No one seemed particularly motivated to form friendships within the program.

The first of these healthy nights apart, Patrick went to meet a fellow law student for drinks, and I perched on the couch, flipping channels. I called Aubrey first, then Carly. On a Saturday night, I had only their voicemails to talk to. Why had I not tried harder, made friends? Why had I moved all the way to Calgary for Patrick?

After he'd been gone half an hour, I took a novel and climbed into bed. It was not quite 8:30. As a kid, I often read myself to sleep, *Sweet Valley Twins* and *The Baby-Sitters Club*, dulled my brain past Carly's tossing and turning and yawning and chirping in the bunk below mine.

Over time, I conditioned myself into drowsiness whenever my eyes met text, which proved problematic when it came to cramming for tests and attempting to comprehend iambic pentameter as an undergrad. I drifted off, too apathetic to take my contacts out.

Kipling leapt up onto the bed, waking me, and began kneading at my yellow blanket. She'd been found without a mother or any siblings. Cats separated from their mothers when they're too tiny will do this, I'd learned from Papi, mimicking the pressing of paws into their mother's swollen belly to expel milk. Right paw, left paw, right paw, left paw. She shut her eyes into squints in rhythmic bliss. Stevie Wonder, playing the piano.

The second night apart, Patrick went to a documentary, by himself. It seemed ridiculous to me; independent movie-theatre viewing was not something someone did when in a happy, committed relationship. We could never agree on movies — on a lot of things, actually. Patrick called mainstream movies cliché, and only ever wanted to go to Calgary's independent theatres. He felt this way about Starbucks, TV commercials, and major chain bookstores.

That morning, during a coffee break, I'd asked a classmate if she wanted to get together that night to study, to keep each other motivated. She told me she had plans with her husband, adding, "It sounds like fun though, maybe next week?"

I borrowed Patrick's too-big University of Toronto sweatshirt and rolled up the sleeves, laced up my running shoes. If it worked for Aubrey. . .

I jogged once around the entire campus, breathing heavily in the dark, finally stopping, gasping for air, bent over, my hands on my thighs, wondering how Aubrey ran every day. I walked home under the slanted streetlights. Cars sped past the intersection of Crowchild Trail and 24th Ave, and I stopped at the crosswalk to wait for the lights to change, watching faces blur by. I didn't want to check my phone for missed calls, sure there would be none. Pathetic. With distance preventing me from taking care of Carly as much as I was used to, my downtime from school gaped in front of me.

In our still-dark apartment, I stripped down to my underwear and threw Patrick's sweatshirt into the laundry hamper.

By November, I could make it all the way around campus and back home without stopping.

& I'd grown up on streets where people walked and paced and shopped and ate, had conversations in different languages, played drums and handed out free samples on corners, swirled in the smells of sunscreen and Thai food and dank sewers. The humidity lifted the hot scents onto the crowded streets. A perpetual block party, a multicultural family reunion.

And then in Calgary — nothing. I walked the streets to campus and back, surprised at their emptiness. When the snow began to fall, shockingly early, and a cold crept up behind my sinuses, I skipped my last class and made a pit stop at the Dairy Queen before going back home to finish an assignment. The man behind the counter had sagging eyes, like a basset hound. He lifted my Blizzard and turned it upside down, the mandatory way to prove the thickness of the ice cream. Me and him: the only two people in the store.

At home, I ate the bits of crushed Oreo cookie from the bottom of the cup, black and gritty in my teeth.

& Of all the things Carly feared as a child — and there were many — church was not one of them. At St. Peter's, with its lurid organ music, its giant stained glass depictions of saints and martyrs clutching their hemorrhaging hearts, she sang sanctimoniously, the syllables to gory lyrics she didn't know blending into gibberish. She shook hands with all the shrivelled raisin ladies and let them kiss her pious little cheeks, telling them, "Peas be with you."

I found Church confusing, found its messages bipolar. God was supposed to be unconditionally loving and benevolent, but the Bible said, "It is easier for a camel to go through the eye of a needle than for a rich person to enter the kingdom of God." The smiling parishioners, singing along with the choir, seemed off-kilter with the actual words coming out of their mouths.

Unless you eat
Of the flesh of the Son of Man
And drink of His blood,
And drink of His blood,
You shall not have life within you

Aubrey attended Catholic school with me because her mother had been baptized as a young girl, and so she had an in. "I'm only here because of the gifted program," Aubrey informed me. "I have to do religion class because the school says I do, but my parents are atheists. That means they think God is just make-believe." Aubrey had assimilated her parents' views about Catholicism, relentlessly questioning religion, questions I had no answers to. "He *rose* from the *dead?* Doesn't that sound a little freaky? Like zombies, Darcy. It's like Zombie Jesus in his loincloth. Dreenk my blooood. Eeeeat my flesh." She walked towards me with her arms outstretched sideways, as though nailed to a cross.

And yet, Aubrey called the church and planned Carly's funeral.

A set of automatic doors and a "Do Not Enter" sign separated baggage claim at Pearson International Airport from where family and friends could wait for arrivals, but Aubrey had ignored the warnings and had a luggage trolley already lined up beside the carousel before our bags started making their way down. The plane ride itself was early morning blurry, Patrick having booked our tickets and arranged everything. But when we landed, there was Aubrey in a red blouse. I felt heavy, saturated like a sponge, and Aubrey's round face and red blouse let something loose inside me, like I was being wrung out. She held me against her. When I pulled away, I'd left wet patches on her blouse, like when Kipling kneaded and suckled on my T-shirt before bed.

Patrick collected our luggage, dragging it off the lazy carousel. I didn't remember packing. On the drive to my mother's, Patrick sat in the back seat with Aubrey and the suitcases.

Mom and Dick still hadn't fixed the water damage on the ceiling, yellow stains like urine. What did it matter? The house smelled like tomatoes; two greasy boxes of pizza gaped open on the kitchen island, but no one had eaten any. My mother looked skinnier than I remembered, and she clenched her arms around me, all bones like a bird. They both had puffy, swollen eyes, my mother and Dick, our stepfather, our stupid, Mack truck of a stepfather, a man's man with a bald potato head, what was he crying for? As though he'd loved Carly. He took a slice of pizza, holding it in his hands without a napkin. Aubrey had a manila folder with her, and she opened it and started reading from it — details for the funeral. My mother excused herself and went upstairs. Dick took the folder from Aubrey. The grease from his fingers left stains on the pages. I'd already turned down the option to go to the funeral home. How many hours had passed since? A day and a night and a day. Not even.

I heard the toilet flush. My mother came back down, her skin jaundiced under the light. She held up her car keys as though she didn't exactly know what they could be.

"Okay, I think we should go," Aubrey said, encouragingly. I felt my hand constrict and looked down. Patrick was squeezing it.

When the garage door began to close behind them, Patrick said, "I think you should eat something."

"I can't," I said. Carly liked her pizza with pineapples and hot peppers, which made her sneeze.

I went downstairs to my old basement room and lay there, on the bed, a spinny, seasick feeling. I took out my phone and dialled Ryan. When he answered, I heard a little girl in the background. A little girl laughing.

&T Carly learned to read late. She struggled through picture book after picture book, labouriously sounding out the words. My teenaged attempts to help her seemed to only frustrate her further. Cross-legged on her bed with a hard-backed Dr. Seuss, she ran her finger limply across the title, "If. . .I. . .r. . . r-an the. . ."

"Circus," I supplied, "S-er-k-uh-s."

"But — " she scrunched up her face, "but S says sss!"

"Right," I said, "But sometimes C says sss, too."

"C says -k-k-k! Like cat."

"Well, yeah, but — " I didn't know how to explain. "Letters sometimes, like — different sounds can — different letters can sometimes make different sounds." I took her hand in mine and ran her finger along the underside of the title, "See, this C says sss and then this one says -k. And then the S here — " I pointed to the word's terminal letter, "this says sss, like the first C. See?"

"But how do you *know*?"

"How do I know what?"

"When C says sss and when S says -k?"

"Well, S doesn't say -k."

She flipped the book over in her lap. "Too hard!"

Shortly after her tenth birthday, I found Dick in the kitchen, the phone cord strung hazardously across the kitchen to where he sloppily scooped leftover mashed potatoes out of a Tupperware container for our dinner, prattling off a voicemail.

" — just letting you know that we're not interested in having Carly do any, you know, learning tests or whatever. We think she's fine. So, um, have a good day."

Usually, I stayed in my room when Dick was home, under the radar, whereas Carly somehow found a way to always be *in* Dick's way. She turned the volume on the stereo too loud. She spilled juice when she tried to pour it. She *needed* to show them something — the dance she'd created, the painting she'd done at school.

Dick would swat at her, tell her to "scat." When she cried, he'd say, "Nobody loves a pussy."

"Why do you care what he thinks?" I'd ask, having been enticed by her crocodile tears into braiding her hair or painting her nails.

"He's our dad," she argued, incorrectly.

His voicemail completed, Dick hung up the phone.

I needed to know. "Tests for what?"

"Oh," he said, casually, untangling his massive chest and stomach from the coils. "The stupid teacher thinks Carly's a retard."

"What?"

"You know, the teacher thinks Carly has some sort of learning problem. Wants her to do a bunch of tests. IQ tests and that kind of shit. I mean, Jesus, if she can't figure it out, they should just make her repeat Grade Five, then she'll wise up. Nothin' gets fixed by giving kids more attention. They're all dipshits at that school." He pinched his nose between his thumb and forefinger and then wiped the snot on the hem of his grey T-shirt.

"Maybe she actually needs help," I argued.

He turned away from me, towards the microwave, its dull drone. "Stay out of it. What are you, her mom?"

& *I need you to stop talking to her.*
It's hurting her too much.
Well, then you have to let her go.
You're killing her.

& Ryan did not go to the funeral. The day before, I threw up violently, once, and then an hour later, again, and then I couldn't stop. Patrick, who'd taken up his old bedroom at his parents' for the week, drove back to my mother's and took me to my old GP, Dr. Martin, who diagnosed me with food poisoning and took some blood, sliding a needle into the fragile skin on the back of my hand when she couldn't find a vein in the crook of my elbow.

"What did you eat?" she wanted to know.

"Nothing," I said, truthfully. I knew better: I was not rotting from the outside in, but rather from the inside out.

Aubrey made me go to the funeral, physically zipping me into one of her dresses, dark grey and with a pink sash that tied in the back. Carly loved pink. The hem hung long around my knees. I felt like a clothes hanger, bones holding up the dress' frame.

The manner of death necessitated a closed casket. Bronzed pink, the coffin clashed with the darker fuchsia roses on top. I thought of Carly, as a toddler, sitting on the kitchen counter, squeezing strawberry syrup into a glass of cold milk. She'd always used too much, ribbons of red confection swirling in with the milk, the colour of Pepto-Bismol. Her smile — the thin line of strawberry on her upper lip.

I had balled her funeral card in my fist without realizing it. I smoothed it out across my lap, across the grey silk of Aubrey's dress.

Carly Michelle Nolan
September 5, 1987 – February 15, 2007

&T Ryan could not — would not? — go back into the apartment. Looking confused, he handed me his keys, the whole set, then said, "I mean," and took them back. He worked the key he still had for Carly's apartment off the ring. He had clumsy hands, and it took a moment. He drummed his fingers against the doorframe, glanced back into the hall, shifted from one foot to the other. His hair looked greasy; he raked his hands through it, and I could tell he'd been doing it all day. His beard had grown longer than I'd seen in the pictures Carly had emailed me, longer than I remembered. He looked shorter, too, leaning up against the wall, as though he'd shrunk without her. But then, I barely knew him. Maybe he'd always been less than Carly made him out to be.

Inside my sister's apartment, I needed to pee. I danced a little, indecisive. Would it disturb the peace? I put my things down — bulky jacket, backpack, cell phone — in a pile in the doorway, and crossed to her bathroom. A drop of blood had dried in her bathtub, the edges frayed as if it had fallen from a distance, long, sticky spider legs. A bloody nose? Menstrual blood? Cut herself shaving? I noticed in one corner of the tub a sleek, purple disposable razor. Cut herself? — *Don't go there.* Under her sink I found a nearly empty bottle of cleaning fluid and paper towels. The stain held stubbornly as I scrubbed at it, and then it lifted, suddenly, the bathtub bare.

I didn't know what to look for. Her computer was still on, the rainbow fractal of her screensaver rotating hypnotically. I shook the mouse and the screen flickered still to her desktop picture, the two of us several years earlier on the ferry out to Toronto Island. I opened a browser for her email, but it prompted me for a password. Five minutes of guessing proved fruitless.

The sun eased lower in the sky, visible from the balcony, orange and blue swirling together like liquid, like a Hawaiian beverage. Carly had always wanted to go to Hawaii, made Ryan swear they'd go for their honeymoon. I crossed the apartment into her bedroom, slid open her jewellery box. It made tinkly music at me, a tiny ballerina twisting around and around, getting dizzy. The box had mostly functioned as a junk drawer; I removed a lone button, a smashed tampon, a receipt, a tag torn from the inside of an item of clothing, a discarded battery. No sign of the necklace Ryan wanted me to retrieve for him, the gift he'd given her for their first anniversary, one teardrop pink Swarovski crystal. Carly had called it her "bling" and wore it even when it clashed with her outfit. It had not been recovered with her personal effects. What had she done with it?

I lay down in her unmade bed for a moment and pulled the crumpled bedding around me. The smell of her made my chest ache, made me climb off. Too much! I took her raccoon off the bed and touched the spots where its fur had worn away. When she was small, Carly took her raccoon to school, twisting and twiddling the pink bow sewn to its head. After enough handling, the bow popped off. She carried her bald baby home to me, crying.

I retied the bow and reattached it with my limited sewing skills.

She held it away from herself, examining it. "It's not the same!"

My best attempts at sewing left visible stitches, uneven lengths of ribbon.

"She's a real girl now," I said, manufacturing a story that might soothe her. "That's how you know. Real people aren't perfect."

&T Carly and I were both born on the fifth of a month, six years and four months apart. 5/5/81 and 9/5/87. She used 9587 as the pin number for her debit card, which I'd told her sucked as a secret code. I tried various combinations of this to access her email, but nothing worked. Neither did "RYAN," nor "RYANCARLY," or any combination of their two names. I tried my own name, feeling hot with shame. It didn't work, either. At least I knew the PIN code to her savings account.

In her bank account, Carly left a grand total of $13.84. She had outstanding student loans totaling $32,480.79, and unpaid bills for her cable TV and internet ($74.32), hydro ($63.16) and cell phone (a shocking $698.47, with almost half those calls to Ryan's number, and the other half, long distance to mine). On the last day of her life, she'd left a single voicemail when Ryan failed to answer her last call at 8:01 AM, and then typed out that one last text message to me, shortly after 9:00 Toronto time.

Always blur.

Had she left any last words for Ryan during that call?

Not really, he told me. Just a few seconds of silent lingering, followed by the sound of her hanging up. I'd wanted to listen to it, to see if I could hear her breathing, but Ryan had deleted it before he knew what she'd done.

Did he know what her text message meant?

No, he said, she'd never said anything like that to him.

&T My sixth grade class loved Phys Ed, particularly so because one of their gym periods fell on a Friday afternoon.

I could feel their restlessness by the end of the week as they shifted in their desks, dropped pencils, doodled in the margins of their notebooks, tapped each other, passed notes, giggled, and requested bathroom breaks more frequently. The auspiciousness of the scheduling meant that they could release this energy, shift contentedly into weekend mode a few hours earlier. They loved Phys Ed, too, because of the teacher, Conor Fehr, who had modified the rules of regular dodgeball into something rowdy and complicated that I could not follow, but which had made him a legend at St. Sebastian.

The previous year, he'd taught my students Health and the Catholic school equivalent of Sex Ed: instructions on the signs of puberty and lectures on saving oneself for marriage. I'd applied to both the Catholic and Public school boards, surprised that my mother actually located my baptismal certificate after a week of my nagging. It was hard enough to get a teaching job right out of university, but at least I had twice as many jobs as my secular classmates. When I was offered a position at the Catholic board, I warned Patrick that I'd have to attend church sometimes, and that we'd have to keep the fact that we lived together a secret.

"A job is a job," he said. "I hate my job, too."

Not quite the same thing.

I often stayed after the bell on Fridays to help put away the gym equipment, to chat, to do something other than go home. Conor thought it was possible to teach me how to shoot a layup. He was blond, with a receding hairline, despite being in his early thirties. He had wide linebacker shoulders and broad hands that seemed to suck the ball from the floor into his palm. Conor dribbled for a moment, casually, before tossing it to me. It hit the lacquered gym floor near me and rebounded away. We both watched it for a moment before he loped after it. He wore his University of Calgary T-shirts inside out on purpose, the logo faintly visible through the cotton. Several of my students had started wearing their gym strip shirts inside out in imitation. Patrick would not be caught dead in a U of C T-shirt, even inside out, still bitter that the only law school that had made him an offer was his last choice. When I'd told Aubrey where I had gotten in, she'd said, "There's a university in Calgary?"

"I don't think I'll die if I can't shoot hoops." My voice echoed in the empty gymnasium. Conor lobbed the ball at me again, one-handed, and I caught it against my chest with both hands.

"Better," he said. I bounced it back at him, first against the floor.

"Let's pack it in and get coffee," I suggested. "Or a martini. I could use a bit of a buzz."

"I would, but I have to go renew my driver's license. I went to buy wine the other day and the clerk pointed out it's already three months overdue. If I get pulled over, I'm screwed." He faked a pass at me, then rose up on the balls of his feet and let the ball loose, sinking a basket.

The ball hit the floor and rolled in my direction. I picked it up, held onto it. "Want company?"

He gestured for me to pass to him, smiled as though I'd just said something funny. "I won't make you come stand in line with me. I'm not that cruel."

Later that fall, Conor's car crapped out, and I offered him a ride home. Not only had my students taken a liking to him that year, but so had the single mother of one of my boys. "She actually asked me whether you were single," I teased, turning on the windshield wipers.

Conor removed his gloves and held his hands towards the hot air. "What'd you tell her?"

"I said I didn't know. I mean, *are* you single?" Conor didn't wear a ring. Sometimes, he arrived at school wearing mismatched socks. No girlfriend would let that happen, at least not more than once.

Conor rubbed his hands together. "I am. And I don't know why I'm telling you this, because really, we don't know each other that well, but I feel like I can trust you."

"Why you're telling me you're single?"

"Why I'm telling you I'm gay."

Being a teacher at a Catholic elementary school in Calgary necessitated his secret. He was right — we didn't know each other that well — but maybe he told me because on some level he realized I, too, had secrets. Patrick hadn't kissed me in three weeks.

& Andrew O'Leary, the other male teacher at St. Sebastian, taught the sixth grade class opposite mine. Mr. O, the one kids hoped to get. He kept sour gumballs in large jars on a rack above his desk and doled them out as rewards for correct answers in a trivia-style game with which he concluded each day. Just the look of those gumballs — pinks and yellows and blues like fluorescent Timbits — made my jaws ache.

Conor suggested Andrew's basement suite to me as an option after Patrick and I broke up. Patrick vacated our apartment as a courtesy for a few days to stay at a hotel. He got custody of the apartment on a technicality: our suite manager was friends with his uncle. However distantly removed, I didn't want to stay, even though I didn't want to live in Andrew's basement either. I packed my things the first night, using garbage bags for my clothes when I ran out of boxes, and then stood, surveying my packaged life in *his* hallway. Around one AM, I needed sleep, but didn't want to be near our bed. I took a set of extra sheets out of the closet and made up the futon. Kipling, in solidarity, slept at my feet.

The basement suite had remained vacant since its previous owner, a woman about my age, in recovery from breast cancer, had moved to Edmonton.

"What is this place?" I asked Andrew, trying to sound flippant. "A basement catch-all for damaged goods?"

He hoisted one of the garbage bags I'd used to gather my belongings over his shoulder. "Nice pack job, Darce."

The first night in the ugly, 600-square-foot basement hole, I allowed myself one long, unfastened cry, obscured by the noise of my stereo. Afterwards, I drank a tall mug of black tea and spread Vaseline on the dark bruises under my eyes.

In bed, I pressed the tea bags to my skin, caffeine to shrink the blood vessels, wet against my raw eyes and cheekbones, attempting to read at the same time. The bags fell off my face, cold and damp against my fingers as I repositioned them.

When I put the book down, my fingers had stained the pages, the evidence wizened and brown, permanent.

& After the funeral, I had only one week to get Carly's things out of her place, to take what I wanted. Her landlord wanted the apartment on the market again on the first of the month. I didn't want to pack up my sister's possessions, but Aubrey told me she would tackle the bathroom and then left me alone to handle the disastrously cluttered living room. I didn't know where to start. Aubrey thought this was a possible feat.

When we moved into the rental house with Dick the Dickhead, Carly and I got our own rooms for the first time. My basement room had pale, neutral walls, a colour so faded I could not guess at its exact shade. Off-white? Peach? Carly's room upstairs was painted carnation pink, with a butterfly border that ran across the entire midline of the room. I wondered about the previous owner of the room, somebody's very wanted baby, perhaps a much longed for girly-girl after a series of older brothers. Carly loved the butterflies and set to naming them all, her butterfly friends, frozen in flutter, trapped in their eight-inch border, unable to fly away.

Downstairs in my drab basement room, I unpacked just my bare necessities at first, as though perhaps our new living arrangements were temporary. The large window behind me caught me off-guard every time I turned around, the bisected earth: a slice of ground, a slice of blue sky. I stood at the window, eye-level with the grass. I could see each blade, the flecks of dirt, the fallen leaves. I'd spent a long time on the top bunk of the top floor of our apartment building. It was a long way down.

Always blur. Always blur. Always blur.

Not even a sentence, my sister's last message to me. She'd called words or phrases that didn't make sense to her "jibber jabber."

I started with her desk, crammed with stacks of loose-leaf pages, scribbled notes, handouts, bills. In the living room I began a mindless sorting, separating homework from invoices, from art projects, from forms for George Brown, from magazines. Her friends had chipped in and ordered her a subscription to *Cosmopolitan* for her last birthday. "How many new sexual positions can they invent?" I'd asked her the first summer after moving to Calgary, about a month before she met Ryan. We'd been wandering the Toronto Public Library, and when I went to find her again, my arms full of Joyce Carol Oates and Wally Lamb, I found her poring over the glossy publication, an article on how to detect when a man might propose. She was still over a year away from being legal to vote.

She smirked. "What, you don't think Patrick would be impressed with the Joystick Joyride?"

I'd cringed. My baby sister!

There'd been two before Ryan. The first, Jensen, she'd met after joining the yearbook committee. She'd played romantic, idealistic love ballads on repeat, singing along, hideously off-key. She pierced her belly button and began wearing strategically short T-shirts when our mother wasn't around. She repeated his jokes to me, giggling excessively, almost as though he was present. "So, two midgets take a trip to Las Vegas. . .and they see these two, like, strippers. . ." After two or three of these jokes, I'd cut her off.

"Don't you think those jokes are a little offensive?"

She rolled her eyes. "You're such a prude." The wound around her belly button barbell looked infected.

Jensen invited her over one evening, and she couldn't help bubbling about it to me on the phone. "The whole yearbook committee gets to go, but I think he really wants me to come. He kinda flirts with me non-stop. I'm so excited. Were you like this when you first met Patrick?"

A few days later, she called and confessed they'd played strip poker at Jensen's house, and later, she'd let him remove the last items of her clothing once everybody else had left. She was fifteen. It was her first time, but not his. "Was it supposed to feel so — ?" Unable to find words.

The next time she talked about him, she tried to explain. "He says he has baggage from his ex. He doesn't know what he wants right now. He can't be in a relationship. He wants space." It's not you, it's me.

The second, she hadn't even pined for. She just met him at some random birthday party near the end of Grade Eleven. He lived in another province and had flown in for the weekend just to visit his cousin. She'd slept with him that night. She wouldn't even tell me his name.

The heedlessness of it made sense for Carly, but I'd felt a merry-go-round spin in my stomach when she told me. I'd come home for a weekend to visit and she confessed that it had happened six weeks prior. I scheduled a doctor's appointment for her, gave her a few packs of birth control from my own supply, bought her a box of condoms, tore the box open, and popped two in a side pocket of her purse. She seemed more distressed by having a pap smear than having an unprotected one-night stand. Afterwards, we went for coffee, and she'd stirred her hot chocolate noisily, her spoon clinking against the glass, fidgeting in her chair. I closed my eyes for a second. I wanted to stay that way. To fall asleep, right there. The coffee shop, the steam from my mug, smelled like our mother.

Ryan came along, just before she started Grade Twelve. He was one year older, already out working, trying to save money for college, trying to move out of his grandparents' place and be on his own. In her mess of papers, I found a birthday card signed with Ryan's all-capitals scrawl, HAPPY BIRTHDAY BEAUTIFUL! I put the card in its own pile. It sat there, a small rectangle on the floor, alone next to the chaos of the pile beside it.

& Jessa Ryce, Ryan's ex-girlfriend, had been a pageant girl. When Carly told me this, I'd said, "They *have* pageants in Toronto?"

"I guess. You should *see* this girl, Darce, she kinda looks like Barbie."

"Plastic?"

"*Perfect*. I look like a total heifer compared to this girl."

I balanced the phone between my shoulder and my ear, trying to twist my hair into some semblance of a bun, running late for work.

"How do you even know what she looks like? And why do you even care, Carly? Ryan loves you."

"Because!" I could picture her pouting on the other end. "Because she keeps phoning. She left her name on our answering machine and I looked her up in Ryan's yearbook. Listen, Jessa Marie Ryce. Grade: Ten. Activities: Dancing, Pageants — "

I interrupted her. "She sounds pretty dumb."

"You didn't let me finish," she said. "Activities: Dancing, Pageants, Debate Team, History Club. She's gorgeous *and* smart. I'm a cow who may not even pass English. School to me is all jibber-jabber." I'd once tried to explain to her the possibility that she had a learning disability. "That's just a nice way of saying I'm stupid," she'd countered.

"Don't compare yourself to Jessa! Anyway, that's not the point. You shouldn't snoop through Ryan's stuff. He hasn't called her back, so obviously he's not pining over her. If you're worried about it, talk to him."

"The thing is, she's only in his Grade Ten yearbook, not Grade Eleven or Twelve. Do you think they broke up because she moved away?"

"Listen!" I said, "They were fifteen! Nobody stays together at fifteen. He's with you now. You have to let this go!"

She did not let it go. A week later, she was at home alone making dinner. The pasta sauce had bubbled over and spilled chunky tomato onion onto the burner, sending the smoke alarm into a frenzy. She'd clambered up on a chair and taken the battery out to get it to shut up. The apartment clouded over. She'd opened the balcony door to let the smoke out. The phone rang.

When she told me this story, her teary blubbering made it so that I couldn't understand the words. I had to make her repeat it a few times.

"And, and so I answered, and she was like, I'm looking for Ryan Angeli, and I was like, who is this? And she wouldn't tell me, but of course I knew who it was, so I was like, *I want you to stop phoning my boyfriend.* And she was all, *I don't want your boyfriend, I just want to tell him he has a daughter.*"

&⟩ Valentine's Day fell on the Wednesday after I'd told Ryan to stop answering my sister's calls. Carly had a class on Monday, Wednesday, and Friday mornings. When I phoned her on my drive in to work, she answered, breathless and jovial.

"Hey, sis! I'm actually just heading into class, can I call you after? I have good news."

I slowed for a red light.

"Ryan phoned," I said. It came out as a statement, a fact. I squeezed the wheel, my cell phone pinned between my ear and my shoulder. The car slid forward, just slightly, with the loss of traction.

"Nah. But he will. I mean, it's Valentine's Day. I know we're kinda broken up, *technically*, but he wouldn't — he hasn't called me back for a while, but I mean, it's Valentine's Day, and, well, anyway, whatever. I can't really talk. How about I call you at lunch?"

I agreed, the thought occurring to me that I'd left my lunch — leftover Hawaiian pizza from the previous night's dinner — sitting on the counter, slowly warming in a Ziploc bag. I wondered whether Kipling would gnaw her way through it. The light wouldn't change. I sat, gripping the wheel, my stomach warming sour.

&⟩ Papi died the day before Patrick and I were to celebrate our first anniversary. I found out when his niece Frances called. Papi kept his phone numbers on sticky notes on the wall by the phone, but he refused to rely on the single side of adhesive to get them to stay, taping down all sides with scotch tape in neat little squares. He had several numbers for me, as I'd changed apartments or cell phones, each crossed out and rewritten in his shaky hand against the grooves of the tiled backsplash.

He died in his sleep. A nurse, who had been coming to check on him and help administer his insulin shots, found him. I hadn't even known that he'd hired a nurse, or that he'd been diagnosed diabetic. I pictured him in his faded blue striped pyjamas, of which he owned four pairs. I pinched my jaw shut on the subway over, breathed through my nose to keep from crying. My eyes stung, holding the tears back. Frances told me that she'd given the landlord at Papi's building — my old building — permission to let me into Papi's apartment, in case I wanted any keepsakes. Her voice on the phone unnerved me, the voice I'd never heard before, behind all the birthday cards written in calligraphy with chocolate loonies hiding in the envelopes, the shiny ribbons and crunchy wrapping paper.

I called Carly and asked her to take the subway to Papi's apartment after school, but went in first myself, bringing a small empty backpack, not even sure what I wanted to take. I lay on the couch with his rough orange blanket that felt like cuddling carpet.

I tried to picture him, dreaming about his beautiful twenty-five-year-old wife, her picture at his bedside, and then the two of them, reunited, no space in-between. Over time, the cats had reduced in number to a lone, scrawny kitten. Papi's apartment seemed bare without the cats, the way a room feels with the furniture gone, a bare square of floor where a bookshelf should be, a TV stand, a beloved recliner.

"Don't worry, the kitten had plenty of food," Frances told me, and I wondered if Papi had known, if he'd had a feeling. Keeping others safe, as usual. "She's at the neighbours, but they can only keep her for a couple of days. I think someone from the shelter will come take her back." I'd never met the kitten before; he'd acquired her over Christmas, during my final exams. I'd talked to him, but hadn't visited for several months. My stomach turned inside out.

I called Patrick.

"How does dinner in Little Italy sound?" he asked, before saying hello, recognizing my name on the display.

"My grandfather died," I said, flatly. His sentence and mine hung there, for a moment, awkwardly juxtaposed.

"I thought all your grandparents died a long time ago."

"Well, yeah. Not my real grandfather. My Papi. My adopted grandfather."

He paused. "The guy who used to babysit you and Carly?"

"Yeah."

"I didn't know you were still close."

I pulled the blanket up to my face and didn't answer.

"Darce? You still there?"

"Will you come with me? To the funeral?"

"To his. . ."

"It's going to be in Sudbury where his wife is buried."

He paused, again, "Oh, Darce, I dunno, I think. . .to take the whole day and go up to Sudbury. . .and I've barely met your mom and stepdad. And you haven't even really been that close with him, lately, right? You'll be okay without me. We can meet up afterwards."

"You didn't even ask when it was," I said.

"When is it?"

"You don't care." My voice, not unlike Frances', sounded unfamiliar. Patrick and I had not yet had a significant fight. I hung up. I got up off the couch and studied the Matryoshka dolls on the counter. My phone rang. I ignored the ringing, slowly unscrewing the dolls into halves, one by one, until the noise stopped. In the dolls' bellies were the mismatched babies from the day I'd been home sick and switched them. In all those years, no one had ever checked.

I put the tiny wooden infants back in their correct places and put the dolls back together, meticulously lining up all the patterns. Each, I tucked in the bottom of my backpack, their wooden bodies knocking up against one another, and zipped them away, into the dark.

Then I went next door and knocked.

&T Ryan often teased Carly, telling her she was the only nineteen-year-old he knew who didn't drink. Despite her weakness for anything sugary, Carly refused to drink, saying, "My body is a temple." A temple? So then why did she think fries and a milkshake during a break from work sufficed as dinner three nights in a row? When I started running, she teased, "Why run, unless a bear is chasing you?" I wondered whether the smell of alcohol reminded her of Dick's vodka B.O. Whatever the reason, I didn't argue. I didn't want alcohol on top of everything Carly already brought to the table.

She argued the temple thing about medication, too. When sick — and she often claimed to feel sick — she did not like to take meds, unless they came backed by a legitimate prescription. While I was known to pop DayQuil every four to six hours during a cold to make it through the school day, Carly preferred to call in sick, to miss class, to wheedle Ryan into buying her wonton soup and red-white-and-blue popsicles, the kind we'd suckled on when we were little, to make it through the humid Toronto summer months.

All three of us got sick often — Carly, my mother, and me. Illness seemed to run in the family. I remember my mother, sick and pregnant with Carly. I remember trying to scramble into bed with her, curling around her massive belly.

"Stay away from me," she warned. "You're going to get sick. Go play with your dad."

She pulled the blankets around herself, despite the late summer humidity. She smelled of sweat, and had forgotten that my father had gone out. I spent the morning playing ponies. During her pregnancy, my mother often pointed out that soon I would have a playmate. I stashed my ponies on the highest shelf in my closet, where no baby could reach.

Mom gestured me out of the room. Irritated, I wandered into

the bathroom. One of her lipsticks lay open on the counter, the lid popped off. I twisted the bottom and smeared the tube across my lips, dark red. I smacked my lips together. It tasted kind of gross. I wiped it off across the back of my hand.

My parents' toothbrushes sat side by side in a glass, their bristles rubbing up against each other, kissing. I pulled them apart, made them face the other way.

The next morning, when I woke up hot and nauseated and about to start a week of day camp, my mother felt my forehead with the back of her hand. Still sick, she couldn't feel my fever.

"I'm okay," I said, "Cross my heart."

Later, after a game of freeze tag at the park, supervised by two teenagers in matching bright red CAMP SPADINA! T-shirts, I slipped behind a tree and threw up. My mouth tasted like breakfast, backwards. No one noticed.

& And so, Ryan's history spilled out, like spaghetti sauce bubbling over the pan, sticky and scorched, smoke rising from the burner.

Jessa Ryce, as it turned out, moved away because she'd been pregnant. Her parents had packed up and packed her up, and moved to Kingston, 244 kilometres from Toronto.

She'd delivered their daughter, Autumn, without ever telling Ryan. Autumn Ryce. It sounded like a Thanksgiving recipe. I didn't voice this opinion, though. I could barely think it over the sound of Carly's sobs. The very energy of the conversation drained me, even over the phone. Ryan had to work a late shift; when Carly finally conceded to going to sleep, I went to my own bed and lay there, my eyes open, my body humming. I got up and laced my running shoes, slid my mittens inside the sleeves of my hooded sweatshirt. I wanted to feel the cold. Novocaine for my nerves.

&⌐ Conor obsessed over the Calgary Flames and still ranted about how they'd been robbed in the 2004 Stanley Cup playoffs when, in the final game against Tampa Bay, their final goal during double overtime didn't count. Patrick and I had lived in Calgary for eight months, and though I had no interest in hockey, I watched the game with some classmates on a big-screen TV, squeezed into a booth at Bob the Fish. Despite being a new Calgarian, I found myself actually watching, cheering when the Flames slapped the puck into the net. Like everyone else in the tavern, I believed the Flames would bring home the coveted trophy. Patrick stayed at home studying, accusing me of being a "follower." I took a cab home after the anticlimactic night, and Patrick pulled away when I tried to kiss him, saying I smelled like booze, and to go brush my teeth.

Happy for a day of warm weather in March, Conor, Andrew and I elected to eat lunch outside. Conor leaned against the trunk of a large tree, his mouth full of ham sandwich. "I just think the Flames were robbed. I mean — "

"Look, Man." Andrew noisily slurped reheated chili from a Ziploc container. "The Flames are like my last girlfriend. Every season, they put on a little show, do well in the first couple of games, pretend like they're going to do something, and then, as soon as you get close, bam! They freeze up. It's hopeless; they're never going to put out. Speaking of. . .I got tickets to this singles event tonight down at the Hyatt. You want to come? Come on, dude, singles event. . .desperate women. . ."

&⌐ I do not know quite when my father left us; I could not narrow it down to a day, an argument, a specific memory. I knew with certainty only when the framed picture in our parents' bedroom, two identical girls with heavy bangs and corduroy dresses, went missing from its place on the wall. I was seven, and Carly was just about a year old.

Mom said we girls needed a pyjama party — which became a seemingly endless string of days and nights in itchy pyjamas in Mom and Dad's lumpy bed, the sheets sweaty and sticky and smelly like Carly's hot diapers. And through it all, Mom slept. I stared at the blank spot on the wall, at the patch of paint cleaner than the rest, the way I'd often stared at the two girls. Identical bodies, but asymmetrical expressions. The girl on the left appeared somber, almost bored; her mirror image sister had the faintest smile.

Our father had been a twin, too, but the other twin arrived stillborn. Their names were written in the family Bible my father left behind. *Dell Edward Nolan. Date of Birth: April 12, 1955. Max Jonathan Nolan. Date of Birth: April 12, 1955. Date of death, April 12, 1955. Stillborn.* The picture of the two little girls, he took. The family Bible, he left.

The corduroy twins didn't look at all like the postured family photos of Carly and me in matching outfits, grinning at the camera, my hair twisted into neat French braids, Carly's yellow-blonde tufts tied off with ribbons. Mom took the few blurry shots herself.

The photo of the twins seemed impulsive, the snap and flash too soon, before both girls had a chance to pose, to say cheese.

My father told me stories about the photograph. "Do you know what the lady who took this picture said? She said, 'A photograph is a secret about a secret.'" I couldn't remember his face, but I remembered those words.

Missing secrets — how I knew my father didn't live with us anymore.

The itch of the pyjamas, the empty square.

& In undergrad, while others studied at the library, I carried my heavy knapsack and laptop south on St. George Street, past the construction site for the new graduate student residence, to the U of T gym. Sometimes, before important exams, I had to turn my phone off so that I wouldn't get distracted by Carly's incessant calls. I told her the gym didn't get good reception. High in the bleachers of the pool, I read my textbooks and made dutiful notes to the soundtrack of splashing and whistles, the hoots and cheers, the raucous gossip of college athletes, their wet hair pulled into sloppy ponytails and tucked beneath swim caps. It lulled me: the noise, the chlorine.

& I met Patrick in an art history class, the only class that fulfilled my fine arts requirement and fit my timetable. Aubrey and I rushed in late, having gone first to pick up cinnamon buns. My period had come that morning while I slept, a day early and heavier than normal, soaking through my pyjama bottoms. I'd tossed my sheets into a bathtub of cold water and tied my hair into a loose ponytail, gagging down two aspirin. I'd donned two pairs of underwear, a trick of Carly's, whose menstrual cycle came at different times each month, always irregular. My fingers, sticky with icing, left sugary smears on my jeans when I tried to brush them off.

Aubrey and I slunk into the lecture theatre. Two seats sat available in the back row, on opposite sides of a boy, who smiled at us but did not make the effort to move, perhaps because the lecture had already started. We reluctantly took the seats, reaching across him to pass the cinnamon buns and napkins. Not the kind of day to be sitting next to someone so attractive. He had dark hair, a little on the long side, and wiry glasses. Despite the cold weather, which had produced a sort of rainsnow, he wore only a grey T-shirt, with words in a contorted font that I couldn't read without making it obvious that I wanted to look at him.

The professor droned on, reviewing the assignment he'd just handed out. The boy in between us slid his towards me, diagonally on his desk, so that I could look on. *Select a piece of artwork that has special meaning to you and research its origins and significance.*

When class ended, Patrick introduced himself, offered to accompany us to the photocopier and make copies of the handout. I rooted in my wallet for dimes.

"I think I'm going to do Katsushika Hokusai," Aubrey commented.

Patrick asked, "Who?"

"My parents have a really giant painting of his hanging in our living room."

I remembered the painting — a giant wave poised, about to crash, its white foam edges spiky, like claws. The Satos also kept a hardcover book of Hokusai's art among the other books on their shelves. At age ten, Aubrey had pulled me into her bedroom and flipped the pages open. "Look!" Among the paintings of waves and mountains was the depiction of a two-headed octopus performing oral sex on a naked Japanese woman. One of the octopus' tentacles snaked around her left nipple.

I looked away, burning. "Aubrey! That's bad. We're not supposed to look at stuff like that!"

"I dunno," Aubrey said. "She looks like she likes it."

The light slid across the photocopier.

"At least your parents kept art in the house," Patrick commented. "My parents were about as artistic as a paint-by-numbers. Unless you count Anne Geddes. Maybe I'll research the famous piece, *Baby Losing Its Dignity.*"

Aubrey laughed, "You should."

"Nah," Patrick said, "I'll probably do Monet."

"Really?" Aubrey scrunched up her face. "Don't do Monet. That's so *traditional*."

Patrick shrugged, "I'm a traditional guy. I take a multivitamin, I've read *Crime and Punishment*, I get my hair cut once a month, I like dogs more than cats, I drink red wine, and I can't cook particularly well, though I do make a mean mashed potato."

That evening, I typed "Twins + Famous + Photograph" into my search engine, and there they were, looking at me, doubly exposed.

&   After our fight, I didn't talk to Patrick until after Papi's funeral. A four-day record. I drove the four and a half hours back from Sudbury in a little rented Toyota without stopping, despite a growing urge to pee. Carly slept in the back for three hours, across the seat like an infant, with her bum in the air. Our mother had elected not to make the trip, saying she couldn't get the time off work. "Plus," she'd added, "I haven't talked to Elliot in years. If you want to go, you go, but don't try to guilt me into it." I hung up.

When Carly finally roused, she had the seat pattern indented on her left flushed cheek. "I have *so* much homework to do!" she moaned. "The Cold War is complete jibber-jabber, I don't understand it! You're going to edit my essay when I'm done with it, right?"

"Sure. Email it to me."

By "edit," we both knew, she meant "rewrite the majority." Whatever it took to get her to pass.

After dropping her off, I doubled back to the rental lot. I parked the car and dropped the keys in the after-hour box before realizing I should have prearranged a cab. In the rain, I sprinted to the nearest convenient store and dialled my cell phone with wet hands. Back home, I slept fitfully, dreaming of Papi, sick and trying to care for an apartment full of cats.

The next day, after catching up on my errands and feeling renewed, I emailed Patrick, simply, *I'm back.*

He replied minutes later while I was buttering toast, *I missed you.*

I dialled his number.

"I'm coming over," he said.

"I guess," I said, trying to make it sound like a concession.

When he came over, he hugged me longer than usual, smelling my hair. When he pulled away, he said, "What's that?"

Kipling lay stretched across the top of my futon, her ears alert. She'd spent the first two hours in my apartment exploring each corner and crevice, sniffing out the dust under the radiator, working her way inside the box-spring of my mattress to find a cave. More confident now, she sniffed the air, sensing this new person.

"That's Kipling."

Perhaps knowing she'd be his last kitten, Papi had named her after the subway station farthest West, the one closest to Pearson International Airport. The shelter had been glad to let me take her after Papi's funeral. My roommate for one day, she'd already destroyed my Ikea lampshade.

"Whose is she?"

"Mine."

As Patrick approached, Kipling ducked off the futon and skittered underneath it, just white whiskers and the tip of her nose visible.

"Okay. . ."

"She belonged to my Papi. I'm keeping her. It's what he would have wanted."

Patrick watched her scuttle out from under the couch and dart around the corner into my bedroom. "She's cute. You hungry?"

"Sure."

He made pancakes, telling me he'd been craving breakfast.

He attempted one in the shape of a D, but, overzealous with the batter, it ran together, as did the heart he attempted next. He put them and a plate in the oven on low to keep warm. I kept waiting for him to ask about the funeral, about Papi. Instead, he took the remaining eggs from the carton and scrambled them in the pan, the way I liked them, with pepper, without milk.

"I missed you," he said, as he had in his email, now with a mouthful of eggs. "I'm sorry your grandpa-guy died."

    After I moved out of Patrick's place and into Andrew's basement suite, Andrew and I began carpooling to work. We'd driven in together a few times when Conor pulled into his parking stall at the same time as Andrew, just a few spaces down.

"You probably don't want to let admin know you live with Andrew," Conor pointed out when I went over to say hello. He struggled to pull a mesh bag filled with basketballs from the bowels of his messy backseat. "In case they think there's something more going on."

"Like what?"

"Like living in sin — and with a co-worker!" He reached deep into the car again to retrieve a set of multicoloured hula hoops. "Just be careful. I don't want either of us to get canned."

"They never found out that I lived with Patrick," I reminded him. "And you're the one who came up with the idea that I take the basement suite, anyway."

He cocked his head. "I thought it would be temporary."

Temporary. But, a year later, we stood outside by the school's front entrance on the last day before Christmas break, watching the kids depart for vacation. Conor lifted a mound of snow with his bare hands and began packing it together.

"So, are you going to get a place of your own one of these days?"

"I'll look for a place when I get back from Toronto. Seriously, how can you do that? I'm freezing over here." The dry cold settled in my bones, making me sleepy.

"I'm Calgary born and bred," he reminded me, "I'm like a seal. I have a giant layer of fat under my skin." He was big, but it was all muscle.

"I don't think I'll ever acclimatize."

"Poor, weak Easterner." Conor's gaze tightened, and he shouted "Hey, Rachel!" across the playground.

The student looked up, a second-grader I vaguely recognized, with dark pigtails tucked under a striped knit toque. She held the hand of an older man in a puffy ski parka and a black baseball cap who had her backpack slung over his left shoulder.

"Gimme a sec," Conor said, and jogged over to them. I lifted my chapped hands to my face and blew on them, then shoved them into my pockets. Conor exchanged a few words with the man, then waved over Rachel's teacher.

"Merry Christmas, Ms. Nolan!"

Momentarily distracted, I turned to the grinning face of sixth-grader Katie Ross.

"Merry Christmas! Have a good break, okay?"

"You too!" She smiled again and then skipped towards the entrance.

"What was that about?" I asked, when Conor returned.

"Oh, I just freaked out a little bit. That kid, Rachel, her parents are in a giant custody battle and I didn't recognize that guy."

St. Sebastian policy dictated that children were only supposed to leave with a parent or a caregiver listed on file at the main desk.

"So who is he?" I asked.

"Her uncle. Her mom called the school this morning and let them know he'd be picking her up. Her teacher was in the know. I just wanted to double check."

"When we were kids, our school just let us leave with anybody. My sister and I walked home by ourselves, until my mom got us a babysitter, this man who lived in our building, and he just started coming to pick us up and no one questioned it. Two girls going home with an old guy nobody knew."

"Yeah, my brother and I walked home alone, too, right through a ravine. Easy target for kidnappers."

"Actually, when I was a kid, there was a kidnapping right near my school."

He raised his eyebrows. "No kidding? Scary shit."

"Hey, watch your mouth," I joked, gesturing to the kids running past us, happy and eager for the extended break.

It had started snowing again, just faintly, reminding me of summertime in Toronto, when the air was so heavy and humid you couldn't even feel the rain at first. You saw it before you felt it, the freckled sidewalks in front of you.

"Do you think you would have freaked out if Rachel was leaving with a *woman* you didn't recognize?" I asked.

Conor seemed to consider it. "Maybe." He glanced back at Rachel's uncle, now helping her into his minivan. "Why?"

"People always see men and little girls and think pedophile. But our babysitter — we called him Papi — he was like, my beloved grandpa. He was the one functional grown-up in my life."

Rachel's uncle's car pulled away from the curb.

"I guess," Conor mused. "I mean, anyone can be dangerous." He smiled. "You, in particular, are a total creep. I wouldn't trust my kid with you."

I rolled my eyes, too cold to be amused.

& This is how I imagined it happened.
Stefany lay on her back in the grass in the dark. The sun hung low and slimy in the sky, its runny yolk spilling out across

the horizon. Stefany had tried to get Kristen to play outside with her, but Kris had been painting her nails and had squealed at Stefany to get out. Their mother had permitted Stefany to play outside by herself but only as far as the little island of land right beside the apartment. A balmy breeze dawdled across her face. She thought she could smell a late dinner stewing from the open window of one of the ground floor apartments nearby. The scents danced across to where she lay on the island, warm tomatoes and beans, yeasty bread with garlic.

Outside, she didn't have to be Stefany Beale, who, earlier in the day got her math test back — a first C. She imagined herself tingling and dissolving, re-emerging, a butterfly. She spread her arms out, fluttering her wings. For her fifth birthday, she and her mom and her sister went out to Toronto Island and Stefany and Kristen tried to catch butterflies in the palms of their hands. Stefany came close to one that had settled feather light on the lip of a leaf. But then, she'd come too close, and it flickered away, sparkling pink and purple into the sky. Kristen ran fearless into a flock of fat pigeons.

Stefany waved her arms and legs, making snow angels in the grass. A couple strolled out of the church next door, laughing and talking, and spilled into a nearby car, taking their clamour with them. Stefany lay still, her wings spread and bright, waiting.

And then, the hand closed over her mouth.

"Stefany!" She heard the noise in the distance, a mother on a balcony, calling her daughter home. She fought against the pressure — a butterfly screaming.

"Stefany!" Her mother called again, the word carrying slight annoyance. Stefany heard her own name as a man pulled her to her feet. Instantly she felt tired, her body shutting down, cocooned.

She could smell him, strong, like mouthwash.

She knew, then. She was already gone.

&T While I kept my boyfriends away from our mother and Dick, Carly started bringing Ryan over to the house, which I understood likely made being there more bearable. When I called and asked for Carly, Mom told me she and Ryan were hanging out in her room.

"You let the two of them be alone together in her bedroom?"

"You worry about everything," she retorted. "They're just kids. It's puppy love."

Puppy love. I'd grown up around animals, felines weaving in and out between my scrawny legs, rubbing their chins and foreheads against my shins and the furniture, their deep contented vibration a motor, propelling them to love and lick and be loyal. Puppy love — exactly what she needed.

&T When Carly turned three, she became old enough for Sunday School at St. Peter's, so we went together, Carly with the little kids, me with the eight-to-tens. I asked to go because my Grade Four teacher, Mrs. Reiner, volunteered as the Sunday School teacher, and a couple of my classmates went every week. Mrs. Reiner had a picture of her two little boys on her desk at school sitting on Santa's lap. I wondered what kind of presents they had under the tree. I imagined Mrs. Reiner was the kind of mother who baked gingerbread men and read *Love You Forever*. The previous Christmas, Carly and I received matching baby dolls. What did I need a doll for? I already had a baby sister. At least my doll didn't cry. When Carly tantrumed her way through the terrible twos, my mother closed her in the closet and told her to come out when she stopped crying. Being trapped in the dark only intensified Carly's screams. Years later, she claimed claustrophobia.

The same gift as my whiny little sister. I'd written out our lists for Santa: a Barbie for Carly and a Nintendo for me. Mom eyed the letters and took a large bite of her tuna fish sandwich.

"Barbie's a slut," she told Carly. I could see the chewed fish as she talked. "Why don't you just ask for a boob job for Christmas?" But she let Carly keep the hand-me-down Barbies Aubrey passed our way, never one to pass up a freebie.

After Mass ended, I'd drag Carly up the church stairs by her chubby little wrist and try to find my mother in the congregation. Sometimes I spotted her in the vestibule, waiting. Sometimes we waited for her until she returned, sweaty and smelling of coffee. I began to think that she just dropped us off but didn't actually stay for Mass — just wandered the nearby streets to get an hour to herself.

I, too, craved some time away from Carly, some time with kids my own age. Thank God for age-segregated Sunday School classes.

We were learning about saints. A lot of the kids at Sunday School had saints' names — Alexander, Dominic, even Hillary. But Saint Darcy did not show up in any of Mrs. Reiner's books. No Saint Freddie, either. For two Sundays in a row, Freddie Owen had the Batman symbol buzzed into his brush cut.

"I'm not named after a saint," Freddie announced. I wondered what it would feel like to touch the back of his head. "I'm named after my mom's favourite actor, Freddie Prinze. He was on *Chico and the Man*. And you know what? He *shot* himself. Dead."

We gave Freddie wide stares.

Mrs. Reiner waved her arms. "Boys and girls! Listen! You must never, ever take your own lives. Not ever. This is a very, very bad sin. If you ever take your own lives, you will never get into Heaven. Never."

Across the church basement, I could hear Carly crying. Her Sunday School teacher carried her over to me. She reeked of urine; I could see a dark stain on the bum of her overalls.

"Darcy, can you go find your mom? Your sister had an accident."

Years later, the older cousin of one of my Grade Six students, Matthew Ross, also killed himself. Matt's desk stood empty while he attended the funeral. He came back over the lunch hour, dressed in a grey suit.

"Who's Kirk Cobain?" he asked, while we waited for the other kids to come back into the classroom.

"Kurt Cobain?" I said. "A singer. Why?"

"My mom said my cousin Zach killed himself because of Kirk Cobain. She said Kirk Cobain did drugs."

"Well," I said, "Kurt Cobain had a very hard life."

Matt fiddled with the buttons of his blazer. "Did he kill himself?"

"Yes," I said.

"My mom didn't even come with us this morning. She stayed at home. She said Zach killed himself, so he had to go to Hell. My dad wouldn't talk to her."

I put one hand on his shoulder. "That sounds pretty hard."

"Yeah. My mom said Zach did drugs, too. But I liked him. I liked playing PlayStation with him, even though he always beat me." The bell rang, loudly, signalling the end of the lunch period. "Do you believe that?" Matt asked.

"Do I believe. . .?"

"About Hell. Because of what he did."

I thought of Mrs. Reiner. How to give the correct Catholic Schoolteacher response without crushing the kid?

"What do you think?" I asked.

"Maybe Jesus would forgive Zach, because of his problems and stuff. Maybe Jesus let him into Heaven anyway."

My other students started filing in, distracted by recess conversations, shedding their coats.

"I hope so," I said.

&, Diane (pronounced Dee-Ann) Arbus, the photographer behind the lens that shot a pair of identical twins in itchy corduroy dresses, looked just like my grandmother, my father's mother. This I noticed when I began researching Diane for my art history paper.

I have but one memory — sitting on the countertop in our kitchen, watching her cook. She'd taken the food out of the frying pan and went around the corner to put the dish on the table. From my roost, I watched the bubbles of oil leap and spit. Then, suddenly, with a whoosh, flames leapt up from the pan. Grandma rushed back into the kitchen and picked up the frying pan by its handle, holding it straight out in front of her. I put my hands on the counter behind me and scooted back, backing into the cabinets, too small to get down by myself.

Grandma then began to wave the pan back and forth by the handle. The flames swished and surged, but did not die down. Then, she lurched towards me, towards the sink, and dropped the pan into its belly. The flames blazed only a foot to my left, raging hot, the oil sputtering angrily. I cried out, "Grandma!"

She leaned forward and turned the tap on. The water hit the oil full force and surged for a moment.

And then, just as quickly, the flames sputtered and extinguished. My Grandma walked out of the kitchen and I heard the bathroom door slam, the muffled sound of her sobbing. I sat on the kitchen counter stunned and scared, until Mom came home, her pregnant belly entering the apartment first, her arms full of grocery bags. When she lifted me off the counter, I felt my baby sister's eager kick.

I took a book of Diane Arbus' photography out of the library for my art history project. In one of the photos, an emaciated blond boy grinned maniacally, the strap of his overall shorts falling off one shoulder, one hand clutched tightly around a toy hand grenade. His knobby knees reminded me of the flamingos in *Alice in Wonderland*. The look on his face suggested he thought the toy was perhaps real, that it might wreak irrevocable damage, if wielded correctly.

I thought back to what Patrick had said about his own mother's taste in artwork, the photographs of babies dressed like bunnies or squished into flowerpots. Why would Diane Arbus photograph something so unnerving? Sure, Anne Geddes' work was cheesy and repetitive, but it didn't make my stomach contract. I flipped back to the photo of the twins, the one my father had hung on my parents' bedroom wall.

Identical Twins, Roselle, New Jersey, 1967. The twins in the picture were probably still alive. I thought of them walking around, somewhere out there in the world. My father was walking around somewhere out in the world, too.

A photograph is a secret about a secret, one of the books on Diane Arbus read. *The more it tells you, the less you know.* Just like my father had told me.

"I feel like I'm doing a psychology paper more than an art history paper," I confessed to Patrick during our next class. "My artist named her daughter Doon, took pictures of kids playing with weapons, and then offed herself with pills and a razor blade."

Aubrey had stayed home to finish a paper for another class. I'd taken the same seat near the back.

"Well, you know, with creativity comes madness. Look at van Gogh. Sliced off his own ear." Patrick took off his glasses to clean them, and I could see the weird mottled grey of his eyes. His chosen artist had gone blind in his old age, his paintings becoming more and more impressionistic.

The whole project made my skull ache, reminding me of all the crazy in my family. My sobbing grandmother setting the kitchen on fire, my loony mom yelling at telemarketers, my disappearing

Dad. "I need a break from it," I said. "I don't even want to think about this project."

"You know what?" Patrick said. "I could use a break, too. Do you want to have dinner with me on Friday?"

I didn't realize what he meant at first. When I didn't respond, he added, "I promise I won't talk about the paper."

"Oh!" I said, "Oh, yeah, okay, sure."

&   When I returned to Calgary after Carly's funeral, I sat at my computer, scrolling through pictures I'd saved on my hard drive of Carly, pictures of the two of us together before I'd moved, and then pictures she'd sent me of her and Ryan. Between how many photos she'd emailed me, and how Patrick preferred to be behind a camera versus in front of it, I had more pictures of Carly's relationship than my own.

Carly's seventeenth birthday, the two of us at a Jays game, Carly's hair in pigtails under her ball cap.

Carly posing in front of the Christmas tree, wearing the new jeans I'd bought her.

Carly in Calgary, holding a squirming Kipling under the armpits.

A self-portrait of Ryan and Carly, around which Carly had photo-edited a pink heart. Underneath it, she'd typed "4 Ever!"

Sleep became blotchy with intrusive dreams.

She grinned. Dimpled cheeks, Pigtailed hair. Fingers outstretched, the flaming orange of Cheetos dust on her fingers. She'd gotten into the pantry. Mom was going to kill me.

Carly! Carly!

My chest, my lungs compacted. My eyes wide, pupils distended in the dark, drowning in my duvet cover. I struggled to breathe. My heart flipped over, searing, in a frying pan.

& After my last day of seventh grade, Aubrey and I got permission to take the subway to Eaton Centre to spend our allowance. Aubrey's mom met us there, bought us veggie dogs, and drove us home. I'd purchased a new Ace of Base cassette and planned to spend the afternoon listening to the songs I hadn't yet heard on the radio, provided Carly would relinquish her beloved Raffi tape, which she should have outgrown.

When I got home, I let myself into the apartment to find Papi and Carly playing Go Fish. Papi still walked Carly home from school, but Mom had called in sick that morning, having dragged herself around the apartment for several days. She'd asked me to get Carly ready for school, and I'd done so, rushing to get it over with, telling Carly to shut up and hurry. Still, Carly sang the entire time I tried to brush the tangles out of her hair, and I'd had the tune to "Bananaphone" in my head all day. Mom got up only to brew a pot of coffee, then took a mug of it back to bed with her. I filled my own mug with the dark brew when she wasn't looking, took a gulp. I almost choked, coughing the hot liquid from my throat.

"This song drives me *bananas!*" Carly exclaimed, as I ushered her out the door.

"Where's Mom?" I asked Papi.

"Um, do you have any. . .fives?" Carly asked. She held her Garfield cards splayed too far forward; Papi could easily see them.

"Your mother went on vacation," Papi said. "I'm going to stay with you for a little while."

Vacation? She'd barely woken up that morning. I set my bag down on the floor beside me and kicked off my shoes.

"Vacation where?" I asked.

Papi's words sounded well articulated, intentional. He tilted his head towards Carly while speaking. "Mexico. She'll be back in a week or so."

I clenched my jaw. "Mexico?"

"We baked a cake!" Carly announced. "I licked the beaters." She hummed the opening verse to "Bananaphone."

"Car — cut it out!" I snapped.

"A chocolate cake!" Papi said, loudly. "Right, Carly?"

"Can we eat it now?" Carly asked, "Can we, can we, can we?"

"What do you think, Darcy?" Papi asked.

I dropped my backpack at my feet. "Sure."

When Carly darted up and towards the fridge, scattering her cards on the floor, I said quietly to Papi, "She's coming back, right? She has to come back. She can't leave Carly."

"She's coming back," he said. "I promise you."

In my bedroom, I crossed the day off my dry erase calendar, X'd out the happy words, LAST DAY OF SCHOOL!

What day would I die? Each year, I passed it, over and over, unaware of the anniversary of my death. Maybe I would die young. Maybe a car would hit me on the way to the bus stop before I even graduated high school. Maybe I would get cancer. Or a rare mystery illness that no one could diagnose until it was too late. Maybe it was the anniversary of my death, right then. Maybe —

Carly bounded into my room, her mouth smeared with chocolate. "Come! I cut you a ginormous piece!"

&⎯ Carly's proclamation that she had "good news" that last Valentine's Day distracted me all morning. While teaching Geography, I listed Austria as one of the continents. Freya Nichol's hand shot up. "Ms. Nolan, don't you mean *Australia?*"

"Right!" I said, a little too loudly. "You caught my trick! Good job, Freya!" The kids were eager to fill the baskets we'd made earlier in the week with their red and pink paper valentines.

On my recess break, I got Carly's voicemail the first time I called, and then the second time. Where the hell was she? Why wasn't she answering? Was she okay?

She picked up the third time, while I had a mouth full of carrot.

"Hey," she said, so nonchalant. So nonchalant? What the fuck? I swallowed too quickly, the carrot rough in my throat.

"Hey," I said. "So what's your good news?"

"Okay," she said, "okay, so. . .you won't believe it." She seemed to be stalling, purposely, for dramatic effect. "I'm gonna be a model."

"What?" I crunched hard on another carrot.

"A model! There's this guy in the art department at U of T, photography department, I mean. A friend of Heather in my class, and he's doing this project on nudes, right?"

"Wait, wait — " My brain struggled to catch up. "You want to be a *nude model?*"

"Kinda! It's not pornography, it's art. And it's tasteful. Like, with my hands covering my nipples and stuff like that."

"I'm confused."

"I think it's a cool idea, his project, he says it's about like, *fatalism* or some jibber-jabber."

"You're going to pose naked for this guy? Is he your age?"

"Couple years older. Twenty-five or something. He always wears hats, isn't that funny? Every time I see him, he's wearing a hat. Maybe it's some sort of political statement."

I noticed Conor in the doorway to the staff room, and he held up a student's file, reminding me that we'd agreed to conference about a bullying incident between two Grade Six boys. I held up one finger at him. He grinned and held up two fingers back at me, a peace sign.

"Car — " I said, interrupting her. "I'm glad you're feeling better, but I actually have to run to a meeting, can we talk about this later?"

"Sure," she said, "I'm going to go have drinks with this guy. He said he might be able to get the studio so we can do the shoot this afternoon."

"You don't drink!"

"Yeah," she said, "I know, relax, I'll have a Red Bull. Maybe go for a quick run, get rid of some water weight. God I hate running."

"You're not fat," I said. "We'll talk about this later, okay? Make sure this project of his is legit. Maybe you should talk to me again before you take any pictures. This guy could be a creep. Don't do anything I wouldn't — "

"Heather!" Talking to someone else, already one step ahead. "I'll be there in a sec! Thanks, Darce, talk to you later!"

&T During our mother's "vacation," Papi rented a car and took us on a surprise field trip. Carly often fell asleep on car rides, but this time I fell asleep in the back seat to the low drone of Papi humming along with a cassette tape of classical music. When I woke up, the music skidded along, fast and foreboding.

Papi had set up a makeshift bed on our couch, and when I awoke to go to the bathroom, his presence reminded me of our mother's absence like a slap. I wanted her back. I didn't want her back. Papi slept flat on his back, rigid and still, like a corpse in a coffin.

"I'm sorry, did the music wake you?" Papi asked, making a left turn.

My shoulder ached from where I'd jammed it against the window to nap. "I'm fine."

"I love classical music," Carly chirped. Carly awoke from naps fully recharged, sundrenched. "Papi, make the radio do the bumblebee song again."

"Ah!" Papi glanced over his shoulder and smiled at us. "Rimsky-Korsakov, 'Flight of the Bumblebee.' Coming up." He hit rewind, and the tape deck purred.

When we arrived, my stomach growled. Carly happily munched on the peanut butter granola bars Papi had packed, getting crumbs everywhere, but the drive had made me motion sick. When I stood up out of the car, I bent over for a moment, hands to my thighs, trying to settle my stomach.

"Birdie!" Carly shrieked. I cringed. She sounded like a toddler.

We were in Mississauga, I discovered, at a wildlife veterinary clinic. It had a large bird painted on the outside. Carly flitted back and forth from Papi to the clinic entrance. I dragged my feet along the gravel path. Seriously? A wildlife veterinary clinic? I shuffled inside. "Cool, Carly, huh?" I gave her the widest smile I could.

Inside, a chubby woman wearing pale blue scrubs came over and gave Papi a squishy hug. She looked to be probably ten or so years younger than him, and had round, ruddy cheeks. She should have been a baker, I thought. She had a small multicoloured bird appliquéd to the pocket of her shirt.

Carly stood up on her tiptoes. "I like your bird."

The lady grinned. "Did you know lots of female birds are brown or grey? It's the male birds that are all pretty and colourful. It's so that they can attract a mate." She smiled at Papi. "So this bird would probably be a boy."

"This is my friend Laura," Papi said. "Laura is the veterinarian here."

Laura took Carly to another part of the clinic to visit a chipmunk with a cloudy eye. Carly put her face right up to his cage. I wandered off on my own, drawn to a small cage at the back of the main room. In it, a small bird was huddled by itself in the corner, its slick black beak tucked into its chest, masking its reddish throat. It had a long, dark back. Its eyes flickered open and closed, open and closed.

"It's a swallow," Papi said. I hadn't realized he was behind me. "A barn swallow."

"It looks sad," I said.

"Maybe. It's probably recovering from being sick." He squatted down a bit to become eye level with the bird, which perched on one of the lowest rungs of the cage. "Did you know, Darcy, that swallows mate for life?"

I didn't say anything. The swallow rustled its feathers for a moment, settling.

"Maybe you've seen people with tattoos of swallows before. It actually dates back to sailors, who often had to go away for long journeys. Swallows symbolized hope for their safe return home, back to those they loved. And if someone didn't survive, if a person drowned at sea, legend said that swallows would find the person's soul and carry it up to Heaven."

"That's depressing," I said, not looking at Papi. The bird seemed to agree with me, tucking further into itself, as though it wanted to dissolve. It looked nothing like the perky, winking bird stitched onto Laura's pocket. If swallows mated for life, where was its partner? Would it mourn forever, like Papi? What happened when part of you was gone for good?

"I'm hungry," I said. "I'm going out to the car to get a snack."

&⎯ When we got back to Calgary after Carly's funeral, Patrick began coming over every day around six PM, letting himself in. Oftentimes, he found me still in bed, having lain awake all night and then finally passed out, exhausted, at dawn. Those days, he would crawl in beside me, his chest to my back, his arms around me like a cocoon. A little boy in kindergarten at St. Sebastian had been diagnosed with autism, and we'd had a staff meeting about the disorder to increase awareness, during which his teacher had demonstrated how the boy liked to be hugged; the deep pressure calmed him. With Patrick pressed up beside me, the pressure on my lungs released, the air letting out slowly, like a hissing balloon.

He came over one day, at the end of the second week, with a casserole dish smelling strongly of onions. I had actually slept somewhat the night before. The small pocket of energy that afforded me had resulted in all my towels being washed and folded.

"I had leftovers," he said.

Patrick had leftovers? "Did you make this?" I asked.

"Yeah. Where do you want me to put it?" He held it out. I seemed to have missed him learning how to cook. I wanted to cry, not knowing if it was because of how foreign he suddenly seemed, or because of the giant onion stink. I took it and thought, *Never take food from a stranger.*

"I'm not very hungry."

"Okay. Well, you'll have it for later. You look skinny. I'm worried about you."

I didn't know what to say. "Okay," I mumbled. We looked at each other before he took the dish back from me, as if he recognized his responsibility in keeping up the momentum. Like a metronome; he moved and I moved, matching his pace. I didn't know how else to function. Patrick put the casserole in the fridge. He settled on the futon, reached for the remote. "Do you want to watch a movie or something?"

Do I?

"What is this?" I asked.

Patrick's brow creased. "What's what?"

"This." I couldn't explain. I thought of Carly trying to converse with Papi in Polish, his native language. He tried to teach her, but she remembered only a very limited repertoire of words.

Hello, my name is. Witam, mam na imi.

"Okay," Patrick said. "Come here. It's okay. What are you confused about?"

I stood still in the kitchen. "Us." I motioned at the space between the two of us, "This. Are we? I mean. . ."

"Darce. . ." He let out a long exhalation. "I don't think now is the time to really be talking about this, do you? I mean, you've got enough on your plate with. . .with. . .what your sister. . .did."

What your sister did. As though she *voluntarily* wrote Aubrey's number down on a slip of paper, tucked it and her ID into her pocket, walked out of her apartment, turned left at the end of her street, walked north, walked down the stairs into the subway tunnel, slipped her token into the slot, pushed the revolving doors, walked to the platform, paced the platform a few times, listened for the rumble of the train, laid her jacket on the floor, and jumped. As though I had nothing to do with it.

& Our mother came back from her "vacation" skinnier than she had been, and more agitated, restless. She began to drink coffee out of a clear water bottle, straight and black. Her tongue took on a perpetual brown sheen. In the months prior, she'd been sluggish, exhausted. After returning, she moved nervously around the apartment, picking at the skin at the creases of her elbows, tearing paper and napkins into shreds, cleaning invisible spots on the walls and the carpet. She started yelling at customer service agents again, over the phone. But she could keep up with Carly better than before, taking her for long walks up and down Bloor Street, repetitively pushing her on the swings at the park. After tagging along for one or two jaunts, I gave up. I lay on my top bunk with the ghetto blaster loud enough so that I couldn't hear my thoughts anymore. She didn't explain where she'd been, and though I wasn't buying the vacation story, I didn't ask. She didn't have the money to jet off to Mexico with a friend. And, on top of that, she didn't have any friends close enough to jet off to Mexico with. When Aubrey's mother had gone to Las Vegas with a girlfriend for her birthday one year, my mother had called her a "rich bitch."

I didn't know *where* she'd gone, but I knew *why*. To get away from her kids. Sure, Carly was a handful, always singing and shrieking and crying and dancing, climbing and clamouring for attention. But what was wrong with *me*?

My mother also joined a book club that met every Thursday night. I hadn't seen my mother read a book except for *Goodnight Moon* and *Green Eggs and Ham*. She'd finished high school, but barely. The book club was just another excuse. Where was she going now?

> *I would not like them*
> *here or there.*
> *I would not like them*
> *anywhere.*

Aubrey had gone with her parents to their cabin in Haliburton for an entire month — half our summer vacation. I wrote her a letter the week she left, splurging on pink stationary and a purple ink pen. Aubrey's letters would make my month of babysitting Carly more bearable. I listened for the postman outside our door, sorting through the mail that came through our slot, waiting for Aubrey's reply. Nothing.

Aubrey returned berry brown and bursting with confessions about having kissed a boy a whole year older than us who also spent his summer at his parents' cabin. "The first kiss was kind of weird," she told me, "but it definitely got better with practice." I hoped she wouldn't meet anyone she wanted to kiss during the school year. I didn't want to lose her again.

Aubrey didn't, but my mother did: Richard the Dick. Not much taller than my mother, Dick was bald, and had a beer gut and excessive eyebrows. He wore the same faded black T-shirt with a pinkish bleach stain on the seam every time I saw him and drove a burnt red 1987 Buick LeSabre. He called Carly "squirt," liked to catch her and rub his fist on the top of her head. "Knuckle sandwich!"

My mom started setting the table, serving meals that involved multiple ingredients and required heating on the stove or in the oven, not the microwave. When the phone rang during dinner, I hoped the call was from Aubrey. I'd been trying to get her to come over when Dick was around; I needed her opinion. I stood up.

My mom put her hand on my shoulder, pushing me back down into my chair. "No phone calls at the dinner table." Since when? I glared down at my food. She could play pretend all she wanted. Make Dick think we were a real family, the kind who ate together and liked each other. How long would that last?

Aubrey eventually did get a chance to meet Dick when she came to pick me up to go for Slurpees. She sucked back her half-orange crush, half-root beer as we walked back to her house. I kept quiet, waiting for her to volunteer her opinion.

"What do you think?" I finally asked, once we'd arrived back at her house.

She yawned. "He looks uneducated."

"He's a plumber," I said. Aubrey had started painting her nails. Condensation built on the side of her abandoned Slurpee, a puddle pooling at its base on her dresser. "He would have had to have done some kind of school," I added.

Aubrey blew on her fingers to get the paint to dry. "Not university. This summer I'm going to start my own babysitting company to save up for university. I'm going to do a master's degree, like my dad."

"My real dad has a university degree," I told her. "Business school." I didn't know whether he'd actually finished or not. As far as I knew, my parents hadn't spoken since he left.

Aubrey held her fingernails out, posed, like red claws. "Really? Well, your mom should have hung onto him, then."

I asked Papi what he thought of Dick, too. Carly had built a fort out of Papi's floral couch cushions and throw blankets. When she ran out of blankets, he'd given her a folded stack of his sweaters.

"He makes your mom happy," Papi said.

"I'm happy, too," Carly said, from inside her fort.

"It's very difficult to be without a partner," Papi said, softly. "I still miss my wife very much."

If he missed her so much, why did he only have one picture of her in his apartment?

I decided Papi couldn't give an informed opinion. Carly still went over to his apartment after school sometimes, but I didn't need a babysitter anymore. And Papi was never around when Dick the Dickhead was around; when Papi watched Carly, my mom and Dick went for coffee or to the movies. I volunteered to walk another tenant's golden retriever, a job that kept me out of the apartment *and* helped me start a small savings account. I would go to university, too, far away from Toronto. I'd live with a roommate who would make me forget how much more sophisticated Aubrey was compared to me. My mom and Dick could have their stupid, happy little family.

By New Year's, they were engaged.

&   I intended to go back to work after Carly died, I really did. My principal insisted I take at least a month off. I'd told him my sister had "been killed in a motor vehicle accident." Vague, but technically it wasn't a lie. Nobody, no matter how Catholic, was going to tell me that Carly had committed a mortal sin.

I drove to St. Sebastian to meet with the substitute who'd been teaching my class — a tall, recently retired woman, perhaps ten or fifteen years older than my mother. I wondered how she'd kept up with my rowdy bunch. They'd taken surveys of each other's food preferences and made them into bar graphs, labelled the province capitals on maps, built contraptions to drop eggs from the top of the school without having them break. The substitute teacher pulled out their writing portfolios. Since September, I'd had them free write for fifteen minutes every day, usually to a prompt I provided.

> *If my house were burning down and I could only save one thing,*
>   *it would be _____, because. . .*
> *My favourite family tradition is. . .*
> *The best thing about me is _____, because. . .*

The prompts helped the slower writers in the class generate ideas. The sub had photocopied a few samples of her own prompts, explaining that she'd started to see some real progress in their work.

> *If I could change one thing. . .*

I excused myself and went to the bathroom. I closed the stall and sat down on the floor, kicked off my shoes. The tile beneath me looked grimy. The metal bathroom door felt cold through my blouse.

I'd have to get a doctor to write a note explaining why I couldn't go back to work yet. Why I needed longer.

& Or maybe —
Even though she wasn't allowed to venture past where her mother could see her, Stefany wandered down to the grocery store. Her mother was on the phone with her new boyfriend, anyway.

Stefany's hands felt slimy; she lifted her hair into a ponytail, wishing she had an elastic, then let it drop back down against her neck. The sky looked heavy and full, about to rain. Stefany opened the doors in the frozen food aisle, squished her face against the ice creams, the frozen peas. The back of her neck, the backs of her knees felt sweaty. She followed a woman wearing cutoff jeans and a yellow tank top. The woman squeezed avocados and tapped cantaloupes; Stefany could see the straps of her bra.

Stefany wondered what it would be like to be a grown-up, to have her own apartment and buy her own groceries, steer a tall shopping cart. She would buy the corn chips that went in the little rolls like a tongue. She would check labels for grams of fat, and go, "hmm." She would have a silver credit card. And she would go to restaurants with her friends and order strawberry mousse and have a very curly signature on the bill and say, "Remember when we were kids? Seems like just yesterday."

The woman moved to the counter to pay, loading her tomatoes one at a time, fat and in a line, as though they were schoolkids, lining up for the water fountain. Stefany's throat itched. The soda machine had a piece of paper taped to it that read "Out of Service," but she didn't have any quarters anyway.

Outside, it started to rain. Stefany pressed her face up against the glass door and watched the rain stream down, a tumbly feeling in her stomach. Mom would send her to her room without TV if she came home soaked. She needed to go to the bathroom. She stood on one foot, then the other, a tiny rain dance, a need-to-pee dance.

Someone came up behind her, bumping into her with grocery bags.

"Oops!" he said. "I'm sorry. I almost bowled you over, there."

He was very, very tall.

But then, she was very, very small.

"Where's your mom?" he asked.

Stefany tried to stand up straighter, to look older than she was, not like a nine-year-old out wandering by herself. "She's at home. I'm allowed out by myself. I'm ten. I just live around the corner."

When she got home she might watch a video, maybe *Honey, I Shrunk the Kids*, even though she'd seen it four times. If Mom didn't catch her for being out.

"Do you want a ride home?" the very tall man asked. "You'll get soaked walking home in this rain. My truck is in the parking lot. Why don't I load my groceries and pull up to the door?"

Stefany thought that sounded like a great idea. Maybe Mom wouldn't notice that she'd snuck out. And she *really* had to pee.

"Thanks," she said.

When the tall man pulled up to the curb, Stefany dashed across to his truck with her arms over her head. The rain splattered hard against her head and back. The man opened the front door for her. Stefany wasn't allowed to sit in the front in Mom's car. Kris was, which meant Kris got to pick the radio station all the time. Stefany hopped in and shook her hair out a little bit.

The very tall man had a head that was mostly bald and eyes that went down at the corners. He pressed a little button and all the locks went down. "What's your name?" he asked. He put the truck in reverse and backed away from the curb. The inside of his truck smelled like mouthwash. Stefany scrunched her nose. Oh well, she would be home soon enough.

"Stefany," she told him.

"Stefany," he repeated. "That's a grown-up name."

There was an old lady who swallowed a bird.
How absurd to swallow a bird!
She swallowed the bird to catch the spider,
that wiggled and jiggled and tickled inside her.
She swallowed the spider to catch the fly.
I don't know why she swallowed a fly.
Perhaps she'll die.

& I set up a counselling appointment at Aubrey's urging.
The counsellor looked younger than me, perhaps only by a year or so, but the gulf was obvious in her apprehensive giggle, her vehemently purple eye shadow, her stumble through the informed consent. She notified me that, should I indicate suicidal thoughts, she would have to break confidentiality. What advice could she possibly give me? She asked if I was taking care of myself, eating right, sleeping okay. She was the kind of girl, I hypothesized, who nannied her way through undergrad, got all As and A-minuses on her transcripts (except for that one B-plus), the kind of girl who threw her parents a twenty-fifth wedding anniversary party and drank a little too much, gave an animated flush-cheeked toast and whined to her boyfriend of seventeen-and-a-half months for an aspirin to cure her hangover headache until he finally conceded and got her one.

"I think it's important that you try to keep your life as normal as possible. What kinds of things did you like to do before. . .this happened?"

"I don't know." My memories eclipsed. I tried to put myself back there. "I was working; that took up a lot of time."

She fiddled with her pen. "What about for fun?"

What had fun felt like? "Sometimes I went out with some colleagues for drinks, if it was someone's birthday or something. Some of the girls from school set up a monthly dessert date, but I was so busy with work I didn't make it very often. I volunteered after school to do the school newspaper with the kids. I went running. Sometimes, I went to the gym, when it got too cold out to run." Pathetic.

This sparked her attention. The gym? She was probably a spin-class addict. "That could be a great thing for you, if you took up exercise again. Not only would it be getting back to normal activities, but exercise increases the production of dopamine in the brain, which can elevate your mood." My lack of response seemed to make her feel like she needed to elaborate. "You know, happy juice."

I went to a drop-in step class with the small flicker of energy I had left. At the end of the warm-up, I stood at the water fountain, tried to slow my jagged breathing. My reflection looked gaunt in the mirror as it raised its knees. Up, down, up, down. When Patrick and I broke up, Carly commented on the fact that I'd shed a few pounds, calling it the "Break-Up Diet," telling me she would set me up with her good friends Ben and Jerry. Carly hated the gym, and had a shameless sweet tooth. She floated Gummi bears in chocolate milk and called it "bubble tea," sucked the chocolate off Glosettes and spit the raisins into a bowl the way some people discard the broken shells of pistachios. Her hunger to be enthusiastic and bubbly and love-y made up for her lack of exercise, though. The energy to keep herself in smiles all day long was enough of a workout.

The morning after the step class, my hamstrings yelped at me when I climbed out of bed. I'd left the class as soon as it ended, not bothering to stretch, sweaty and panicked to be away from all the naked belly buttons and breasts in the change room. I'd clocked my time, stepped up and down off my platform methodically for a full fifty minutes.

I eased onto the couch and probed the backs of my knees with my thumbs, trying to loosen the muscles. The pain felt gratifying. I pushed my thumbs into the crevices until they started to burn. At least I could still feel.

& I have vague memories of the day Carly was born, the pickled smell of antiseptic, holding someone's hand and being pulled down the maze of hospital corridors.

My mother's belly had bulged large, a summertime watermelon, and I'd imagined one day the baby would just burst out of her. The week before Carly's birth I'd watched a balloon fill, fill, fill with air until it could not possibly hold any more. Who'd blown up that balloon? A memory of puffed cheeks, a chin grazed with stubble. The balloon exploded. Scraps of purple plastic speckled the carpet.

"Darcy! Pick up the pieces."

My father.

Was it my father?

My baby sister would burst forth like this, too big to fit in the world.

Screaming, fists balled in fury against my mother's bluegowned chest.

"This is your baby sister." My mom looked deflated. "You're going to be the little mommy, okay? I'm counting on you."

&J Like with the media coverage following Stefany Beale's disappearance, I couldn't stop reading about suicide. About what my sister did, about what I made her do.

Jumping in front of subway trains actually has a high failure rate; subway cars approaching station platforms begin to decelerate, and may either lack the momentum needed to cause enough bodily harm, or may allow the driver to witness the event and slow down in an attempt to stop it.

According to the articles I read, failure rates for subway suicides reached 67 percent, though survivors often suffered injuries, such as limb amputations, which resulted in long-term social, functional, and financial difficulties. Several survivors reported to one study that they'd selected the method because they incorrectly imagined that the method would be lethal. Ninety percent of survivors claimed they were sure they would die.

Over half, then, did not die. Over half. Yet, despite often struggling to be successful in a number of areas her whole life, and despite the odds against her, my sister achieved what she'd set out to do that morning. What I'd set into motion.

Behaviours noted by observers prior to a suicide attempt included removal of shoes, sudden dropping of belongings as the subway approached, having sentimental personal items in one's possession, and avoiding eye contact with other commuters.

When I wouldn't stop calling, the constable in Carly's district finally referred me to the medical examiner, who told me that Carly died after being crushed by the wheels while the stunned driver tried desperately to stop.

"Knowing the details aren't going to bring her back," the ME said.

Carly was dead by the time paramedics removed her body. The

security guard at her building told the police that, on February 14th, Carly had returned to her apartment, alone, shortly after six PM, and did not leave until the next morning, at 8:58 AM, just minutes before she sent me her final text message. No other individuals entered or exited her building during that time period. The police said they'd confirmed his story with the apartment's video surveillance footage. I wanted to see the tape, to see her again, the way her ponytail swung when she walked, the way she carried plastic grocery bags over her shoulders instead of in her hands. I requested a copy of the footage, but the constable told me they'd released it back to the apartment superintendent. The superintendent told me it had been recorded over.

When I'd suggested Carly and Ryan move to an apartment with video surveillance, Carly had said, "Seriously? I think it's creepy. Like, who's going to be watching me when I'm doing laundry, or taking out the trash? What if the security guard is a pervert?"

In the background, Ryan said something muffled. I wanted to have the conversation with her face-to-face; over the phone, her attention span wavered. But then, she'd accused me of the very same thing, of multi-tasking instead of giving her my undivided attention.

"It's actually safer," I protested. "You don't have to worry about break-ins and things like that. What if you're home alone and Ryan's working late?"

When Carly and Ryan started looking at places, they'd wanted to rent a basement suite to keep their expenses low. I'd nagged her to at least look at buildings, making arguments about lighting, amenities, and space, until she'd finally caved and agreed, likely just to shut me up. "I'm your big sister," I told her, "I know." She conceded when I told her I'd pay her first two months rent to help them get started. I filled out an application for another student loan.

Her blood tests came back negative for drugs or alcohol. It didn't surprise me. She didn't need substances to her over the edge. She had me.

  When I moved to Calgary, I wanted her to come with me. "People in Calgary are hicks," she insisted. "You're going to come back saying *y'all.*"

"You hate living with Mom," I pointed out.

"Yeah," she countered, "but I would hate living in Calgary, too. I don't want to go to a new school and have to make new friends."

I held back from suggesting that she might actually benefit from a fresh start. "I hate the idea of you being alone with Mom and Dick."

"So maybe you should stay here, then. They have teaching schools in Toronto, you know. We could move in together. Like when we were kids."

"Calgary is where I got in." I didn't tell her that I'd been accepted by U of T, but had turned them down.

"You're just going because of Patrick. You're abandoning me for him. You don't even care about me."

I still thought she would change her mind, and browsed online ads for two-bedroom apartments that I could possibly afford, despite my mounting student loans. It would be worth it in the long run, I figured, not to leave Carly behind. How to tell Patrick, though, that I wanted my sister to live with us?

Patrick and I scheduled a coffee date in Kensington market, but he called to say his class had run late and he would be another ten minutes. I jotted down some numbers on a napkin, trying to figure out if we could afford an apartment I'd read about online.

Patrick loved the individuality of mom-and-pop shop coffee houses. I scanned the menu, unable to find any of the flavoured lattes I ordered whenever I stopped at the chain coffee shop on my way to class.

Patrick came in and kissed the top of my head. "Math homework?"

"Budgeting. I'm trying to see if we can afford this two-bedroom place in Capitol Hill. It's fairly close to campus."

He shook some coins loose from his wallet. "You think we need two bedrooms?"

I didn't tell him about Carly. She still hadn't said yes. I needed to convince her first.

I asked Carly again, at our mother's house, over sundaes. She stirred her ice cream, the whole thing a smeary mash of hot fudge and candy bits. That morning, her history teacher informed her that she'd failed another exam and would have to do a make-up assignment just to pass the course. I wished she'd told me before I'd arrived. Bad timing.

"I'm not fucking moving!" She slammed her spoon down on the table; it bounced, flicking ice cream at me. "And if you move away, I'm never going to speak to you again." When she got up and stomped off to her bedroom, I sat at the table, watching her sundae melt into soup.

"What's your sister so pissed about?" My mother shuffled into the kitchen looking like a potato sack in one of Dick's faded long-sleeved T-shirts, which hung mid-calf.

I picked up Carly's ice cream dish and brought it to the sink. "She doesn't want me to move." The hot stream of the faucet sucked the remainders of her dessert down the drain.

My mom leaned back into the counter. "She's going to miss you. Richard and I are, too."

"Right," I said.

Mom pushed up the sleeves of her shirt. "You think you're too good for this family? Ha! You're one of us, whether you like it or not. Just wait until you come crawling back."

Carly's threat lasted two and a half days. She knocked on my apartment door, her hair frizzy and damp from the rain, and several inches shorter than when I'd seen her last. "I forgot an umbrella," she announced, dropping several large shopping bags onto my floor. "Do you think my hair's too short? The hairdresser told me to get a bob. She was like, *They're so trendy*! But I miss my long hair!"

"What's all this?" I'd missed her; put my phone on vibrate and at the loudest possible volume when I took showers or blow-dried my hair to be sure I wouldn't miss one of her calls. Apparently, I'd worried for nothing. But all the shopping bags — what the hell?

"I decided you needed some new clothes for Calgary. I can't send my sister out west looking like a Toronto hipster." She squatted down beside the bags and began rooting. A shiny, colourful blouse with metal buttons; a pair of shimmery animal-skin cowboy boots.

"How did you pay for all of this?" I asked. She was too young to get a credit card, and no way in hell would our mother or Dick co-sign. Then, I knew. Papi had left us each two thousand dollars in his will, with the instruction that it be used towards college. I'd taken Carly down to the bank and started a savings account. Made her promise not to touch the funds until she was eighteen, until it had some time to accrue interest.

"I don't even know if I'm *going* to college. I'm not smart enough," she'd insisted.

"You *are* smart enough. Papi believed in you. That's what he said this money is for."

"I'll get a job, I can make lots of money between now and

then. I really don't think Papi would mind if I spent some of it on back-to-school shopping."

"Trust me," I said, sliding open the door to the Royal Bank. "You're going to want this money when you move out."

I wondered how much of the original two thousand was left. If any. If this was the first time she'd dipped into her stash.

Standing in the entrance to my apartment, Carly grinned at me, dangled the bags. "So? What do you think? Am I the best sister or *what?*"

&T "I think you should see someone." Conor had his feet up on my coffee table, and I noticed then the thin layer of dust punctuated by Kipling's paw prints. When had I last cleaned?

Conor had with him several containers of Chinese food. I had on one of Patrick's thin white undershirts, one I'd kept after we broke up. That morning I realized it was the only clean shirt I owned, and I technically didn't even own it. I pulled a blanket off the couch and wrapped it around my shoulders. I'd spun my hair into a greasy ponytail. It was getting long, my bangs had grown out. I pushed the strands behind my ears.

I exhaled. "Do I really look like I'm in any condition to date?"

"Not dating," he corrected. "A counsellor. I'm worried about you."

"I went to a counsellor," I said. "A couple weeks ago. She told me to start exercising."

"So you quit?"

I looked away. "Well? Wouldn't you?"

"Maybe. But I wouldn't write off psychologists altogether. Some of them actually know what they're doing. Like my brother, for example." He hopped off the couch and began dishing out the stir-fry onto plates.

I pulled the blanket closer around myself. My stomach growled, waking up to the smell. "But wouldn't it be weird if I started seeing your brother?"

"Well, yeah." Conor surveyed the mess of dishes in my sink. "Not to mention that it's a dual relationship."

"What?"

"Psychologists aren't supposed to work with people they're connected to. It's in their code of ethics. Plus, he's a child psychologist. But I can ask him to recommend someone good."

"Maybe." I lifted my hair up off my neck, then dropped it. "I'll think about it."

& As a girl, Carly had loved to play the shadow game, copying everything I said until I blew up at her, screamed at her, called her a little brat, a little shit.

Carly, I'm serious now, stop it.
Carly, I'm serious now, stop it.
CARLY! Leave me alone!
CARLY! Leave me alone!

& Just before the Halloween after Carly turned seven, our mother said that she felt sick and needed to rest. For a week, she sat in the bathtub, her flesh white and goose-pimpled, until the water had turned cold and scummy.

Mom banished Carly from the bathroom, Carly's animated chatter too much for my mother's listless brain to bear. Papi had left town for a friend's funeral. When the lasagne he'd stocked in our fridge ran out, I scraped enough peanut butter out of the bottom of the jar to spread a sandwich for Carly, cut a blackening banana lengthwise, and folded the bread around it.

"Here, kid, a dessert hot dog."

She spun in circles on the living room rug. "I love it, I love it, I love it love it love it love it. . ."

I thrust it at her. "Take it."

I knocked on the bathroom door. No response. I turned the knob. Mom hadn't even bothered to lock it. She had dark hair on her legs, under her armpits. Her breasts hung down, openly miserable.

"Who's going to take Carly out for Halloween?"

I sat on the closed toilet seat, waiting for a response. Nothing.

When I came back out of bathroom, Carly had fallen asleep in the middle of the rug, fists clenched, face smeared with peanut butter, as though she'd collapsed mid-spin. She had a pattern of falling asleep in unusual places, like Papi's kitchen table once, while waiting for cookies to finish baking, and another time in the cart at the grocery store while Mom stacked loaves of bread and boxes of crackers and cans of ravioli around her.

That night, Mom moved from the bathtub to her bedroom, leaving a trail of damp footprints on the carpet. She stopped in our room, hovered in the doorway in her towel. "G'night." But Carly had fallen asleep again, despite her afternoon nap. I'd carried her there, tucked her in, still in her clothes, all arms and legs, skinny from her endless energy, her constant kinesthesia. At least she'd gone to bed early. I pretended to be asleep, face towards the wall, lips pressed into a line. When my mother left, I flicked the light back on, pulled my battered copy of *The Giver* off the dresser, and read myself to sleep.

In the morning, my alarm hadn't gone off, but Carly was jumping so violently my bed shook with exhilaration.

"I got a Halloween costume, Darce, look!"

I rolled over. She had taken her magic markers and drawn stripes of colour on her skin. Red, orange, yellow, blue, green, indigo, violet. The lines extended up her arms and legs and disappeared beneath her nightgown. Her face was a scribbled mess.

"Darcy, Darcy, I'm a rainbow!"

&⏐ I remember the ribboned water, her slippery shoulders, how she reeked of magic marker, the scents mixed with soap: black licorice, cinnamon, evergreen. She'd fought me, splashing vigorously.

"You're wrecking my costume!" The bath wasn't working anyway. Some of the marker had come off her skin, but still, rainbow ink stained her blonde hair. I pulled her out, wrapped her in a towel.

I couldn't let her go to school like that. People would think. . .

"I have a surprise for you!" I told her. "We're going to have a special day, just you and me. But you can't tell Mom."

"I have a parade!" she insisted.

"I know. But this will be totally better, I promise."

"Ten hundred times better?"

"Ten hundred times better."

I took two twenty-dollar bills from our mother's wallet. A zombie mother, perfect for Halloween. At the Shoppers Drug Mart on the corner, I bought Carly a witch's mask with a hood. Behind the plastic, you couldn't see the rainbow chaos or her streaky hair.

My mother and I had a similar voice, which made it easy to get us both out of school. Two quick phone calls. Two twenty-four-hour flus.

I bought Carly a real hot dog, let her smother it with mustard. She raised her cackling witchy face and took an overzealous bite.

I had enough money left over to take her to the ball pit. Our mother had never taken us to one. I tried to explain. "You know, it's like a swimming pool, except instead of water, it's filled with coloured balls." I couldn't see her expression behind her mask, but I knew she would love it.

"This *is* ten hundred times better!" she bellowed, drawing a few stares from fellow subway riders.

She stayed in there for four hours, bouncing around, while I read my science textbook to make sure I wasn't missing anything important before my test on Monday.

"Darcy! Darcy! Look at me! Look at me!"

Carly, behind the glass, a blur of colour. I held her mask on my lap, a plastic shell. Inside the ball pit, her messiness didn't matter.

We stayed there until it was time for dinner. I used the last of the money and a few dollars from my own wallet to buy her a Happy Meal.

"Can we go trick-or-treating now?" she begged, her mouth full of fries.

"Yup." I stole a sip of her 7UP. My hunger coiled around the sugary tease.

I hoisted Carly's heavy loot bag. I'd told her she wasn't allowed to eat any candy until I got home and checked it out for her, but I'd caved and allowed her to eat a few, sneaking chocolate bars out of the wrappers as she ran up to each house. Candy for dinner. Great.

"I'm cold," she whined. Her mask started to slip. I'd forgotten to grab mittens that morning. She slipped her cold little hand into mine.

On the street in front of us lay the broken, pulpy remains of a Jack-o'-lantern, his skull bashed in.

"Okay," I said, "time to go home, little witch."

She cackled at me behind her mask. "Mwahahaha! I'll boil your brains in my cauldron!"

& I didn't have a GP in Calgary. While doing my Ed degree, I'd gone to the on-campus clinic for two bad sinus colds and a yeast infection. But getting a family doc meant suffering through lengthy waitlists, and I'd used walk-in clinics since graduation.

Back in Toronto, I had Dr. Martin, my mother's doctor. Her husband, also Dr. Martin, had been our pediatrician. Our mother saw Dr. Martin frequently at her office, which happened to be walking distance from our apartment. First, she took us both with her. Then, for a while, just Carly. Then neither of us.

Dr. Martin says I pulled a muscle in my neck. I'm supposed to rest, so keep quiet and don't bother me. Stay out of trouble. No running around in here!

Dr. Martin ran some tests. She thinks I have fibromyalgia. That's what happens to moms when they're worn out. Christ!

Dr. Martin says those headaches that I've been getting are actually migraines. That's why I feel like I'm going to puke all the time, too. She said I should stop eating MSG and take more naps. So, if either of you bother me, you're going to get it. Keep the TV off!

I have irritable bowel syndrome! Gives me the runs! I'm not supposed to get stressed. Keep your sister out of my hair. I mean it.

Irritable. Was that all?

I wondered what kind of random diagnosis Dr. Martin would have slapped me with.

The school board referred me to an employment physician, who I met with to gauge my readiness to return to full-time work. I told him that I'd slept two hours in the past three days.

"Ativan should do the trick," he said, scrawling his dark signature onto a requisition. "I'm very sorry about your sister's accident." *Motor vehicle accident.* Still not a lie.

&T That Halloween was not the only time I took off with Carly to get a break, even after our mother remarried. Once, Carly climbed onto the countertop, trying to reach the sugary cereal mom hid in the cabinet on top of the fridge behind Dick's extensive stash of cheap liquor. From my bedroom, I heard the smash at the same time as my mom did. Red wine slithered along the linoleum, soaked into the carpet.

"Why did you do that?" our mother sobbed. "Richard's going to kill you! Why do you have to be like this?" Dickhead was working late on a jobsite; he wouldn't be home for another day.

"It was an accident," I said. Shards of glass mingled with the ruby liquid. Our mother covered her face with her hands.

"I'm sorry! Don't be mad!" Carly cowered like a baby rhesus monkey on top of the fridge.

"Get down!" I instructed her. "Come here."

My mother surveyed the mess, not moving. "Clean it the fuck up!" she screamed, and stalked off. I heard the slam of her bedroom door.

Carly bawled. I helped her down off the fridge, but left her perched on the counter. I didn't want her bare feet anywhere near the glass.

In high school science class, my teacher had shown us how pouring white wine on red neutralized the stain. But I wasn't about to open another bottle of Dick's booze. Most of the spill had stayed on the lino. The carpet was dark enough, the stain fresh enough, that a few paper towels soaked it to the point where I could barely see it. Carly cried. I used the whole roll soaking up the fluid from the kitchen floor. Carly cried. I swept the glass up and dumped it in the kitchen garbage.

I grabbed both our coats and then Carly's scrawny wrist and got us the hell out of there. I tossed the garbage out back. We rode the subway as far east as it went, and then back, as far west.

Eventually Carly's hiccupping sobs subsided, and she fell asleep, her little body hot against my lap. Our fucking mother. "Fuck you," I said under my breath. In our subway car, a teenager rolled a sleeping infant back and forth in a worn stroller.

Next stop Spadina Station.

Arriving at Spadina Station.

When Carly sat up, my zipper had pressed its zigzag imprint into her flushed cheek. It looked like a scratch.

&⊤ Supposedly the Ativan would help me sleep. There'd been a small bottle of Ativan in the bathroom cabinet when I lived with Patrick. In law school he'd begun to have difficulty falling asleep. Sometimes I would get up in the night to pee and he would be lying awake, staring at the ceiling. I'd come back from the bathroom, my toes cold from the linoleum, and he would roll over, irritable.

"I have to be up in four hours and sixteen minutes," he'd mutter.

The Ativan, when Patrick finally caved and got a prescription, did not seem to work. It was supposed to calm him, supposed to make him drowsy enough to sleep. He moved from our bed to the living room and began to read his textbooks there, by the light of a single bulb.

"You're going to ruin your eyes," I said, the first time I woke up alone and wandered out to find him. He had his back to me, his hair askew. I stood behind him for a moment, at the desk, wanting to hug him. Then I changed my mind.

&⊤ On our first date, I got stitches. As Patrick pulled up to a red light at the corner of Yonge and Dundas, he said, "So I found a spider in the shower last week. I turned the tap on and flushed it down the drain, but every morning now I'm lathering up, and I can't stop thinking it's going to crawl out of some crevice." He had the radio on, the window partially unrolled. He drummed his fingers repetitively against the steering wheel, onetwothreefour, onetwothreefour.

I put my palm down on his thigh. "You're afraid of spiders?"

Then the car leapt forward, on impact, thrust into the intersection. I put my arms out, slammed my elbow and my chin into the dash. I touched my hand to my lip. Blood in my palm made all the lines and grooves of my hand stand out.

"You okay?" Patrick tried unsuccessfully to push away the airbag. I couldn't see him.

"I'm okay," I said. "Are you okay?"

"Let's get you out," he said. "Can you open your door?"

When we met on the street, he said, "Shit, you're bleeding!" He pulled his T-shirt off and told me to hold it to my face. It smelled of spring and sweat and exhaust. His skin had goose pimples.

At the hospital, I clenched my fists around his bloody T-shirt while they stitched invisible threads into my lip. He sat beside me on the exam table, his arm around my waist, protectively, which I felt more than I felt the needle inside my lip. The doctor taped the x-ray of my wrist up to the wall and flicked a light on behind it. "We'll have to put a cast on."

I nodded, my lip puffy, my jaw tingling with painkillers.

When the stitches dissolved, a small purpleblue scar lingered in their place. Carly thought the whole thing was unbelievably romantic.

"I'm jealous," she bemoaned.

"You want a broken wrist?" I asked. I knocked my cast gently against her head. "I have to wear this stupid thing for three weeks, numbskull."

"Still jealous," she repeated. "I want to be rescued, too."

&⎯ I memorized Patrick. His disdain for receipts ("such a waste of paper"), his regret over an upper back tattoo he got in high school (the Celtic knot for strength and protection). How he liked the window open to cool down the bedroom before falling asleep. How he touched the ceiling of his car every time he drove through a yellow light. How he kept the volume dial of his car only on even numbers. How he drank red wine — dry reds, so bitter they made me shudder. Red wine; good for the heart.

&⎯ When Patrick and I moved to Calgary, I promised Carly I'd talk to her daily, promised I'd pay the long distance bill. We rigged up our computers with webcams and arranged a standing date, which coincided with one of Patrick's classes. Carly talked too fast for the computer to catch up; I often missed parts of the conversation. She liked sending things in the mail, but she liked receiving the things I sent her more. I collected all her favourite things: candy corn, pink tank tops, fuzzy socks, chocolate-covered pretzels, tiny capsules of perfume. I hadn't been able to delay my departure date to be in Toronto for her sixteenth birthday, but I'd promised to pay for her to come visit once I'd saved up some cash. I had to dig deep into my student loans for the trip.

That fall she accepted a job babysitting two afternoons a week for a couple who lived around the corner. I liked that she was out of the house more, and she certainly had the energy to keep up with the couple's two-year-old boy, but I knew it couldn't be good for her grades.

"Actually, I get lots of studying done," she told me, "because they don't have cable. When Brody sleeps, the only thing to do is homework! Hey, did I tell you I met a guy from Calgary the other day?"

"No, where?"

"He's the new barista at my Starbucks. I told him I had a

sister who lived out west. He made me a custom mocha caramel frappuccino."

"Really?" I scrawled a note on a piece of paper to add a Starbucks gift card to the next package I sent her. Flat gifts definitely cut down on costs.

"He said one time he was camping, and he and his buddies took some shrooms. . ."

"What?"

"You know, mushrooms. Anyway, he told this hilarious story about how — " She started laughing. She couldn't get the words out. "About how he had an argument with a mountain, because he thought it was Jabba the Hutt."

Whatever, I thought. She was going to school, she'd move out of Mom and Dickhead's place soon. Whatever kept her laughing instead of ranting and sobbing. Whatever kept her on track.

& Midway through my first teaching practicum, a set of twins transferred into my class. During a meet-and-greet, their mother confessed that they'd been honeymoon babies, conceived in Italy, which explained their hideously unique monikers: Amalfi and Sicily. They came to school dressed in identical inappropriate outfits, too fancy for the classroom: white wool dresses and white stockings.

Though my host teacher figured out a way to tell them apart, by Christmas I still accidentally called each of them by her sister's name. Even the other students had figured it out.

"Miss Darcy, can you help me?" I didn't know which one I was talking to.

Twins.

My father had been a twin, a lone twin, the surviving half of a divided egg. What did you do when you were only half of what was supposed to be a single person?

& Despite the disrepair that they'd kept the house in, the previous tenants of the home our stepfather rented kept a well-maintained garden in the backyard, a small rectangle of dirt oddly tucked on the right side of the house, between the wall and the fence that ran between our property and the neighbour's, in a place where the sun never reached. The blossoms had started to droop, their edges brown. At the very corner, I found a dangling stem, heavy with a row of teardrop petals, obscenely pink, in the shape of hearts. I plucked one off and pinched it between my finger and my thumb, applying pressure until it cracked open.

& When he broke up with me, Patrick made perogies. The grease in the frying pan sizzled, agitated. Papi often made perogies smothered in butter and onions. He'd taught Carly and me to cut vegetables by rocking the knife back and forth. We cut the onions and laughed and then cried, our eyes watering with a mixture of pleasure and salt.

"Hey Darce," Patrick said, "you hungry? I found these at Safeway on sale; there's lots of extra, I put them in the freezer."

Patrick rarely cooked. In retrospect, maybe I should have seen this generous gesture on his behalf as evidence of premeditation. He was, after all, a lawyer in progress. He started ranting, stalling. Already thinking about how to soften the explosion. Instead, I thought he was trying to apologize for an argument we'd had the previous day.

I said, "Those look really good."

"I tried to get them golden, but I burnt a few." He slid four onto a plate and handed them to me.

"That's okay." I sat down at the table, speared one with my fork. "Is this about yesterday?"

His face washed greenish in the harsh kitchen lights. "I'm

sorry." But he seemed distracted when he said it, as though look-ing for something else in the room. Kipling, maybe.

I speared a perogy with my fork.

I don't remember what he actually said. Or maybe I don't want to.

Just that, when I bit into the dough, the potato inside was still frozen.

&
"Did you know I was adopted?" Carly asked me one day, shortly after our mother remarried.

"Dream on," I informed her. She held one of her Beanie Babies, twisted its head nervously, her poor unicorn, dying by manual strangulation. "I was there, remember? I remember Mom being huge. You want proof? Go look at her c-section scar."

Mom had told me about my natural birth: a full day of labour, a full head of dark hair. I appeared more frequently in the family photo albums, likely, I reasoned, because of the novelty of first-borns and because my parents had still been young and hopeful, not yet tainted by sleep deprivation, runny noses, and temper tantrums. Carly, on the other hand, was the result of an emergency c-section, her massive head becoming lodged in the birth canal, the umbilical cord looped around her neck.

Once, we rode the elevator downstairs with a woman in our apartment and her just-weeks-old infant, asleep in a stroller.

"You're so slim already!" my mother exclaimed, almost as though it were a bad thing. "Did you push it out all natural? With this one," she gestured to Carly, "they had to carve me open like a pumpkin! I've still got that nasty scar." She ran her knuckles across the top of Carly's head, making my sister squirm. "Hear that, kiddo? You made me ugly!"

And, when my mother had friends, in those unapologetic con-versations (which Carly could have easily overheard, had she been paying attention versus off in some fairy dreamland or dancing to *Sesame Street*): "That c-section messed with my head. Dr. Martin said it was hormones. I was a basket case for weeks after Carly was born." Understatement.

Carly twisted her unicorn's head the other direction. "Then I was switched at birth."

"Go away, Car." I shifted on the couch to see the TV better. I didn't really like *The Simpsons,* but it beat playing Hungry Hungry Hippos with Carly ten times in a row. I picked at a scab on my knee from shaving my legs. A spot of blood welled up behind it.

"You look exactly like Mom," Carly continued. "I look the total opposite of you guys. The TOTAL OPPOSITE!"

"You look like our dad," I said. This both was and wasn't true. She would have to, I reasoned, look somewhat like our dad, what with her being 50 percent his DNA. But I could not remember at all what he looked like, my image of him distorted by men I saw in line at the grocery store, at the bank, on the subway.

Adding to my confusion, our mother had taken scissors to the family photo album and cut him out of all the snapshots. Then, perhaps because she had shitty self-esteem, cut herself out of the family photos, too. She took the cut-out Mom and Dad and chopped all the heads off, then threw both heads and corpses in the trash.

Our childhood photo albums seemed to suggest, not necessarily inaccurately, that we'd raised ourselves.

&⏄ At first, the cops thought Stefany had run away. On the news, they said she'd bickered with her sister; she'd left the apartment voluntarily. She was nine years old, old enough to know how to navigate the subway. Her face didn't start appearing in the paper, on posters, until a few days after her disappearance.

MISSING CHILD: Stefany Erin Beale
DATE OF BIRTH: July 19, 1983
MISSING SINCE: September 27, 1992
MISSING FROM: Toronto, Ontario, Canada
EYES: Brown
HAIR: Red
HEIGHT: 3'8"
WEIGHT: 59 lbs
Last seen wearing a pink and purple windbreaker,
jeans, and purple high top sneakers.

One week after she went missing, the community hosted a vigil in the park near our apartment. I saw the flickering lights as we walked home from Dominion, a bag of apples bumping up against my knees. Carly had her shoes on the wrong feet, her thumb in her mouth.

"What's that?" Carly asked, taking her thumb out to point.

"It's nothing," our mother said, sharply. And then, "Darcy! Stop gawking!"

Six months later, I stood outside the music store on Lawrence Avenue, waiting for Aubrey to finish cello lessons. I'd run to the Mac's to get us some five-cent candies: cubed caramels wrapped in cellophane, sugar-crusted cola soda bottles, sticky blue sharks with marshmallow tummies. We had to build a model of an eco-system. We'd already made one attempt, but ate all the wildlife. Aubrey liked to decapitate Gummi bears with her teeth, affixing their heads to other bears' bodies.

There, in the window of a boutique: Stefany's grainy greyscale face. She had a missing tooth in the picture, on the upper right side. Behind the photo, through the glass, the store mannequins shivered, their bare shoulders exposed, decked out in halter tops and sundresses. The new spring merchandise seemed out of place, not ready to face the world. *Last seen wearing a pink and purple windbreaker, jeans, and purple high top sneakers.* I put my hand in the bag of candy, put a Skittle on my tongue, and swallowed.

& Ryan left Carly.
Ryan rode the Carly rollercoaster with a salesman smile and his arms up in the air, waving. In contrast to my own white-knuckled ascent, the drop in my stomach at the beginning of a big plunge.

I assumed, at first, that their break-up would eventually fix itself. He would leave, but then return, likely with flowers, store-bought and slightly limp multihued carnations over which she would make a big, excited fuss, kissing him sloppily.

Except that he did not come back. He had a kid now. Parents who abandoned their kids — like his own mother — didn't deserve beautiful little girls like Autumn. Didn't deserve kids at all.

I heard it all through Carly. He didn't want to drag her into it, he said. He needed time to focus. It wasn't her fault that he'd messed up. He wanted to see his daughter, get to know her. He needed to sort things out. I wondered how much Carly had distorted the real story due to her own distress. I didn't tell Carly that Ryan's reaction didn't seem that bad. He just wanted to see his little girl.

At first, Carly assumed that he was leaving her for Jessa. "He's sleeping with her. I *know* he's sleeping with her. When he talks about her he can't even look me in the eye. That means he's lying, right?"

But Jessa, she said, didn't even want to see Ryan, let alone let him see his daughter, until he could pay the child support she felt she deserved. It seemed a tad vindictive — letting him know he was a father, but withholding Autumn. Jessa had sent a picture, but Ryan had not let Carly see it, telling her only that he thought Autumn looked just like him. Carly sobbed — but then, she always sobbed.

"He said kids need a mom *and* a dad." I could picture her, on the other end of the phone, just by her voice; runny nose, bed head, raccoon circles under her eyes. "It's not like *we* had a dad, and we turned out *fine!*"

Just fine.

"Plus, it's not like he can't be with me *and* have a kid. I told him, go over there, see the kid, fine, whatever. I kinda don't even care if he drops out of school. He doesn't get it. Darce, you have to phone him and explain it. Tell him to come back."

"He'll come back," I said.

& One anxious week during their relationship, Carly insisted she was "late" and then discovered, instead, that she had simply miscounted. Her ineptitude at math combined with forgetfulness meant that she often missed a pill. I stayed at their apartment during one visit home, crashing on their couch instead of sharing living quarters with my mother. While brushing my teeth, I discovered her pack of pink birth control, four days behind.

"Carly!" I admonished. "You have to be careful with this stuff!"

"Oops!" She popped them out of the pack one by one and into her palm, then tipped her whole hand into her mouth, as though the progesterone were Tic Tacs. "This is still going to kill all the sperm, right?"

"No," I said, "don't you read the instructions? If you forget, even for a day, you have to use a back-up method."

She frowned. "I don't like condoms. They're all slimy."

& A few days before Carly died, I sat in the staff room grading math tests while the children were in an assembly. I got up and poured myself a coffee, put my lips to the edge of the cup. Lukewarm. I popped it in the microwave, stretched.

A female student sat in the main office on a chair opposite the secretary's desk, clutching a mass of Kleenex to her nose. She had a few specks of blood down the front of her sweatshirt. She swung her legs back and forth, unperturbed, waiting for the flow to die down.

The microwave chirped. I reached for my coffee, sliding the sleeve of my shirt down over my hand to protect against the heat of the cup.

The little girl watched me, her legs just dangling, her bangs brushing her eyebrows.

I remembered sitting on the edge of the bathroom counter, my legs dangling. My mother had combed my wet hair over the front of my face. She snipped away, bits of hair tickling my eyes. Then I could see again.

"Look, Baby! You have bangs, just like Mommy!"

I put the coffee to my mouth again and almost burnt my tongue.

&⸂ There were a number of public service announcements in the nineties, when Carly and I grew up. The Ninja Turtles explained why, instead of succumbing to the peer pressure of smoking marijuana, I should tell a parent, or order a pizza. Louie the Lightning Bug reminded me never to fly kites where power lines go. Two fuzzy blue puppets sang about the dangers of consuming unknown products: "Don't ya put it in your mouth." Hal Johnson and Joanne McLeod encouraged me to get active and take a Body Break. Cartoon rollerblading rabbits Bert and Gert reminded me to "Stay Alert, Stay Safe."

Public service announcements instructed kids to stay away from people they didn't know. Strangers could look like normal people. They told kids never to get into cars with strangers, never to look for lost dogs or give directions. Never to answer the door to a stranger when home alone. Never tell the person on the other end of the phone that your mom and dad weren't home. I already knew all that. I could be smarter than Stefany Beale. Carly feared stupid things, like Rataxes, the cartoon rhinoceros on *Babar*, and the sound of balloons popping. But she always wanted to show off her cute high tops. She would offer to sing the alphabet to people at the park (out of tune). She asked about their gadgets and pets. Once, when she could have been no more than three or four, we walked past a man with a pit bull. This dog had a giant boulder of a head and pinched, feline ears. Carly walked right up to it, patted its rump, and crooned, "Nice pib-tull."

Maybe I was smart enough not to get snatched or killed by a stranger, but my trusting little sister wasn't. Carly had a power-ful set of lungs. I tried to teach her to kick and scream when approached, to raise a holy fit. But when I approached her, say-ing, "Okay, Carly, remember, I'm a bad guy," and then, in the smarmiest voice I could muster, "Hey, there, little girl, want some candy?" she just smiled up at me and said, "Look! This rock looks like a bum!"

Something bad was going to happen to her, I knew it.

I knew the public service announcement slogans by heart. *Remember, kids, always trust your instincts about a situation. If some-thing feels wrong, it probably is wrong.*

&   Patrick lay asleep beside me, the tips of his fingers dang-ling on my arm, imperceptible, as though make-believe. My sister. Dead.

Sometimes I had panic attacks, through which Patrick slept, unaware, and I lay shaking, unable to breathe, my thoughts tying knots in my brain. I didn't take my medication. I didn't deserve any relief. When the crest of the panic began to subside, I'd look over at Patrick, my fingers and toes tingly, like they'd fallen asleep. His snoring occasionally gave way to breathing that sounded like blowing bubbles. He looked like an infant: pink cheeks, rising belly, deeply rested. I thought back to the nights when he'd been unable to sleep, when he'd been a twitchy, nocturnal creature.

He never made any advances. I kept waiting for him to. We lay side by side in the bed like siblings, the way Carly used to cuddle up beside me when she had a nightmare. Patrick a hard, heavy sleeper, who couldn't wake up. Me, light and fizzy, drifting away.

&　For several days I couldn't figure out why Kipling sat, waiting, facing the corner where my bookshelf met the wall, her ears alert. Finally, I dragged the shelf away from the wall out of sheer curiosity. One of my framed pictures from on top, Aubrey and I in matching dark sunglasses, clattered to the floor. The glass shattered. Kipling emerged, tangled in my feet, a fuzzy purple mouse caught between her teeth, her tail erect, triumphant. *See?* she seemed to tell me.

&　Winter became spring became summer. In late August, the leaves began to change colours, falling in pairs, angels committing suicide, their airy summer souls departing, leaving their wings behind to rot. Reckless sleep. Phone calls to Aubrey. Walks in circles around the block. I left a bag of garbage in the bin but forgot to put it out for pick-up. When I finally lifted the bag out, white maggots squirmed in a slimy pool underneath where it had sat. I had all my photos of Carly printed, and flipped through them, one at a time, counting each. Three hundred and twenty-seven. Not even a full year's worth. The photos marked her life from fifteen to nineteen. I wondered if I would stop re-membering, at some point, what she looked like as a little girl.

Carly's birthday was coming up, which I always associated with the start of a new school year. I was supposed to start teaching just days before Carly would have turned twenty. I'd missed watching my class graduate elementary school. The Calgary Catholic School Board emailed me my new class list.

On the first day of second grade, Carly spilled chocolate milk down the front of her new pink blouse. On the first day of fourth grade, Carly stepped in dog shit in her new purple sneakers.

She had a red lunchbox shaped like a bus that she carried until age nine, when one of her classmates started singing "The Wheels on the Bus."

"The babies on the bus go wah wah wah. . .wah wah wah. . . wah wah wah. . ."

Late in August, I emerged from my basement with a bag of garbage to put against the fence for pick-up, and noticed a skinny-looking woman on the step, leaning backwards, as though relaxing. Large sunglasses shaded her eyes. She took them off when I came out, perched them on top of her head. What did she think of my sweatpants? Of my giant, uncombed knot of hair?

"Hi," she said, and stood up. "Are you Andrew's tenant?"

I put down the garbage. "I rent the basement."

She smiled, "Oh yeah? I used to rent the basement."

Cancer girl, I thought, then felt a flare of guilt. It was the kind of comment my mother would have made.

"I'm Leah," she said, when I didn't respond. "Andrew said he had some of my mail, but he's not home. Anyway, I hate to do this but — can I use your bathroom? I really need to pee. I was debating coming to knock, but I didn't know if that would be weird. . ."

I unlocked the back door and she followed me down.

"It's kind of a mess," I warned her.

She headed down the stairs, unperturbed. "You should have seen it when I lived here."

I waited on one of the kitchen barstools. The size of the apartment didn't afford very much privacy. I often heard Andrew upstairs walking around. I wondered whether he could hear me. The first day I'd moved in, I turned the radio on before I cried. Now I'd both stopped caring *and* crying; a cactus, prickly on the outside, water on the inside. I'd swallowed all my feelings.

She came out of the bathroom wiping her hands on her jeans.

"My landlord just hiked my rent. Makes me miss living with Andrew."

I nodded.

She pushed some hair out of her eyes. "So, you're a teacher, right? That's how you know Andrew?"

"Yeah," I said, "Well, I'm on leave, right now, I had a — there was a, a family thing."

"Right."

We stood there. She rubbed her ear. My knowledge of her story made it highly likely that she had knowledge of mine. The two of us, a bad joke: cancer and suicide walk into a bar —

"So, Andrew says you and your boyfriend got back together, how's that going?"

"Andrew said that?"

She looked a little sheepish. "Sorry."

"It's okay," I said. I didn't know what to say; were Patrick and I back together? What was I supposed to do with her? Give her something? Make small talk? "Do you want some tea?" I asked. I probably had some tea bags at the back of the pantry. Tea bags didn't expire, did they?

"Sure," she said, but then Andrew's front door opened, and we heard his feet stomping on the front mat.

& J "Carly never talked about suicide before?"

My cell phone felt hot against my face. I hadn't talked

to Aubrey in over a week. "Never. Don't you think I would have mentioned that?"

"Not even, like, stupid threats?"

"No. Obviously she felt like shit, but she never said anything that would have made me think she would have. . ." What *had* she said? I swallowed. "In the couple days right before she did it, she seemed to be doing better."

"How so?"

"I don't know, Aub, she just — she sounded happier on the phone. I called because I figured, Valentine's Day, she was going to lose it again, without Ryan. But she seemed fine; she started telling me about this new scheme of hers, she was going to be a model."

"I remember, you told me about that, after. . .did she do it?"

"I don't know. I couldn't talk at work, I told her I would talk to her about it later."

"And you didn't?"

"No. She didn't pick up that night, but she sent me a goodnight text message right before bed."

"So, maybe you should stop blaming yourself."

That easy.

 After Carly, I started to remember Before Carly.

My kindergarten Mother's Day tea.

The tightness of my party dress that I'd started to outgrow.

The cupcakes on a table in the classroom, the thick pink icing.

Moms mulled around, moms wearing dresses and high-heeled shoes. My mom owned one pair of heels, but didn't wear them anymore, because of the baby in her tummy. Sometimes she let me put my hand on her belly and feel the baby kick. My little brother or sister was coming at the beginning of Grade One, which seemed a long way away.

"Where's your mom?" Someone else's mom asked me.

I was the only one without a mom.

My teacher pulled me onto her lap.

I ate my cupcake.

I ate my mom's cupcake.

Two of them burned my tongue. Too much, too much sugar.

She came in late, when we were all lined up at the front of the room, reading a Mother's Day poem.

The door opened, noisy. Everybody looked at her: The teachers, the kids, the other moms.

I forgot my line.

Afterwards, she squeezed in beside me on one of the little folding chairs.

"Where were you?" I asked, and squeezed up against her.

"I had a doctor's appointment. Stop whining."

& When I think back to that time when Carly's relationship with Ryan overlapped with mine, I remember Patrick pulling away, like an elastic band, stretching until we snapped.

The Christmas before Patrick and I split up, Carly had the idea to go on an all-inclusive vacation to Cuba. Neither she nor Ryan had any money. She begged Patrick and me to come. The brutality of Calgary winters made this a tempting offer. I reasoned that it might be one of only a few holidays left before Patrick started articling and would have even less time off than he already had. Carly found cheap tickets flying out of Toronto, and promised a "terrific" deal for the week after her exams, leading up to Christmas.

"Darce, you have to live in the moment!"

And so I set about convincing Patrick. He seemed into it, at first. I came home from class and he'd made tacos. The meat tasted slightly too spicy. Tacos weren't actually Cuban, but I valued the effort, a nice break from Patrick's usual studying, worrying about his grades. He took out a book from the library about Varadero, asked if I wanted to do a day trip into Havana. Carly texted me asking if I would do an excursion with her where we would get to swim with dolphins. I pressed a layer of grated cheddar into my taco, trying to make it stay in place. Patrick and I had sex for the first time in a month, and he kissed me with an urgency that made me realize I still had a bit of beef in my teeth.

Lying there, afterwards, he mused, aloud, "How well do you think the hotels in Cuba wash their sheets?"

"I don't know," I said. "I'm pretty sure hotels cater to tourists, though."

"You never know." He had a thin glaze of sweat across his lower abdomen. He looked skinny lying on his back, his stomach concave. "You could stay at a hotel and have no idea how many people had slept on those sheets before. They could just pretend to change them. I bet hotels do it all the time, to save on their water costs."

"I suppose."

He shivered. "It's disgusting! Can you imagine all the germs?" He got up out of the bed to pee, and did not come back. When I wandered out later, I found him on the computer, Googling "dirty hotels exposed."

"If you really care that much, we can just bring our own sheets and make the bed ourselves."

"The sheets are just the beginning! Look at the toilet! This is what these researchers discovered with infrared technology."

That night he spent so long in the shower that when he came out, he'd rubbed his skin bright red and raw. He threw both sets of our sheets in the wash — even the spare set, which had been resting clean and folded in the closet. I wanted to sleep, but they still had a half hour to go in the dryer.

"You're being obsessive," I pointed out. He took a textbook into the kitchen. I took a novel into the laundry closet and watched our sheets tumble dry.

&〈 Had Carly actually gone through with her plan to be a model?

I set to finding out, contacting her friend Heather first. Heather had come to the funeral in a short and clingy black dress, with a gaggle of Carly's new friends from school. Carly often tried to initiate "girls' nights" at the apartment she shared with Ryan. They came, but I wondered if they did so because she had her own apartment and had tendencies to purchase large quantities of cookie dough and fruity coolers, never requiring the other girls to contribute. At the funeral, they all sat in a row, with perky, slightly chubby legs and '80s names: Heather, Jessica, Sarah, Christina — their perfect outfits, perfect teeth. I bit down hard on the inside of my cheek.

There were, in fact, a series of photos that had been taken the last day I talked to her, the afternoon before she died. Carly had underestimated the age of Jamie, the photographer, by several years, though when I surfed Jamie's website, he had pictures of himself, in which he, as Carly had correctly reported, sported a hat — a black fedora with a green band, making him look like a mobster. Heather had gone to the photo shoot too, which Jamie proved by emailing me several shots of Heather, wearing only strategically placed pieces of duct tape, including, in one photo, a strip across her mouth. Jamie's cavalier forwarding of Heather's naked photos made me wonder who else had already seen Carly's stripped snapshots.

Though Carly and Heather did not appear in any photos together (or at least none that I was shown), the date stamp on both sets of pictures read the same: February 14, 2007. Both Heather and Jamie said Carly left first, on her own, and Heather had hung out with Jamie longer because she'd had a thing for him.

Heather's over eighteen, Jamie wrote in his email, *I just took their pictures that's it. I'm sorry shes dead. I usually charge for electronic negatives but you can have these ones for free.*

Smarmy, self-celebrated asshole. Had he done something to her? Said something? He wouldn't have told me if he had. He claimed he was giving me the full set of Carly's photos, saying he felt it would be disrespectful to her if he were to include them in his "book."

The photos were not particularly tasteful, as Carly had assured me. She knelt, with one leg crossed in front of the other, exposing the rounded curve of her thigh and bum. She had her hands up and over her breasts but splayed open like stars, with her middle fingers covering her nipples, though some areola was still visible. She arched her back slightly, her hair wild and tousled. I could make out the small scar above her belly button, from the piercing she'd removed. Her eyes looked straight at the camera, wide and gullible. *I'm a model!* She seemed to be thinking. *I hope I don't look fat in these pictures. Ryan is going to phone tonight.*

The last photographs of my sister alive.

&T I sold the car I'd bought after moving to Calgary for less than it was worth and put the excess cash in my savings account. I dreaded having to go back to teaching, having to go back to being responsible for needy children. Wasn't I destined to just fuck them up? When I expressed my concerns, my doctor suggested changing my medication to a daily dosage. I shook my head. The bottle at home still contained the full set of pills. At one point, it had fallen off my bathroom counter and Kipling ran off with it, batting it between her paws like a rattle. I snatched it back from her, glad for the childproof lid.

I walked the full forty minutes to the office, unwilling to take the c-train. So far, the long walk hadn't been an issue. I hadn't thought ahead as far as the fall, or worse, the winter.

Leaving the office after my check-up, I stopped at the café in the bottom of the building to get a bottle of water. Was it — Conor? — in line, ahead of me? Conor wearing dress pants? I had never, in the years I'd known him, seen Conor wearing dress pants. I tried to think of the last time I'd seen him. Was he on a date?

"Conor?" I said, experimentally.

He turned around, cocked his head, as if trying to place me. "Hi," he said. "This is probably confusing — I'm Joel, Conor's brother."

"Oh," I said, and then, embarrassed, laughed. Carly certainly wasn't laughing. Who was I to laugh, when —

I shut my mouth.

"And you are?" he asked.

"Darcy. I teach with — I used to teach with — well, I was on leave last year."

Conor had mentioned his brother, but not the fact that they were twins. My blathering seemed redundant — I'd probably come up in conversations between the two of them before. That poor girl whose sister jumped in front of the subway. What an unexpected tragedy.

Joel stepped away from the counter. I still held the bottle of water I hadn't yet paid for.

"I work in the building." He balanced a Styrofoam container of soup and a croissant in one hand and a rolled-up copy of *The Globe and Mail* in the other. "I'm on my lunch break."

I smiled, trying to be polite. An unfamiliar version of a very familiar person.

"You're welcome to join me," he offered.

I took a step back. "Uh, that's okay, I should get home."

"Okay," he said, "It was nice to meet you. And don't worry about thinking I was Conor. Happens all the time."

When I was outside the café, in the furious sun, I realized I'd walked out without paying for the water, my hands like fists around the stolen bottle.

&⎯ Often, the long forgotten memories would find me, tugging on the edges of my shirts the way Carly used to. *Remember us?* Carly, two years old, wearing a blanket over her head, pretending to be a ghost, slamming into the apartment wall and rebounding back onto her diapered bum, letting out a delayed wail of shock.

Carly, six years old, sitting in the bathtub, drawing hearts on the tiles with bath-time crayons, her hair lathered into a swirl on the top of her head, singing, "Nobody likes me, everybody hates me, I'm gonna eat some worms!" A cat, kidnapped from Papi's apartment, walking along the edge of the tub, sniffing curiously at the masses of bubbles.

Carly, seven years old, having begged me to take her to church because all her classmates went, and Mom had stopped taking us. When the priest began talking about the Holy Spirit, the symbol of a dove, which each person had inside of him or herself, she'd whispered into my ear. "I bet I know where they keep it. In the rib cage."

Carly, eleven, prancing around in her pink polka-dot bathing suit in front of the Victoria's Secret runway show on TV.

Carly, thirteen, caught chatting on the Internet with HOT_BOI664, naively pecking in our home phone number.

Carly, fourteen, the one and only time (she swore!) she'd smoked a cigarette, in her bedroom, as though she wanted to get caught. What was that smell? Why was Carly coughing so loudly? "I promise, I just wanted to see what it was all about!"

Carly, fifteen, Carly, sixteen, Carly, seventeen —

I walked too far past the turn to my apartment and found myself at an intersection, in front of a homeless woman and her doleful-eyed German shepherd. Her sign read "$1 for Good Karma." The dog raised its head at me for a moment, then lowered its chin into its owner's lap, hungry. Hopeless.

There was an old lady who swallowed a cat.
Imagine that! She swallowed a cat.
She swallowed the cat to catch the bird.
She swallowed the bird to catch the spider,
that wiggled and jiggled and tickled inside her.
She swallowed the spider to catch the fly.
I don't know why she swallowed a fly.
Perhaps she'll die.

&T When I graduated high school, a month after my eighteenth birthday, I began hunting the classifieds for apartments near campus. My acceptance letter to the University of
Toronto English department had arrived months earlier, and I'd
originally planned to live at home as long as possible because of
Carly. The six-year age difference was a major problem. I sat in
silent rage at the dinner table while Dick shovelled overcooked
lasagne onto our plates, watching Carly squirm and pinch her lips
together. She often sat at the table long after he and our mother
went to watch one of their sitcoms, crying softly and trying to
swallow bites of whatever gristly casserole he'd prepared that
night — they all tasted exactly the same. And, in the same chair,
gnawing on her pencil, forced to finish her homework before bed.
Often, her notebooks had holes in them from erasing so hard.
the book i am doing my report on is ann of green gabuls a book about

a gril who is an orphun and she cause lots of trubel. I couldn't stay, but I couldn't imagine leaving her there. She would not even turn twelve until September. She wouldn't graduate high school — if she even graduated at all — for over five years.

I met Papi for coffee on College Street, and paid for my cinnamon latte and his black-with-one-sugar. As soon as I'd paid, I regretted it. I'd wanted to demonstrate my maturity as an independent, fully functioning adult so that he would be more likely to go along with what my plan for Carly to live with me. But then I realized I should have demonstrated thriftiness, showing him I intended to save my money to raise my sister, not splurging on frilly, sugary drinks.

I would do a better job than my mother and asshole stepfather. I wouldn't sit in the bathtub all day. I wouldn't go on random, spontaneous vacations and abandon my kids. I wouldn't force Carly to sit at the table doing her homework without help, trying unsuccessfully to cry without making too much noise, using her napkin or the edge of her shirt to muffle the sound. Plus, Carly being in school all day made caregiving arrangements unnecessary. If I had to take a night class, maybe Papi could babysit. He had before our mother remarried. Why not now?

Papi sipped his coffee slowly while I made my proposal. I rambled on and on about how I was totally prepared, how I'd basically taken care of Carly for years already.

When he finally spoke, he cupped his hands around his mug, as if to keep them warm. "Darcy, that's very generous of you, and I think you're a wonderful big sister. But your mother is not going to let Carly move in with you. Carly is *her* daughter."

"My mom doesn't care about Carly," I blurted. "She barely pays attention to her. And Richard treats her like crap. They'd probably love it if I took Carly off their hands. Then my mom could stop bitching about all her headaches and stomachaches and stuff. She resents having kids in the first place."

"That's a harsh assessment."

I sat back in my chair and took a large sip, scalding the top of my mouth. My tongue felt fuzzy. "I can't leave her there!"

"Yes," he said, "I know it feels like you can't move out without your sister, and I know you worry about her. But Darcy, I feel — " he paused. "Please don't be offended by what I am about to say."

My mouth tasted awful.

"Darcy, I'm worried — I know it's hard to picture your sister staying where you think she is unhappy while you move forward. But you need to have your own life, too. It is time for you to move out and think about yourself. As an adult, you need to find yourself, discover what kind of career you want, find someone you want to spend your life with. You can't let your sister hold you back from that. You deserve it, too."

"I can do all of that! *And* raise Carly."

He sipped his coffee again. So calm. My fingers danced in my lap, twisted the edge of my shirt into a knot.

"You're too young to have an eleven-year-old daughter," he added.

"Then *you* take her!" It sounded desperate. I put my hands flat on the table to steady them. "I can't just leave her there."

"I'm too *old* to have an eleven-year-old daughter." He put one of his soft hands over mine. "I know how hard it is for you to watch your sister struggle. And I know you disagree with the way your mother parents. But Carly is *your mother's* child, and like it or not, she gets to decide how to parent her. *You* made it through without the protection of a big sister."

"But I'm not Carly!" I insisted. "I made it through, but that doesn't mean she will."

"Right," he said. "You're not Carly. And now it is time to be Darcy."

& After I was born, I was checked out in the NICU because I arrived prematurely, but the only noticeable symptom was jaundice. Premature, but with a birth-weight of six pounds, and fully developed lungs. Sometimes I wondered whether my mother simply failed to accurately remember my date of conception.

She'd once wished Carly a happy birthday a full week before the actual date. "My birthday came *early?*" Carly shrieked. Explaining that it actually hadn't? *Fun.*

One Mother's Day, Carly woke up early and made a breakfast omelette with a face in it. Mom wandered in, then began picking up all the ingredients: broken eggshells, onion peel, an empty milk carton. She held up the cheese grater. "What's going on? What's wrong? You're not supposed to be in here."

Mom missed work shifts, went at the wrong times. She got fired from one job, and went on unemployment insurance. One Saturday, she ran panicked into our bedroom at five o'clock in the morning, screaming at us, "Get up! Get up! You're going to be late for school."

She couldn't find her keys. She forgot to pay bills and tickets on time. She misplaced Carly's birth certificate. When prescribed painkillers for the various changing ailments Dr. Martin discovered, Mom forgot to take them, despite complaining about how unbearably she ached. She virtually never remembered to give Carly multivitamins, and could not remember the appropriate dosage for over the counter cough syrups. Instead, I poured the purple liquid into our shallow kitchen spoons, trying to balance it so that it wouldn't spill while Carly coughed and sneezed and protested.

In the midst of a common cold that had turned into an ear infection and kidnapped my voice, I thought about Carly, having a hot and humid Toronto summer fling with her new boyfriend, Ryan. Carly, almost the same age as our mother when our mother conceived me. Carly was going to do something stupid. She was already doing something stupid.

I'd finished the first year of my Education degree several months earlier, and worked full-time that summer as a receptionist at a doctor's office to supplement my income and student loans. Probably a bad idea, in retrospect: exposing myself to all those germs with my crappy immune system. I'd started feeling sick the previous Thursday, and the office was closed Friday for the Canada Day long weekend. Patrick had accepted a summer job at a law firm and worked sixty-plus hours a week. Despite the summer heat, the apartment felt unpleasantly cold. I peeled the sheets away from myself and stood in the shower, shivering under the hot stream, chilled to the core. My nipples stood at attention, my body refusing to warm. After a nap, I thought, I would go to a walk-in clinic and get a prescription for some antibiotics. The university clinic wasn't open on weekends.

I settled myself on the couch but couldn't fall asleep, even with two Tylenol and bits of Kleenex shoved in my ears and a towel wrapped around my wet hair. Carly had met Ryan just over a week before, a new hire at The Upstairs Basement, the restaurant where she bused tables, still too young to actually waitress. I wanted her to focus on school, but Dick had told her that he wasn't going to pay for her to go to the movies or buy clothes anymore. He hadn't gone to college, and didn't care if Carly did either.

Carly told me she thought Ryan looked gorgeous — but I couldn't form a mental picture of him, what with all her conflicting adjectives. His hair was both "muddy" and "goldy," he was "short" and "muscly" and "athletic" and "fragile." He had facial hair, she said, and the first time they'd made out it had chafed her skin, leaving her nose and chin red. "I think everybody at work could tell something was going on," she said, clearly thrilled to be the centre of gossip. "My new nickname is Rudolph. Like, the red-nosed reindeer?"

By the end of that first week she told me a story about them passing a jewellery store on Bay Street and how she couldn't stop ogling the engagement rings.

She hadn't called me that day, or the day before, but I couldn't stay awake to phone her, couldn't make my vocal chords work. I drifted off into a tipsy, uneven sleep, dreaming of Carly: pregnant, sweaty, screaming, and in labour. When her baby came out, it looked exactly like she had as an infant, with fluffs of blond hair. But then, the baby writhed in my hands, and I looked down, looked at my infant in my arms. I'd just given birth, to my own sister. Baby Carly screamed, squeezing her eyes together and balling her tiny fists in fury. Love me! Pay attention to me! You're not doing a good enough job!

I woke up to Patrick, arriving home. He dropped his knapsack down on the floor, which startled me out of my mucousy sleep.

"What time is it?" I croaked, disoriented.

"Nine," he said. "How long did you sleep?"

My throat ached. "I don't remember."

He heated some soup up on the stove, and then, while it cooled, drove to the drug store to find something over the counter and stronger than what we had at home. "I don't want to sit with you at the walk-in all night," he'd said. "This time of night, we'd wait for hours. Hospitals have so many germs. . ."

"It's going to get worse," I argued.

"Antibiotics just build our resistance and make infectious diseases stronger."

By Monday, whatever I'd managed to contract seemed to be clearing up by itself, but my boss told me not to come to work, to take an extra day and make sure I was 100 percent. When Patrick went to leave for work around six AM, and I dragged myself to the door with a blanket around my shoulders, stood on my tiptoes to kiss him goodbye.

He turned his face away. "You're still not well enough."

He'd slept on the couch since I'd started sniffling. After my nap, he'd sprayed the couch with disinfectant and quarantined me to the bedroom, hauling in the TV and balancing it on the dresser for me to watch.

"I can't be sick with my job right now," he reasoned. The house stank so strongly of lemon cleanser that I could smell it even with my blocked nasal passages.

Back in bed, I finally gave Carly a call. Four days had elapsed, probably the longest we'd ever gone without speaking. I sensed anger in her avoidance. She'd once gone on a talking strike after our mother yelled at her, refusing to speak, hoping, perhaps, that Mom would apologize. It didn't work, both because our mother simply went on cleaning, and because Carly barely held out half an hour. After pouting around with her arms crossed dramatically, huffing loudly, she finally gave up, exclaiming, "I hate you!" and then came to find me.

"Will you play Candy Land with me?"

"No, I'm doing homework."

"How about Operation?"

"Carly! Leave me alone!"

When she answered my phone call, she said, "Shhh! Ryan's sleeping!"

"Where are you?" I blew my nose.

"Just a sec, I'm going into the living room. You sound like shit! Bad cold?"

"Yeah. Sorry, that's why I haven't called. You mad at me?"

"What?" She sounded baffled, her voice still thick with sleep. "Sorry, we went out last night with Gemma and her boyfriend and then we were up all night talking. Ryan's grandparents went out of town for the weekend. Mom thinks I'm staying at Kelsey's. Did you know Ryan is double-jointed *and* he can make tiramisu? And he's thinking of getting his own place! On Saturday, I had this terrible headache, I think it was a migraine like Mom gets. It was kinda like my head was being pounded with hammers. Or squeezed in one of those things, one of those things that kinda like, pinches — "

"A vise."

"And before that, I'd had a terrible day at work, where a customer spilled wine all over my favourite sweater and then I cried in front of everyone! I think that's why the migraine came on. Anyway, Ryan stayed in bed with me all night, and held a wet cloth to my forehead, and then when my headache had finally got better, he was like, Babe — that's what he calls me, Babe — he was like, Babe, you need some dessert. So — "

"So he made you tiramisu."

She laughed. "No. He didn't have all the ingredients, but he did have these chocolate pudding cups. So we ate these pudding cups, and they tasted *awful* — they'd expired like, six months ago! We were just in bed, sitting there, eating rotten pudding! So funny. Totally cheered me up. I love him *so* much."

& I heard the noise above my bedroom — yelling, name-calling, swearing. Fuck sounded the same through floorboards as it did directly coming out of my mother's mouth. When we first moved into Dick's house, the noises through the floorboards were often directed at Carly: yelling, reprimanding, sometimes a spank or a smack. And always, Carly's cries.

But that night, Carly had already gone to bed, and I was in my pyjamas, studying for a final exam.

Maybe, I thought, if they fight with each other enough, she'll leave him. She'll leave him, and we can go back to —

My mom leaned in the doorway to my bedroom, a jittery shadow. "We're going out."

"You and Richard?"

"Fuck Richard." Her eyes darted away. "Get dressed. I'll get your sister."

Carly slid her flip-flops on in the doorway, pulled back her tangled hair in an elastic band. "Where are we going?"

The sun had started to dangle longer in the sky before descending into night as spring slithered into summer. Carly and I both had major exams coming up before summer could really start; my Grade Twelve final exams and Carly's Grade Six EQAOs. I tutored her in math while struggling to stay on top of my own math curriculum. I'd already decided to major in English. Our father had gone to business school, which I imagined involved lots of math; apparently, neither Carly nor I had inherited his genes. Maybe for the better.

We rode the subway south to King Street, got off, and started walking.

Mom strode quickly on a pair of old high heels I vaguely remembered, almost tripping in a sewer grate. "Three girls going out for a nice meal. Well, look at us!"

Carly trotted behind her, trying to keep up.

I'd eaten at the restaurant where we finally stopped once before, for Aubrey's sweet sixteen. Her mother had ordered sparkling lemon sodas for me, Aubrey, and Aubrey's cousins, and an appetizer platter of prosciutto and brie. All the desserts had Italian names: Frutti, Nocciola, Tiramisu.

Way out of our price range.

"I can't read this menu," Carly complained, as the waiter carried a tray of savoury pizzas past our table. "Ooh, pizza! Do you think they have pepperoni?"

The pizza made its way to a table where a young woman with

long, dark waves of hair sat breastfeeding a small infant obscured by a pink and white appliqué blanket.

My mother scoffed.

Carly looked up from her menu. "What?"

"Breastfeeding in public!" My mother tore apart a piece of bread from the basket in the middle of our table. "I mean, have some decency."

"You breastfed Carly," I pointed out.

My mother put the bread in her mouth. "I breastfed you both," she corrected, while chewing. "But not in public. And not a day longer than I had to. If we'd had money back then, I would have bottle fed from the start."

Her voice carried, too loud for the ambiance of the restaurant. I watched the mother with the pizza to see if she'd noticed. She lifted her long hair and draped it over the shoulder opposite her infant.

"Why?" Carly wanted to know.

My mother raised her eyebrows. "You want a kid chewing on your nipples?" She'd eaten her way through three slices of bread. When our waitress returned, Mom ordered lamb ragout. I cringed. I'd planned to order the same thing. Instead, I ordered what Carly was having.

When the bill came, Carly said she needed to pee — also, too loudly — and sauntered off to the bathroom. My mother rooted through her purse. "You got any change on you?" she asked me.

I had a couple twenties that I hadn't deposited yet from babysitting for a few families Aubrey had outgrown. Aubrey was about to start a summer internship with her father's company; until then, she'd abandoned all part-time jobs to study for finals. Aubrey had consistently trounced me in the grades department since we were kids; all As to my Bs. But I didn't have a father whose company would pay my way through university. After being accepted to the University of Toronto's English program, I'd filled out paperwork for as much money in student loans as I could get approved for.

My mother slid the bill my way. "I think you should pay for your own meal. It's about time you started contributing. You take advantage of Richard's generosity, you know, supporting two kids that aren't even his. I don't think you should feel entitled to a free ride."

I pulled a twenty from my wallet.

"I'm moving out," I said. I hadn't told her yet. "In the fall. For university."

She shoved another piece of bread in her mouth.

Ran her tongue over her teeth.

Swallowed.

"Good," she said.

Until then, I hadn't completely made up my mind.

But then, I'd said it out loud.

    I expected Carly to freak out at the idea of me moving out. Instead, she ran around my empty 500-square-foot bachelor pad. "You should put your desk over here. . .no, the bed over here, and the bookshelf in that corner." Spatially, my furniture really only fit one possible configuration.

Carly helped me assemble my single bed and desk, taped my posters up crookedly, and surprised me by spending her allowance on a tiny potted plant, so I wouldn't be so lonely.

"You can come over whenever you want," I told her.

"I know," she chirped. She flopped down on my bed, starfish style, with her head hanging upside down. "I wish I had my own apartment. You're so lucky."

& Ryan was on the short side for a guy — short and broad, with the kind of brown hair that had faded from childhood blond, and a perpetual five o'clock shadow.

I flew back for a visit the summer they started dating, and part of me assumed they would break up by the time I got there.

Patrick's cousin Anderson had invited us to his wedding, and the bride insisted I come to her bachelorette party, which was on the Friday before the ceremony. Patrick and I booked the Friday and Monday off work and flew out at the ungodly hour of four AM. Friday morning. Patrick hated flying because it meant being confined in a small space with so many people. He claimed that fewer people flew the red eye. I let him sit by the window, because he whispered that the person on the aisle looked contagious. He'd gotten a new prescription for sleeping pills just before the flight, and he popped twice the recommended dosage as soon as we boarded. Before we even ascended, he dozed off, his neck cradled in a semicircular airline pillow. I wondered if the new pills would work once we got back home.

I stayed wide awake.

Carly and Ryan met us at the airport, Carly hugging me while jingling the keys to Ryan's car. Her hair looked tousled, as though she'd ran from the parking lot, and she danced around us, talking loudly, gesticulating with her hands.

Carly didn't drink, but behind the wheel, one would have imagined her to be intoxicated.

"Where's the turn? Did I miss it?" She impulsively pulled a U-turn while Patrick and I tensed our bodies in automatic anticipation of a crash. She sang along with the radio and began to move the wheel in time to the beat without realizing it, causing the car to fishtail.

In the backseat, I cringed, hoping Patrick wouldn't comment. I'd taught her how to drive, for Christ's sake! I'd taught her never to answer her phone while driving or pack more people into a car than the number of seatbelts. My sister, and the rest of the planet, were safer if Carly took public transit.

What was Patrick thinking as she drove? As she sang off-key and dominated the conversation?

"The yam fries at work are better than the regular fries, but they cost a dollar more. But Ryan and I get a 50-percent-off employee discount. Remember how Mom would always bring home fries, Darce?"

I smelled deep fry. "That pedestrian had the right of way."

"I wish Mom had brought home yam fries, back in the day. They're better for you, too, less, um, you know. . ."

"Starch," Ryan supplemented.

Patrick sat fussy and tight-lipped in the backseat, flinching whenever Carly slid through a stop sign, answering questions with single words, squirming because of a discarded, grease-spotted cardboard fast food container at his feet.

"Sorry, we're out of sorts," I explained, trying to make amends for me *and* Patrick, even though technically, Patrick had slept the entire plane ride, and I wasn't being difficult. When we arrived at Ryan and Carly's apartment — Ryan smiling and unperturbed, and me, thankful that we'd all escaped with our lives — Carly lifted our bags out of the trunk. She shifted her eyes first towards Patrick and then towards me as if to say, "What's *his* problem?"

I missed the easygoing Patrick I'd dated back in Toronto. The stress of law school, of living in a new city, of the two of us living together and adjusting to each other's idiosyncrasies would all be over soon. I hoped.

I loved them both. But seeing each through the other's eyes, their flaws magnified. The hot sun beamed too bright against my face.

In all honesty, when I look back on that trip, I don't remember much of Ryan at all.

& Prior to Anderson's wedding, the only wedding I'd ever attended was my mother and Dick's. During the reception, Carly and the ring bearer chased each other around in the basement of the hall with their hands smeared with liquid soap residue, threatening to ruin each others' formal attire. I sat sulking in the corner picking at my plate of smelly hors d'oeuvres, strange hairy vegetables wrapped in shaved meat. I scratched my itchy nylons.

My own parents had tied the knot because my mother had found out she was pregnant with me. Nothing like a shotgun wedding because someone got knocked up. How stupid, I wondered, did one have to be to get pregnant by accident? All kinds of people, like Aubrey's parents, tried and tried for a baby for years. We went to Catholic school, which prohibited education about any kind of prophylactics, but, when we were twelve, Aubrey bought some condoms at the shifty little variety store on the corner where the man behind the counter didn't ask questions. We'd stretched them over a few bananas, then got bored and decided to see whether they would fit over different kinds of fruit. We succeeded with kiwi and apple, but failed with a fairly large mango, our hands slimy with lubricant.

By the time I lost my virginity, Aubrey had already slept with five "boys" whom she often spoke of as packages of ham or containers of yogurt — with expiry dates. "Things are just going sour," she would announce, seemingly out of nowhere, while I worried about whether I would know how to have sex or not. Aubrey took to calling me "Leo," in reference to a children's book about a tiger we'd once read to Carly, *Leo the Late Bloomer.*

"Better late than never, Leo," Aubrey had taken to teasing. The Catholic in me wanted to call her out on her promiscuity.

But, in university together, over coffee or during breaks between classes, she'd talk about her latest assignment and then I'd ask how things were going with her latest guy.

"Oh, did I not tell you?" She'd bite down on her flax/protein/ whole grain granola bar. "Jason's out. What kind of guy wears socks with sandals?"

The day before I had to go back to work for the first time since Carly died, when I was at home in bed having a panic attack about the responsibility of twenty-nine innocent eleven- and twelve-year-olds, Aubrey phoned. She opened the conversation with, "I have something to tell you. I'm engaged."

I hadn't even known she had a boyfriend. She hadn't brought anyone to the funeral.

When I asked, she said, "Well, I didn't tell you about it."

"How — how long?"

"Since February."

The date made things fall together. "You didn't tell me because of — "

"It wasn't the greatest timing."

"It's been. . .six months!"

My sister — dead for six months.

"Seven," Aubrey corrected. "And I was going to tell you, but at first it just felt inappropriate to talk about my love life, and then you got kind of stuck. When I called, you barely talked. I could only get one-word answers out of you. And, you never asked how I was, or if anything was new with me."

I bit my lip, hard. "Stuck? Aubrey, my sister *killed herself*."

"Hey," she said. "when Carly died. . .you're not the only one who was affected. I still get nauseous every time think about her, like all the stupid songs she would sing. They get stuck in my head. But there are other things going on in the world, too. I'm getting married."

I pulled my blanket up over my head.

"Say something," Aubrey insisted.

"I didn't think you wanted to get married. When we were kids, we always said we were going to boycott marriage."

"When we were *kids*," she repeated. "People change."

I could not fathom feeling any sort of excitement or pleasure. The ingredients with which to make such emotions did not exist inside me anymore.

"Thanks," Aubrey said, after a moment of silence. "You know, you could have at least been happy for me. You could have at least tried."

  To try to keep Patrick sane during law school, I started making his lunch every day: bagels with cream cheese, mini Tupperware containers filled with cherry tomatoes and celery, a Ziploc baggie of pretzels. In elementary school, Aubrey's mom scrawled notes on napkins and tucked them into Aubrey's paper lunch bags. Aubrey scrapped them into the garbage can, rolling her eyes. "My mom — the cheeseball."

After work, Patrick spent a good hour cleaning per a daily schedule. Mondays, Wednesdays, and Fridays, he'd vacuum and clean the kitchen; Tuesdays and Thursdays he'd clean the bathroom. After cleaning, regardless of the task, he'd take a shower. I tried to sneak in with him, surprise him. He was surprised, but not in a good way.

"Can I have some privacy, please?" He blocked the entrance to the shower with his arm. Water streamed into his hair and ran into his eyes. He shook his head. The soft droplets tingled cold against my naked skin. I went and lay down in our bed with a book, but not before getting dressed.

I started cleaning the house before he'd get home, according to his chore schedule. Carly called twice while I vacuumed; I didn't hear it the first time, and then only caught the last ring of the second call.

"Why didn't you pick up?" she whined, when I called her back.

"I was vacuuming." I wound the vacuum cord around its base, then wondered if I should have emptied it first. Dust filled only half the canister, but I imagined the dirt still driving Patrick nuts.

"What a waste of time. You should just relax. Vacuuming sucks." She laughed at her own joke.

I opened the fridge, surveying the contents to see what I could put in Patrick's lunch the next day.

"I'm bored," Carly whined. "Entertain me."

Cheese. Bread. Slightly wilted lettuce. "I'm making Patrick's lunch," I told her.

"Boring. You clean for him, you make his lunch. You make a good mom."

Had the ham Patrick carefully sealed in a Ziploc baggie expired? I tried to recall when we'd purchased it. "I like taking care of him," I told Carly, balancing my phone between my ear and shoulder.

Carly laughed. "We're so different."

"How so?"

"I'd just so much rather be the one being taken care *of.*"

&ᴛ Aubrey had said, *There are other things going on in the world, too.* I turned off the TV when the news came on, tore up Aubrey's save-the-date card when it arrived. Walked past last year's lesson plans — boxed in my closet — but refused to take them out, to look at them.

Carly thought the whole world revolved around her. My whole world did. So why hadn't the world stopped?

I couldn't sleep the night before school started. I'd forced myself to go back through the curriculum in August, but teaching sixth grade again meant my lesson plans from the previous year would suffice. "We have a couple weeks before school starts," Conor had reminded me. "Use this time to relax. You're going to need it."

I poured myself a bath, but the water almost scalded my fingers. Distracted by a series of photos of Carly on my computer, by the time I went back to check the temperature, the bubbles had flattened and the water felt tepid to the touch.

On the first day of school, I arrived bleary-eyed, but insomnia had made me get up early, straighten my hair, iron a blouse, and put on makeup. I looked like a human being.

At lunch, I found a seat beside Conor at the staff meeting. He scribbled an illegible note to himself on a notepad in front of him, then elbowed me. "I have to talk to you." Somehow, coming from Conor, it didn't carry the same valence as when Aubrey had said exactly the same thing.

Before Conor could tell me what he wanted to talk about, though, our principal launched into a welcome-back speech, during which he glanced in my direction and commented, "And we welcome back Ms. Nolan, who took leave for the latter part of last year for personal reasons." The one or two teachers new to St. Sebastian glanced up from their coffees. As a new teacher, talk of "leaves" always elicited a strange mixture of curiosity, feelings of superiority, and anxious dread. None of us wanted to believe that we would collapse under the pressure.

Once, when I was in the sixth grade, my entire class had colluded to drive a substitute teacher to her breaking point. The class ringleader, a girl whose glossy chocolate hair I envied, masterminded a plot of pen-clicking, desk-doodling, name changes, seat changes, incessant requests to go to the bathroom, homework refusal, and faking sick. The substitute tried effecting a week of lunch-hour detentions, though that just trapped her with us longer. After a solid week of hoping our regular teacher would recover from whatever ailment had rendered us with this incompetent, overweight twentysomething, Alicia Penner randomly began a chorus of "The Song That Doesn't End," and we all chimed in. Our substitute stood at the front of the room holding a math text to her chest for a good three rounds of the song before slamming the textbook on her desk and darting out of the room. I balled my left hand into a fist, pressed all the nails into my palm until it hurt. What had the substitute ever done to Alicia? Why was I still singing? *Somebody started singing it, not knowing what it was, and they'll continue singing it, forever, just because —*

Conor followed me out of the staff meeting into the hallway, jovially putting his giant basketball dribbling hands on my shoulders, almost pushing me forward into a scrappy fourth-grader with his head down, digging a king-sized Snickers bar out of his lunch bag. "What good are all my lectures on healthy food groups when parents keep packing their lunches with C-R-A-P?" Conor asked.

"You know," I said, "some of these kids can actually spell. At least, I hope so. If I'm doing my job properly."

He released his grip on me. "Sorry."

"What did you want to tell me?" I yawned, lifted my hair off my neck for a moment. It had grown long and unruly over the summer; straightened, it looked even longer. I wished I'd brought a hair elastic.

"Right!" Conor scratched a spot in his ear, "Yeah, that. So, I was talking to my brother yesterday, and he said you guys had lunch?"

I'd run into Joel again, after a follow-up doctor's appointment. After my embarrassing behaviour when we'd first met, I couldn't turn down his second invitation, though I sensed pity behind it. We sat in a corner table, next to a window, and under a surprisingly chilly air conditioner that mocked the summer scene outside. Joel apologized to me on behalf of the Italian wedding soup I'd purchased. He continued to purchase his lunch at the café despite the remarkably pitiful cuisine, he said, because he barely had time to eat in-between clients. He had one client who had an annoying habit of trashing his play room, which forced him to spend his lunch hour tidying for the next client, a little girl with an anxiety disorder who got upset if the toys weren't in the correct places.

"I really have to stop scheduling them back to back," he confessed. Why was he taking an hour-long lunch to eat crappy soup with me?

"So," Conor said, "was it a date?"

"No." A headache had started to build behind my eyes. "He and my doctor work in the same office building."

When Joel had made a joke about the soup, his smile revealing a slight dimple in his left cheek, a tiny physical trait he did not share with his brother, Carly's voice popped into my head.

"He is hot! *You should ask him out."*

Conor absently scratched his ear. "Shame. Don't tell my brother that. You'll bum him out."

"Why?"

"He brought your name up five times yesterday, out of nowhere. *So, how long have you known her? She's teaching Grade Six again this year? Does she have a boyfriend?* I think Patrick should be jealous, don't you?"

& A month after going back to teaching, the school psychologist at St. Sebastian knocked on my door and poked her head in, just as I started packing up my belongings for the day. I slid a stack of ungraded tests into my backpack. Why had she come? Someone on the staff must have mentioned something. Could she tell I'd been white-knuckling my job for the last twenty-two days? I pressed the thumbnail of my left hand into the palm of my right, under the desk.

"Got a sec?" She didn't wait for my answer.

We'd met once the previous school year. Stephanie. Stephanie something. When she'd shaken my hand the first time, I'd thought about Stefany Beale, who adored the colour orange, who loved rollerblading, who had a small strawberry birthmark on her left side, only visible when she raised her arm. Carly had sported a birthmark, too, a pale, watery blotch barely visible, a sun spot on her right inner forearm. Stefany's mom called her Peanut. Stefany Beale: obviously dead. She'd probably been killed within the first day or so. Strangled, maybe. Or stabbed. What was left her after so long? Somebody's Peanut, dead somewhere, probably buried. Maybe people walked over her remains all the time.

Stephanie, psychologist Stephanie, dragged a chair up in front of my desk. "So, I just wanted to drop by and have a quick chat about one of your students. Celina. . .uh, Janik?"

She pronounced it wrong — Yan-eek, not Jan-ick. I didn't bother correcting her, as Celina often didn't. I'd pronounced it wrong the first three days when doing roll call until one of Celina's friends finally pointed it out to me after class. Celina was one of my quieter students, tiny and dark-haired with rainbow elastics around her braces. She rarely raised her hand, but when she did, she always knew the answers. When I'd asked the class on the first day to hand in a paragraph or two telling me about themselves, Celina had written a list of facts about everyone else in her life. Her parents, her sisters, her pet parakeets, Topsy and Turvy.

"Anyway, I got a call from Mrs. Janik — apparently Celina's dad walked out about a week ago. Just up and left, no contact information, nothing. She hasn't been able to reach him, and he disconnected his cell phone. She's pretty worried about Celina, and the younger siblings. Three other kids, I think."

"Two," I said. "Two more girls."

"Right. Anyway, I just thought I'd mention it, so you could keep an eye out for Celina over the next little while, let me know if you notice any unusual behaviour. Sounds like Mrs. Janik has her hands full — three girls! Yikes. Apparently the youngest one has asthma and ends up in the hospital quite a bit. I don't get that. How someone could just walk out on his kids, especially a sick one? How would he know if anything bad happened to her?"

&⏀ Not too long after he and my mother got remarried, Dick got pissed off at Carly because she kept getting up out of bed to use the bathroom and then couldn't fall asleep. After the third time, he took one of his leather belts and laid it across the threshold of her bedroom door.

"The next time you get up, you're gonna get the strap."

In the morning, Carly had a fever and started urinating blood; turns out, she had a urinary tract infection. Dickhead bought her a popsicle and a litre of cranberry cocktail, let her lie on the couch all day watching cartoons. But two days later, he lost it on her again for putting an empty cracker box back into the cupboard.

A month later, he brought home an audio recorder from work and threatened to record Carly during one of her meltdowns, told her he would go play it for Child and Family Services so they could go find someone else to deal with her, and she'd never get to see me or Mom again.

Later, I snuck into her bedroom and told her that if he ever did something like that, Child and Family Services wouldn't take *her* away, they would arrest *him*. She cried into her raccoon. "Maybe not. Maybe I'm just a stupid pussy nobody loves."

"I love you," I insisted. I should tell her more often, I thought. Poor kid didn't hear it enough.

"No you don't," she snuffled. "You would leave me, too, if you could."

& I hadn't slept before Meet the Parents night at St. Sebastian. Under the fluorescent lights of the staff bathroom, I tried to apply makeup to the dark circles under my eyes, but couldn't cover the blotches entirely. I'd worn torn nylons all day without noticing. I peeled them off, running a hand over my shins to see how long it had been since I'd last shaved my legs. One felt smooth, the other, bristly. Good job, Darce.

Someone had left glazed donuts in the staff lounge, which would have to do for dinner. I'd booked my appointments starting right after dismissal so that I could get them over with. The whole parent-teacher thing took up three after-school evenings in a row. I had twenty-seven students in my class, nine of whom had parents in contentious divorces and who'd booked separate appointments. Fifteen minutes each meant an almost seven-hour commitment — and experience had taught me that parents always blabbered over their allotted time. In the past, I'd aimed to have at least one parent show up for each child in the class. This year, the parents who didn't bother put me one step closer to sleep.

"I'm a terrible teacher," I told Conor, my tongue fuzzy with donut sugar. Conor, who taught all the students gym, but did not have a homeroom class, had no obligation to stay.

"Mary Kay Letourneau was a terrible teacher," he challenged. "You need some perspective. I'm going to run grab a sandwich before soccer practice. Want anything?"

"I'm okay."

He eyed my donut. "Nutritious."

Patrick had often mocked my tendency to graze on whatever food I had nearby for dinner or eat at odd times. He insisted, even while in law school, that we had to eat full, proper meals — a meat, a carb, a vegetable. He couldn't really cook, but he always "assembled" proper meals by boiling frozen peas and carrots, browning rubbery chicken in olive oil on the stovetop. Even when we ordered pizza, he often opened a package of carrot sticks to go along with it. His parents did this, too. Carly and I had grown up with haphazard meals that came from a can or could be contained within two pieces of bread. The most common vegetable consumed in our house had been pickles.

I'd acclimatized to grab-and-go food, a source of energy and fuel, for the primary purpose of keeping my blood sugar up, keeping me functional. When Patrick and I moved in together, and he set down placemats, I couldn't stop picking at them, twiddling the edges between my finger and thumb. Sugared donuts for dinner: totally against Patrick's rules.

& It's surprising how easily someone can stay lost when no one looks for him.

And then, surprising how easily someone can be found.

Dell Nolan.

Search.

On the website for an accounting firm in Markham, I read the name *Dell E. Nolan* beside the title "Marketing Manager." Was it my father? My father, who didn't even know his daughter had killed herself.

D.E.N. We had the same initials.

His name lit up blue; a hyperlink. I'd hovered my cursor over it. What if there was a picture of him? I couldn't recall his face. I thought of those twin faces, deadpan. Their itchy corduroy jumpers. When I clicked over, the link revealed just an email address and phone number. No facts. Had he remarried? Had other children? There could be other little girls out there, who looked and sounded just like Carly. Who had Carly's blood. My blood.

I closed the window, closed my laptop.

I didn't want to know. He'd been good at running away. Maybe I could be, too.

    & Because of our age difference, when I played board games with Carly, I cut the kid some slack, played easy and allowed her to accrue points, even win. But later, when we became more evenly matched, I played more competitively, taking the lead in Yahtzee, or Clue, or Battleship. When I beat her, Carly stormed off in a huff. "You're cheating! This game sucks!" Sometimes Col. Mustard and the candlestick got tossed across the dining room.

"I'm not going to play with you again if you're going to be such a poor sport," I admonished her.

"Whatever," she spat. "I QUIT!"

    & Most evenings after the school day ended, I immersed myself in marking, then immediately fell asleep. If Patrick came over, which he often did, he cooked while I marked, and then we ate and fell asleep together, chaste and exhausted. One evening, looking for something with which to mark my students' journal entries, I rooted around in my junk drawer and closed my fist around a pen. Purple. I don't know how long I held it, not moving, until Patrick, unaware and in the kitchen, asked if I had any basil.

Did I have any basil?

Seriously?

Since "successfully" transitioning back to full-time employment, I didn't have any more appointments with the physician. But work — the bare minimum at work — sucked dry any resources I had. My principal stopped by more often than he had the previous year; always with a smile, but hovering at the back of the room, while I staggered through a math instruction I hadn't properly prepped. Certainly I could not replicate the energetic and ambitious teacher I'd been, determined to make my students not only learn, but *love* to learn.

In October, I stopped outside the school to shake an Advil free from my purse. It hurt going down my throat when I swallowed it dry. I hadn't watched the time close enough. My bus had come and gone. Thirty more minutes.

"Darcy!"

I turned. Joel, all smiles, headed across the parking lot. "Long time no see."

I swallowed. "You're here for Conor?"

"Yeah, he has a date tonight — I brought him an actual dress shirt. With buttons and a collar. He's moving up in the world."

"Okay." Conor hadn't said anything about a date.

"You want a ride home?" Joel offered.

"Um, I'm okay, thanks though. I'm fine taking the bus. Do it every day." I noticed the little yellow emoticon faces patterned across his tie.

"Come on, it'll make up for the terrible food the last time I saw you."

In Joel's new Mazda, I picked at my cuticles, one of Carly's bad habits.

"How's work?" Joel asked, as he slowed for a red light.

"Um, kind of crazy. Almost time for report cards."

"Yeah," he said, "I get a lot of referrals following the first report card of the year. Parents freak out when they don't get the feedback that they want. You know, when little Johnny gets a Needs Improvement in Conflict Resolution, or when little Suzy's reading skills are way below grade level."

"Right." Psychologist Stephanie had removed Jacob Bartony from my class that week for a psychoeducational assessment, handing me a stack of questionnaires to fill out. Instead of thinking of Jake's behaviour, though, I kept thinking of Carly, of that call from the school about her reading difficulties and Dickface refusing to give consent for testing. Would special help have made a difference? What if she'd seen a child psychologist, like Joel? How much of a difference, I wondered, could it really have made, given that, at the end of the day, she still had to go home to my mother and stepfather?

I'd moved out on my own. Left her with them. Moved to Calgary. Left her with them again.

"Makes me glad I don't have any of my own," Joel said.

"Any what? Kids?" I peeled away a piece of skin from my cuticle. Felt the sting.

"Yeah. Being a parent, having a kid twenty-four-seven. . ." He didn't finish the sentence. Turned the windshield wipers on. I hadn't noticed the rain. We stopped in front of my home.

"Nice place," Joel commented.

"I live in the basement. I'm just renting. Trying to save money." He probably already knew this information, I thought, just after saying it. Who knows what information Conor had spilled.

When I'd moved into Andrew's basement, the intent hadn't been to save money, though certainly at that point I couldn't afford an apartment like the one Patrick and I had lived in. Twenty-six years old, still renting someone's dingy basement. Every year on my birthday, Carly unfailingly executed some sort of surprise, though she often ruined the surprise first, hinting way too obviously or trying indiscreetly to ensure I would be home between four and six PM. On my twenty-fifth, she'd sent a barbershop quartet to my classroom with cookies for the kids. I thanked God that none of my students had any nut allergies and resisted the urge to admonish Carly for spending way too much money, though I honestly had no idea what a barbershop quartet cost. On my first birthday without Carly, Patrick came over just before ten with a single peanut butter frosted cupcake. He set the cupcake down on the counter and crawled into bed with me, then, suddenly, roughly, kissed me on the mouth. It was the most intimate move he'd made since Carly's death.

"I'm sorry," he said, immediately after. "I should go. I'll call you." He clambered out of the bed, clumsily, and I heard him take the stairs up from the basement two at a time. I lay alone, trying to remember our last real kiss; the last one before he'd broken up with me. Had it, too, been intense? Or just a rush peck at the door? Maybe just two mouths, barely touching. A cursory, unconscious farewell.

In the morning, the whorls of sugar icing on the birthday cupcake's surface had dried stiff and crusty.

Joel put his hand on the gearshift. "Hey — " he said when I unbuckled my seatbelt. "So, I got invited to a book launch this weekend and I think I'd feel a little out of place. . .but a colleague invited me to go. . .anyway, I thought maybe you'd want to come. You have a degree in English, right?"

I hadn't told him about my degree. "Sounds interesting, but I'm way behind in marking. I don't think socializing is on the agenda. Sorry."

Inside my apartment, I phoned Conor. "What did you tell him?"

"I'm driving, Darce."

"What did you tell your brother about me? What does he know?"

"Hold on." Conor and I had eaten lunch together — had sat and chatted about how he'd pulled a calf muscle at the gym and how I'd forgotten to pay my cable bill for so long the company had disconnected my services. Not once had his date come up. Maybe, like Aubrey, he'd started leaving me out of parts of his life, assuming I couldn't handle it, or couldn't show support.

"Okay," he said after a moment, "I pulled over. Basically I just told him you're my friend, you teach at my school. That kind of thing."

"Does he know about my sister?"

"I mentioned that she passed away. I didn't give him details."

"So he knows that's why I wasn't working."

"Yeah. But who cares? He's not the judging type, he works with, you know, families in crisis. When we were kids, Joel had a dog phobia. My dad really wanted a Husky, so my parents sent Joel to a counsellor. We ended up with a cat. He's kind of an anxious guy. I'm sure he could empathize with you. Me, I'm the strong, silent type. Why all the questions today?"

"He drove me home. He saw me in the parking lot and offered me a ride. He said he was dropping something off for you."

"I think you should hang out with him. He's damn good-looking."

"I'm going to ignore that. And, I can't."

"Why not?"

"Because I'm. . .do you really think I'm in any condition to date right now? I can barely keep my own head on straight!"

"That's okay," Conor said. "He's a psychologist. That's his thing, being the hero. All his ex-girlfriends were kinda. . .don't take this the wrong way."

"What?"

"Well, they were. . .you know, *damaged*. Like, one had anorexia. She carried a little measuring cup with her, a quarter cup. She measured everything. She'd eat like, a quarter cup of grapes for dinner. Or, this other one had *major* daddy issues. Her parents had this really horrible divorce — when she and Joel split, she stole his car."

"Sounds intense."

"I'm not saying marry the guy. Just go on a couple dates with him. Try to remember what it's like to be with people again. I don't think he's going to be scared off because you have a shitty life right now."

"I can't, anyway," I said. "Patrick and I are — " I stopped myself. "You know."

He paused. "Do I? Do you, even?"

       My first boyfriend, Alex, the only boyfriend before Patrick, had curly hair and played soccer. Three years older than me, and about to graduate, he happened to take the same English class as me, and was placed in my study group. After the final exam, a brutally long essay test that left our hands thoroughly cramped, we went to Future's Bakery on Bloor and Brunswick and had soggy French toast and split a pitcher of sangria. When he walked me back to the subway, he kissed me goodbye. We slept together, my first time, on my nineteenth birthday. The first few days on the pill, my skin looked green in the mirror, and I struggled not to vomit, knowing if I threw up, the hormones wouldn't do their job.

"Am I supposed to feel like death?" I asked Aubrey, who'd started taking birth control behind her mother's back in Grade Ten.

I never asked how many other girls Alex had slept with. He hadn't said *I love you* yet, but he *seemed* to love me. Afterward having sex, lying in his bed at his off-campus apartment as he slept, I listened to the sounds of his roommates cooking breakfast. When he woke up, he traced his finger along my naked spine.

"Do you want something to eat?" he asked, then joked, "I don't even know how you like your eggs."

That July, a job he applied for in Vancouver came through, and he told me, cross-legged on my bed, that he didn't think we could pull off a long-distance relationship. We'd only been together since the semester had ended, and I still had three years of my degree to finish. Explaining things to Aubrey over coffee, I called the break-up "amicable," then commented on the "hottie" sitting three tables away from us to prove I was fine. But Alex had left a toothbrush at my place, and for several months, I brushed my teeth with it, until the bristles frayed.

The October after I'd gone back to teaching, Patrick began to leave a toothbrush at my apartment. Brushing my own teeth, I plucked his blue Colgate out of the glass where it rested. The Patrick I'd dated was a germophobe, carrying his toiletries in a plastic bag with a zipper, sealing his toothbrush into its own little container, warning me about flushing the toilet with the lid open, how germs spray everywhere and land on toothbrushes, and then people stick their toothbrushes in their mouths. Leaving a toothbrush on the counter was equivalent to drinking water from the toilet. Kipling occasionally did this — drank water from the toilet — which had made Patrick cringe, swat her off the seat and then wash his hands.

"She's a cat!" he'd exclaimed, as she skittered from the room, smudgy paw prints marking the toilet seat cover. "Don't only dogs drink from the toilet?"

Several of Papi's cats had drank water from the toilet, too. "They hear the water running, it's like being in the wild, they think it's fresh."

Patrick the germophobe. His extra toothbrush voluntarily exposed on my counter as though nothing could happen to it. I placed his toothbrush back in the glass, gingerly beside mine.

Eight months. We were friends. More than friends. We were *going to be* more than friends. I couldn't tell. I couldn't tell what he was thinking. I didn't want to ask, either.

  I'd become accustomed to it being snowy by Halloween in Calgary. This meant that kids had to get creative with their costumes and find a way to fit a winter parka underneath. Ultimately, kids often had to go as an obese princess, a corpulent cowboy. My students had started talking about their costumes by mid-October. Halloween also marked Patrick's birthday — twenty-seven.

During silent reading, Jenna Shanlon slipped Celina Janik a note at the back of the room. I walked around the room making sure the kids paid attention, helping sound out any difficult words. I let the note slide. Celina's father had not yet returned. I hadn't noticed her behaving any differently, but I was still being vigilant. Sean Cibley raised his hand and I made my way over to his desk.

"What's this word?" he whispered. Sean's reading skills reminded me of Carly, but he remained dedicated, unfailingly applying strategies he'd acquired the previous summer after his parents enrolled him in private tutoring. Sean pointed — *masquerade*. "I tried to sound it out," he whispered. "Mas — qua. . ."

"Try again," I said, squatting down to his level. "The *q-u* makes a k sound here, like in cat."

Right around the time our mother remarried, Carly developed an imaginary friend, Elemeno P. Eight years old felt, to me, at least, too old for an imaginary friend. At the reception, with some sort of smudge on the front of her yellow puffy-sleeved flower girl dress, she told me Elemeno P. wanted me to read the menu out loud. "Chicken Cordon Bleu," I told her, "or roast beef and gravy. You pick."

She was *so* slow; it took forever for her to sound things out. When learning the letters, she called the lowercase l "one" and the lowercase u "happy mouth." When I'd finally learned about the process of reading — phonemic awareness, visual memory, sight word vocabulary — sitting in a lecture theatre at the University of Calgary — I wondered again about the way I'd tried to teach Carly to read. Repetition, repetition, repetition. And then, near the end, some bribery.

"When you read through *Where the Wild Things Are* all by yourself, I'll take you to get a Slurpee." *Where the Wild Things Are* consisted of surprisingly advanced vocabulary for someone like Carly, with all the signs of a reading disability. . . .*mischief of one kind or another.* Who was I kidding?

Sean stared at the letters on his page, tasted the word for a moment. "Mas. . .ka. . .rade? Oh, masquerade. Like Halloween."

"Right!" I said. "Good effort, Sean."

"For Halloween, I'm going to be a pirate."

"That's a neat costume."

His eyes, blue, like my sister's, had a green ring around the irises. He closed his book. "What are you pretending to be?"

There was an old lady who swallowed a dog.
My, what a hog! To swallow a dog.
She swallowed the dog to catch the cat.
She swallowed the cat to catch the bird,
She swallowed the bird to catch the spider,
that wiggled and jiggled and tickled inside her.
She swallowed the spider to catch the fly.
I don't know why she swallowed a fly.
Perhaps she'll die.

&   I dreamed that I slept in a room filled with Matryoshka dolls — dolls scattered all around me, on the floor, on the countertops, on shelves. I took one and split it in half. Inside lay the tiny, dead body of my sister, curled in the fetal position, not breathing. I reached to my right and cracked open another. Aubrey, in a wedding dress, her eyes pinched shut. I reached for another and another. Papi, Patrick, Conor, Joel, my mother. I held their bodies in the palms of my hands, not knowing what to do with them. More dolls multiplied around me. I couldn't save them. I couldn't breathe.

Kipling purred and pressed her bony head against my face, waking me. She flopped down on the duvet beside me, rolling seductively on her back. Look at me, I'm adorable. My heart struggled inside my ribcage, trapped, fighting to get out.

  Sixth grade, I'd come to realize, was a precarious age, an age at which a new influx of hormones put children off balance — twenty-seven little drunks trying to fumble through social interactions with their classmates, classmates who they began to whisper about, to fight over. Erica Adair and Landrie Anderson had stopped speaking after they'd discovered that Brody Hindmarsh had told them both they were his "girlfriend."

I hadn't even slow danced until the ninth grade, and even then, only at arm's length. Teachers at the school dances had chaperoned carefully, stepping in if students danced too closely, reminding us to "leave room for the Holy Spirit."

On Halloween afternoon, my class squirmed in their seats, antsy for the night's sugar buzz and the chance for sanctioned deception. I squirmed in my own desk, marking vocabulary tests, while they completed art projects, their fingers and clothes smudged with pastel. An audible ripple in my stomach made a few glance up from their projects. Had I eaten breakfast? Karissa Zakary had defined "unanimous" as "when you really hate animals."

Then Celina was beside my desk, or, almost behind my desk, with her back to the wall.

"What do you need?" I whispered.

Her face washed pale. She gestured for my pen, and I passed it to her across the desk, asking, "Are you okay?"

She cupped her hand and scribbled into her palm, then turned it open so I could see.

my period

She closed her hand around the message, making a fist.

I stood up. "Keep working on your art projects. I'll be right back." I moved towards the door, and Celina slid along beside me. Once in the hall, I bent down to her level. "Do you feel sick?"

She nodded, and whispered, "It's my first time. There's blood on my jeans."

"It's okay," I said. "It's normal. It's nothing to be scared about. I'm sure I have a pad in my purse."

She sniffed. "I really want to call my mom."

"Sure," I said. "We can do that."

"My mom's at the hospital." She rubbed her eyes. "My sister had an asthma attack last night."

"Okay. Does she have a cell phone?"

Celina wrapped her arms around herself and squatted down to the floor, curling into a ball.

"Hold on," I told her. I scanned the empty hallway, then ducked into Andrew's classroom. He stood at the chalkboard, copying math problems.

"Gimme a second, guys," Andrew said to his students. At the door, he whispered, "What's up?"

"One of my students is having a crisis," I explained. "Do you know where Conor is?"

"Uh, not really. Everything okay?" He leaned out into the hallway, glancing over to where Celina crouched.

"Can you watch my class for a bit?" I asked.

"We're in the middle of a math lecture."

"Please."

"All right, I'll bring them in here. You going to be a while?"

"I don't know. Thanks."

I helped Celina to her feet. "Let's go to the office and talk, okay?" I slid my cardigan off and tied it around her waist. It hung too big on her small frame, the long sleeves trailing on the ground.

"My stomach hurts." She held the sleeves of my sweater up. "I want to go home. It hurts really bad."

In the office, I asked the secretary to see if she could track down Mrs. Janik and took Celina with me into the nurse's room.

I got my first period at fourteen, the last of all my friends, in keeping with my tendency to be a late bloomer. Carly's periods started at twelve, and she'd called me at my new apartment to tell me the news, thrilled with herself. But, after one month, she bemoaned her period, insisted her cramps were terrible. She had monstrous mood swings, once throwing a bottle of Advil at my head when she couldn't disarm the childproof cap. It whacked me just above my temple.

I found a pad in the nurse's office and handed it to Celina, ushering her into the staff bathroom, aware of my inadequacy, her yearning for her mother, for her father, for anyone, really. Only after she'd shut the door did I think I probably should have shown her how to use it.

My mother hadn't shown me how to use sanitary pads, either. Papi had proven a great substitute parent, but the workings of a teenage girl's menstrual cycle were out of his range. When I'd told my mother I'd gotten my period, she said, "And?"

And?

What, exactly, had I wanted her to say? What, exactly, did I need her for?

"You know where the pads are," she snapped, and then, "Great, now I have to buy double. Thanks, Darce."

When Celina emerged from the bathroom, her eyes looked bloodshot, her eyelids heavy. My sweater hung, still knotted, around her waist.

"My stomach hurts," she repeated. "I want to go home."

"Do you want to lie down in the nurse's office while we track down your mom?" I suggested.

Celina rubbed the back of her hand across her face, smearing a few tears. "Okay." The secretary nodded, still on the phone, as I guided Celina to the nurse's office and shut the door.

The secretary hung up. "I'm getting voicemail on Mom's cell.

Look, Celina will be fine. Girls get their period. Give her a few minutes to calm down and then take her back to class."

& Halloween night I just wanted to sleep. About twenty minutes after I'd arrived home, just as I'd decided to take a shower, Patrick came to the door carrying three hefty grocery bags. After the kiss, he'd called, but hadn't come over for three weeks. I piled the bed with extra stuffing — spare sheets, pillows, blankets, and a couple of towels. With my futon pulled into couch position, the sleeping portion was half its possible size, and with the extra mass it felt a little like someone else was laying beside me. I distracted myself to sleep, alternately counting happy memories of Carly and Patrick, along with the tiled black-white-black-white ceiling pattern above my bed.

One. Carly, just learning to crawl, grasping my Cabbage Patch Kid doll by the neck in her teeth, the way a mother wolf would carry a pup.

Two. Patrick, at the driving range, super serious in a pressed polo, adjusting his golf stance, fine-tuning the placement of his hands on the club.

Three. Carly, hanging upside down off the edge of her bed, scrubbing at her wet hair with furious fingers, telling me, "If I do this for an hour every night, my hair will grow an extra inch."

It often took me into the twenties to fall asleep. But after a week without Patrick, memory seven turned into a memory of my mother; she'd slept clutching one of her pillows, the way Carly clutched her tattered raccoon. In Toronto, after dark, I'd seen raccoons slip between the garbage cans on the streets near our apartment on more than one occasion. Carly had said she'd like to take one home and raise it as a pet.

"If you touch one of those filthy animals I'll slap you on the mouth," our mother had told her. "Do you want rabies? Huh?"

I'd taken a stack of blank CDs from Carly's apartment when Aubrey and I cleaned it out. Carly had filled them with songs — happy, upbeat pop music, with lyrics about falling in love, about partying all night. She'd drawn Mickey Mouse's face in purple permanent marker on one, and when I pressed play, out blasted the Disney theme "When You Wish Upon a Star." She'd dressed as a different Disney princess for Halloween three years in a row. In Patrick's absence, I'd played Carly's CDs, one after another, on an old Discman — plugged in my headphones and turned up the volume.

I'd lived without Patrick before. I could do it again.

Twenty-one days, exactly. Then he'd started coming back. Less frequently than before, but enough. He hadn't kissed me since my birthday. Hadn't talked about it. That Halloween night, *his* birthday, he descended the basement stairs, bags in hand, smiling.

"Happy birthday," I said, and yawned.

"Trick or treat," he said, grinning. "I brought candy."

He spilled the contents out onto the counter. Twizzlers, peanut butter cups, candy corn, Tootsie Rolls. He'd even brought my favourite, foil-covered chocolate coins, and when I bit into one, I tasted the crispy rice centre. They had skulls and crossbones printed on them, faces with hollow eyes and ossified teeth. He'd brought way too much.

As a kid, Halloween had always overshadowed Patrick's birthday, and his mother had never let him go to houses that she didn't trust, fearing that her only child would come home with razor blades hidden in his Oh Henry!s. Patrick compensated by taking the leftovers out of his own family's dish, he'd told me, but thirty of the same chocolate bars got sickening after awhile. When his classmates compared candy in the lunch room the following day, Patrick would sit alone with his Ziploc container of leftover birthday cake. Over the years, his mother's paranoia made Patrick wonder if sinister strangers really did inject poison into children's treats. "It turned me off candy," he confessed when we first started dating.

And yet, he'd already started to sort through the pile on the counter. He split open a bag of licorice and put one end of a sugary string in his mouth.

"Kids trick or treat at the front door, not the basement apartment," I said. "Let's shut the light off and go to bed. I had a rough day."

He picked up a bag of M&Ms and split it open, poured a few into his open palm. "What happened?"

"Crisis with a girl in my class. There's stuff going on in her family — awful day."

"Poor girl," he said.

Poor girl.

I could have taken her into the staff room, made her a hot chocolate, told her about my first period. I could have let her stay in the nurse's office, kept trying to reach her mom. Instead, when her mom didn't answer our calls, I'd just told Celina to buck up, to go back to class. I couldn't even comfort a twelve-year-old. No wonder I couldn't comfort myself.

& Carly fidgeted before falling asleep, changing positions, wriggling around. Usually, Carly went to bed first, and I would change into my pyjamas, do my homework out in the living room, and then sneak in and climb up to my top bunk when I felt tired. But she'd demanded that night that I stay in for story time, and my mother had, surprisingly, actually read to her, so I'd agreed. My mother read stories fast, skipping sections as though trying to get them over with so she could go do whatever she needed to do. Carly had chosen *The Mitten*, a story about a boy who drops his mitten and one by one, a series of animals, including a bear, sneak inside it to stay warm, stretching the mitten out. I stared up at the ceiling, irritated by this obviously implausible sequence of events. The bear sneezed and all the animals tumbled out of the mitten into the snow.

I could hear it raining heavily, the steady spill against the windows. At first, the drops fell far enough apart that it sounded like horses galloping outside our window. Then they got closer together, sounding more like trains rumbling by. I kept interrupting the story to point out these details, until my mother snapped, "Let me finish the goddamn story." The rain began to pour so hard and fast that it blended into one long stream.

"You know what I think it sounds like?" Carly interjected. "I kinda think it sounds like angels, peeing."

  On November 1st, Conor's phone rang in the tiny office off of the gym where he worked, since he didn't have a classroom. He perched on his desk. "Hey, how's it going?" he said, into the phone, and then, to me, he mouthed, "It's Joel."

Conor had come to me earlier in the week and asked for help organizing his office. He had large stacks of paper in various places throughout the room, though the content of the piles didn't seem related. I flipped through a workbook on puberty.

It's normal to start to be interested in members of the opposite sex.

The opposite sex. Thinking about Conor talking about this with his students made me groan internally. Within a Catholic framework, no allowances were made for mentioning anything to the students about starting to have feelings for members of the same sex. When Conor told me he was gay, I'd asked why he'd applied to the Catholic school board.

"Not a lot of openings at the time," he admitted. "But I wanted to work at a Catholic school. I'm still Catholic. The Catholic church is against homosexuality, but I'm pretty sure God still loves me."

From his perch on his desk, Conor held out his phone. "Joel wants to talk to you."

I took it. "Hi."

"Hey, Darcy. I hope this isn't weird. Listen, I finally finished some of the renovations on my place, so I'm going to have some people over on Saturday. Really low-key. Conor said he might be bringing someone. You should come."

I stalled. "This Saturday? Or next Saturday?"

"This Saturday. The third. Sorry, I know it's kind of late notice. You probably have plans."

"I'm not sure yet. Can I let you know?"

"Sure. Just give me a call. Get Conor to write down my number for you."

When I hung up, Conor slid off the desk and took the phone back. "Are you going to come to the party?"

"I told him I'd think about it."

"You should. You need to get out more, be around people. Stop hiding in Andrew's basement. You're becoming a hobbit."

"I'll think about it."

Conor scrawled his brother's phone number down on a scrap of paper and folded it into halves. "Seriously. Even if you don't want to right now. Just do it."

 Carly had the same eighth-grade teacher as I'd had: Mrs. Wong, who had taught the gym self-defence unit and had previously taught ESL and Special Ed. When Mrs. Wong called the house to talk to Mom about Carly, she often asked to say hello to me, too, remembering details from when I was her student years earlier. She'd provided notes for Carly, who had messy scrawl and couldn't seem to copy from the board at the same rate as her classmates. I didn't need to worry about Carly with Mrs. Wong. High school, however, was different.

I'd promised Carly an ice cream get-together after her first day of high school, and when she arrived, forty-five minutes late, she announced, "What a shit show!" She dragged a backpack already marked with purple pen doodles and removed some course outlines, already tattered and stained with purple fingerprints, not yet organized into binders.

A month into the school year, the few close girlfriends who had gone to the same high school had fit nicely into a clique of ninth-grade girls. Carly began coming more frequently to my apartment under the guise of doing homework, but she chattered rather than studied, distracting me from my own assignments. She began borrowing my clothes in an effort to look more sophisticated, returning them wrinkled and dirty.

She wiped her runny nose with the long sleeve of her sweatshirt. "They want to phase me out."

"Who?"

She'd borrowed her friend Chelsea's math notebook because she'd lost a worksheet, and rooted out a note tucked into one of the pockets. In the note, one of the new girls wrote:

Why R U even friends with Carly? She's so crazy! Hello drama queen!

Chelsea's response: *I know. Maybe we should just phaze her out?*

Totally! The new girl had written back.

"What'd you do?" I asked.

"Nothing! I mean, God! You don't say anything to these girls. They do what they want."

"Sometimes girls are just mean. . .maybe you should focus your energy on some of your other friends. If Chelsea's going to be a bitch like that to get attention, she doesn't deserve to be friends with you."

Carly picked at her cuticle. "Yeah, right."

The next time she came over to my apartment, I lectured her

on the main themes in *Romeo and Juliet*. When I paused to ask her a question, I noticed that she had stopped listening. Instead, she'd doodled a giant caricature of a heart, broken in half, crying tears of blood. She stopped socializing with her friends after school, and began falling asleep when she got home, then waking up, eating dinner late, and doing her homework until dawn. She gained ten pounds, started tying her hair into greasy ponytails instead of washing it.

"Yesterday, at dinner — " She stopped and yawned. "Yesterday at dinner, Richard said, *You know, guys don't date chubby girls.*"

I suggested she come to my apartment directly from school, made promises to help her with her assignments. She stopped talking about Chelsea's new boyfriend, or about Mom and Dickhead, brushing me off, wanting to talk about my life instead: how hot were the guys at U of T? What was the best part of having my own apartment? Was it weird to go to a big school where I barely knew anyone? Did I wish Aubrey was in more of my classes? What did I want for Christmas?

Sleepily, one evening, she dribbled spaghetti sauce on the cuffs of her sweatshirt and pushed her sleeves up so that they wouldn't get in the way. Small scars cross-hatched the insides of her left wrist, a teeny, tiny Tic-Tac-Toe board. Red and inflamed.

I snatched her by the wrist and lifted her arm up off the table, in front of her face. "What the hell?"

She pulled away from me, crossed her arms in front of her chest. "Nothing."

"You're cutting yourself!"

She glared at me, "So?"

"So?! When did things get this bad?"

"You don't get it," she said. "You didn't have trouble in high school. You always got good grades. Aubrey didn't go behind your back."

"You know what I was doing in high school?" I put my elbows on the table, laced my fingers. "I was raising *you!* You think it was easy to study for tests with you chattering away to Elemeno P.? Or having to rescue you from Dickhead all the time? Or how about — "

"I get it!" She pushed her plate away. "Sorry I ruined your life."

& I didn't often take baths. I associated the bathtub with my mother, who, before she met Dick, spent hours sitting lifeless in the water. When she climbed out and fell asleep in her bed, sometimes wearing only a threadbare towel, she usually left the basin full. I cringed, reaching into the smelly, cold water to pull the drain. The water swirled away, leaving the bathtub ringed with soap scum. Because of my tendency to catch colds, I also avoided getting water in my ears, preferring the dull purr of the shower, the way the noise of water hitting chrome could blur out my thoughts.

The basement bathroom at Dick's house had a deep, wide soaker tub with a metal handle attached just above the wall, the kind intended for someone elderly or disabled to ease themselves in and out.

For my fifteenth birthday, Papi had given me a set of three bath bombs. Wide, round, and chalky, they sat on top of my dresser for almost six months. Then, on a day when temperatures dipped and I'd gotten soaked in a slush rain on the way home from the bus stop, I decided to take a bath to warm up. I held them up one at a time, smelling them through the crinkly cellophane. Raspberry vanilla, lavender, and citrus burst. I settled on the lavender. *Slip away into the calming sensations of lavender,* read the label tied on with coily ribbon.

I ran the water and peeled my wet clothes away from my skin. When I first stepped into the tub, the tips of my cold toes burned, my nerves trying to acclimatize. I leaned on the wall brace for a moment, then let myself sink down into the water.

The basement acoustics meant I could hear everything that went on upstairs; with my bedroom just under the kitchen, I'd wake to the sound of my mother, the insomniac, shuffling around at two or three in the morning. Sometimes, I heard the whir of the coffee machine starting up, and then fell back asleep to the monotonous sound of the drip, drip, drip. Other times, there came the whomp, whomp, whomp of my stepfather's heavy feet on the linoleum. When he came in from working the late shift, he would lumber into the kitchen with his boots still on. Then came the sound of pots and pans banging around, pantry doors swinging open and shut. He preferred midnight macaroni and shots of vodka. In the mornings, there would sit fluorescent orange noodles glued cold to the side of a pan, and his liquor bottle, the cap and shot glass beside it. I could smell the alcohol when I screwed it back on and put it back in the counter, out of Carly's reach. I don't know how many shots he took a night.

Sunk deep and warm in the water, the silence stretched out like the soundtrack to a normal family. Carly had gone to play at a friend's house after school, and when I'd checked, I didn't see Mom and Dick's car in the garage. I sank into the warmth of the aloneness, unwrapped the bath bomb from its cellophane shell and set it gently into the water in front of me. It began to fizz, swirling a little, as it interacted with the water. I could smell the lavender. The water began to take on a purplish foam. The edges of my hair touched the water; I pulled an elastic band off my wrist and tied into a messy knot on the top of my head.

Then, above me, the front door swung open, and with it came crying and yelling. I flinched at Carly's wail and Dick's roar, competing for who could scream the loudest.

"Why would you do that? Maybe you're stupid! Nobody except a stupid, little brat would do something as dumb as — "

Carly pleaded, "I'm sorry, I'm sorry!"

"Stop crying, you little pussy!"

I tried to listen for my mother, but I couldn't hear whether she wasn't physically present, or she had simply clamped her mouth shut and chosen to be a spectator.

I lay back in the water, put my ears below the surface. It muffled the sound, but didn't erase it. I could still hear the mixture of anger and misery all swirled up together, like in a blender. I sat back up, feeling the water in my ears, the water from my hair running like fear down the back of my neck.

The bath bomb had fizzled and dissolved.

& My mom dragged Carly and me with her to the mall to get her hair dyed. Carly was seven. I'd been forced to come along to keep an eye on her. Carly behaved like the Tasmanian Devil at the mall, overstimulated by the noise and colour and squish of people. The last time my mother had carted both her daughters to the mall, Carly had spied a plush beluga whale, just like her beloved Raffi song, and thrown herself to the tiled toy store floor when my mother snapped, "You think toys grow on trees?"

"She's just a kid," I argued.

Mom put her hands on her hips. "Look at you, judging me," she barked. "Just wait until you have your own screaming brat." She waited until she'd dragged Carly out of the mall and into an empty subway tunnel before giving her a firm slap across the back of her head. "You scream in public like that again and I'll smack that mouth of yours right off. I don't care who's lookin'."

When I tried to convince Carly we should both stay home while mom went to the hairdresser on her own, she stuck out her bottom lip. "But I *love* the mall!"

The clerk told us that it would take about two hours before Mom was finished. So, we couldn't afford for me to wear earrings, but suddenly Mom could have a fancy new dye job? Why couldn't she do it herself at home? The boxes at the store only cost fifteen bucks, and the poster on the store wall told me that a professional dye job was $70+. You know what else costs seventy dollars? I felt like telling Mom, a new winter coat for Carly, and a new pair of jeans for me. The zipper on Carly's current coat had stuck, and my jeans were close to splitting at the knees.

Carly flitted about the salon. "What do you think Mommy will look like with yellow hair like me?"

"She's just getting highlights," I corrected her. "It's not going to look like your hair. It's going to look stupid and fake."

"I think she'll look like a princess," Carly continued.

I sat slumped on the waiting room sofa, flipping through a magazine of different cuts and styles, wishing my hair didn't snarl into knotty curls, wishing I had nicer curves like the models in the pictures.

Carly came back out into the waiting room and started fiddling with a machine that dispensed Skittles for a quarter. "Do you have any monies?" she asked me.

"Cut it out," I snapped at her. "Can't you sit still for a half a second?" I craned my neck so that I could see into the salon; our mother's hair was still in foils. She wouldn't be able to see Carly being a brat, or me ignoring her. I slid to the edge of the couch and slouched down even farther, turning my body away from my sister.

"Let's go to Toys R Us," Carly suggested. She stuck two fingers up the mouth of the machine.

"Mom said we had to stay here."

"Yeah, but I'm *bored*."

"Leave me alone."

The model in my magazine had an angry face, dark kohl-rimmed eyes, and clenched teeth.

"Uh oh. . ."

I looked up again. Carly had managed to bugger up the machine; it spilled multicoloured candy into her open palms and beyond, rainbow tears falling to the floor. Her face revealed a mixture of excitement and panic.

"What did you do?" I admonished her. I started gathering all the Skittles up from the floor.

"I — I. . ." Her hands trembled, still holding the sugary beads. "Don't tell Mommy, okay?"

    They happened exactly a day apart.

Patrick went first. The Halloween candy should have tipped me off. The excess of it. The day after his twenty-seventh birthday, Patrick came over, as usual, around five-thirty, with a Tupperware container full of meatloaf.

"I hope you're hungry," I said.

"Not really." He ran a hand through his hair, then reached into the bowl of leftover candy and tore open a package of licorice, withdrew a strand, but didn't put it to his mouth. Instead, he began pulling it apart. Kipling, who had readjusted to his presence, hopped off the second ledge of the bookshelf where she'd been sleeping in a shaft of reflected sunlight. She hopped up onto the countertop and sniffed at the container, but when Patrick turned to pet her, she pulled back, hopped down, and trotted off.

"What's going on?" I asked.

"I need to be honest with you," he said, and reached for my hand. I didn't reach back. My hand stayed limp. He took my wrist. "Come sit on the couch."

"I don't want to," I said. Maybe he had a girlfriend I didn't know about. He'd kept it a secret the whole time. I'd never asked.

Why had I never asked? Conor had started dating without telling me; Patrick probably had, too. Carly's death made me fragile, the kind of person who too much information could shatter. What other secrets —

He started talking, standing in the kitchen, still holding my wrist.

He'd been accepted to do a study abroad program at Oxford, to write his Master's thesis on the psychological history of T.S. Eliot while writing *The Waste Land*.

"Stop — " I said, "What? You're a *lawyer*."

"I dropped out of law school after you and I broke up. I never finished my final semester."

Patrick not finishing law school. Patrick couldn't even start a game of Scrabble and not finish it.

He made eye contact. "You made it pretty clear you didn't want me to contact you after we broke up."

"Why? Why did you stop?"

"When we moved to Calgary, I started having panic attacks. First, just once in a while, then they started getting more and more frequent. I couldn't sleep. Like, at all. Sometimes I'd go for days."

I remembered; a feeling recalled from the base of my intestines, guttural. Deep guilt; my fault.

Patrick continued talking, his thumb on the ulnar veins of my wrist. I'd learned in the CPR training St. Sebastian staff had to take that you should never check someone's pulse this way, because you could feel your own pulse through your thumb. I wondered which of our hearts was throbbing faster; impossible to tell whose beat was whose.

"I couldn't stop thinking about all these bad things that could happen. I worried that I would fail school, that there were germs in the house that would make you sick, that maybe I'd left the screen door open and Kipling would get out. . .I kept trying to do everything perfect, keep everything exactly clean, double-check everything. . .but it didn't help. Then, the less time I spent sleeping the more I became convinced that I would just drive home from the library one day, exhausted, and hit someone with the car. I'd crash and fall asleep for hours — I started missing class, and falling further and further behind. I thought I was making all kinds of mistakes, that I was going to do something terrible, and I couldn't catch up, I couldn't figure out — "

"You never told me any of this."

"You would have thought I was crazy."

I pulled my wrist away.

His arms hung at his sides. "I couldn't take it. I couldn't be around anyone. Especially you. We fought all the time. I couldn't take the stress."

"We weren't fighting," I challenged. "You weren't communicating."

"You weren't really communicating either," he countered.

"I tried!"

"Darce, I don't want to fight about this. I'm trying to tell you — will you just listen to me?"

I crossed my arms over my chest to hold myself in.

He sighed. "The same week we broke up — that week, I dropped out. Well, actually, first I thought I would just take a leave and go back, finish that semester later, when I felt, you know, so then I went to one of the counsellors on campus and told her how messed up I felt. She made a referral to a psychiatrist at, at the hospital, at Foothills, and I started seeing her."

He didn't normally stumble over his words. But I hadn't heard him talk at length in a long time, either. Kipling batted at the window, at a fly fluttering behind the screen. Her tail swished, preparing for the kill.

"She diagnosed me with OCD — obsessive compulsive disorder.

Anyway, I started weekly therapy, and she prescribed some meds. . .I felt so unhappy, you know, in law school. . .in life. I thought if I quit everything. . ." He trailed off, as though remembering something, or trying to forget something.

"You should have told me. I could have done something."

"When I started getting better, I wanted to, but I felt like. . .I dunno, maybe, maybe you were better off without me. Maybe we were both better off. We just stressed each other out. Afterwards, with the therapy and everything, I had some time to think about things, just me — I left the program indefinitely, took some time off, worked. . .then I applied to go back and try something else, see if maybe I couldn't find a better fit. I started my master's this fall, when you started teaching again."

"So this whole time, you were just. . .?"

"No, before that, I had a job — at a marketing firm. . ."

He kept talking. A marketing firm? Patrick? Who thought commercials were cheesy and catered to the idiot masses?

". . .because I needed to get out of my own head, you know, so that I didn't hate everything in my life — myself, you, everybody. I started reading a lot of T.S. Eliot. He actually had a nervous breakdown himself, he was hospitalized for a period — back then they called it *nervous disorder*." He stopped. "You look like. . .this is a lot to take in. I'm sorry."

"When?" I said.

"When what?"

"When do you leave?"

I wanted him gone, right then.

& Carly's voice rambled in my dreams, talking to me in her Carly dialect. She said the word *kinda* all the time, as though not 100 percent sure of the content of what she was saying, betraying her confidence. Instead of saying, "He said" and

"She said," Carly would say, "He was like," and "She was like."
And she always interrupted.

In the morning, I could never remember what she needed to tell me, everything garbled. Her silly, mixed-up songs played over and over in my head.

I like to eat, eat, eat, eepples and banee-nees
I like to oot, oot, oot, ooples and banoo-noos
I like to oat, oat, oat, oapples and banoh-nos

& No way I could go to Joel's housewarming party. I didn't want to have to make happy small-talk. *How are you? I'm fine.* Did anyone ever answer that question with anything but *fine* or *good?*

But that meant another night alone, just me and myself. Every time I heard Andrew's footsteps above, I kept thinking it was Patrick, walking down the basement stairs. I was being dissected, piece by piece; first Carly, and then Patrick. Kipling brushed up against me, butting her head against my legs.

I forgot that I owed Andrew rent, but when I went to root in my drawer for cheques, I realized I didn't have any. Going to the bank gave me something to do. After work, I zipped up my boots and shooed Kipling away from the door. I hadn't eaten lunch, but had no appetite.

A few of my neighbours lingered on the street, scraping raw snow off their driveways, chipping away at the frozen ground with the tips of their shovels. In Toronto, the city trucks just dumped salt on the ground, salt that gnawed at the undercarriage of cars and left the bottoms of jeans bleached white. Why shovel, I thought, when it will just snow again tomorrow? Why not crawl in, give up, and let Mother Nature melt it all in the spring? Let it thaw on its own time? My hands felt dry, chapped. I picked at a hangnail, making it worse.

My phone rang in my jacket pocket. It took a few seconds of groping around with cold hands to retrieve it, and by the time I pulled it out the call had gone to voicemail. I'd walked a couple blocks from home already, halfway to the bank.

I pinned the phone between my ear and my shoulder so I could listen to the message but put my hand back in my pocket to warm it up.

"Hello, this is Sheila Stratton from Mount Sinai Hospital in Toronto. This message is for Darcy Nolan. I'm calling to inform you that your mother has been admitted to the psychiatric ward following a suicide attempt. She asked us to call you. We were hoping you would be able to come in — "

&T In kids' television shows, there were the good guys and the bad guys. Cartoons seemed to generally have a good life, aside from the terrible evil force, lurking. At some point, inevitably, the bad guys would do something bad, and the good guys would try to stop them. Sometimes the situation looked touch-and-go. But ultimately, good always triumphed over evil. The bad guys eventually slinked back to their lair. But then the cycle repeated itself in the next episode. The evil never really vanished; instead, the good guys had to face the bad guys over and over again, day after day. The good guys could never just relax or enjoy life, because the bad guys were just going to pop out again.

After these messages, we'll be right back.

&T By the time I arrived at Mount Sinai and got to talk to a doctor, it was almost four in the morning, Toronto time. My stomach gurgled. I bought a Styrofoam cup of coffee from one of the machines on the floor. Afterwards, I felt more awake, but the coffee's bitterness gnawed at my empty stomach. I'd maxed out my credit card buying a last-minute, full-price airline ticket to Toronto. I'd filled three bowls of food and water for Kipling not knowing how long the trip would take and how long it would be before I'd get a chance to talk to Andrew, my cat sitter in a pinch. Andrew and Kipling had bonded after Carly's death, when I'd flown to Toronto for her funeral. When I returned, Kipling stayed wary of me for a week, sleeping on the other side of the room rather than at the foot of my bed.

It wasn't the first time Kipling had to fend for herself with an overflowing bowl of food, I reminded myself, picturing Papi, lying still, in striped pyjamas. The hospital corridor smelled like antiseptic and death.

Finally, the psychiatric resident requested I follow her into one of the rooms. She had small flecks of blood on the cuff of her sleeve. "I'm Dr. Garza, I'm the on-call resident tonight. I have some questions for you about your mother's psychiatric history."

"Okay." I pressed my fingernails into the palms of my hands. "I can try. We haven't really been in much contact — I've lived in Calgary for the last several years, so. . ."

Dr. Garza rattled her pen back and forth between her thumb and pointer finger. "Your mother has signed consent forms allowing me to go over her file with you. I'd like to get as much information as I can. Do you know when your mother's depression started?"

"I — I didn't really know she had. . .I mean, I guess you'd have to be pretty depressed to. . .but she never really told me for sure. . ."

"Let's talk about symptoms. Fatigue?" She paused, waited. "Sleeplessness? Physical slowness or agitation? Weight loss or weight gain? Loss of interest or pleasure? Prominent feelings of sadness? Irritability? Hopelessness? Excessive guilt? Any of those sound characteristic of your mother?"

I couldn't catch it all, rattled off like that. I wondered how many other patients Dr. Garza had to see. She seemed to want to get this over with, fast. Well, so did I.

"I haven't really seen very much of her. I live in Calgary. When I call. . ." When *did* I call? "We don't talk about feelings. We barely talk at all."

"What about when you were a child? Does she have a history of any of the symptoms I described?"

"I. . .say them again?"

"Fatigue, sleeplessness, physical slowness, weight fluctuation, prolonged depressed mood, physical complaints. . ."

I rubbed my left temple, feeling a headache brewing behind it. "She used to sleep all the time. She complained about being sick. Things got better after she married my stepfather. Did you talk to him?"

Dr. Garza consulted her notes. "Upon admittance, your mother gave us your name as the contact person."

The symptoms, all rattled off like that, didn't just describe my mother, but described Carly, too, in the last weeks of her life, but even before that. My mother, Carly, and me, too. Not just since Carly's death, but in the months after Patrick first left. Unhappiness was, apparently, heritable.

"Your mother reported her marital status as separated," Dr. Garza added.

"Separated?" Since when?

"She didn't mention it to you?"

"We haven't really been in contact." My mother had swallowed a bottle of Paxil and a handful of OxyContin and her daughter, her only surviving daughter, hadn't even known that she'd separated from her husband.

"Your mother has signed a release indicating that you have full access to her health records. Now, I understand that you were a child when she first began exhibiting symptoms — "

"I don't know that I want to do this — "

" — but I'd like to do my best to verify as much as I can about her psychiatric history and fill in the information I don't have on file so I can make an informed decision in terms of to what degree she at risk of harming herself again."

"It's a lot of pressure. I mean, I didn't know she was at risk of harming herself in the first place."

"Why don't we try?" Dr. Garza flipped open my mother's chart, a battered manila folder as thick as my wrist.

I rubbed my eyes. "I guess."

"What information can you give me about her parents?"

"Um, single mother, who died in. . .in '88 or '89, I guess."

"Siblings?"

"No. Only child."

"Partners?"

"She married my father at age nineteen; they were married until. . .she must have been twenty-five or twenty-six. I'm not sure. She married my stepfather about seven or eight years after that. I didn't know they had split up."

"Children?"

"Two — me, and my younger sister. . .she died about a year ago. In February."

Dr. Garza looked up from her notes.

"I'm sorry to hear that. Do you mind my asking the cause of death?"

"That's not in the file?"

"We don't have information after November 2006. It appears your mother stopped seeing her psychiatrist."

Her psychiatrist?

"My sister uh. . ." *Motor vehicle accident.* "Uh. . .suicide."

Dr. Garza scribbled this down. I wondered how much exposure to trauma one had to have before it no longer stabbed in the sternum. She brushed her hair away from her face. "Your mother spoke of missing her daughter, but, she was quite upset and incoherent, with the information we had I assumed that she meant her third pregnancy."

"Two pregnancies," I said. "Just me and my sister. Two daughters, two pregnancies."

Dr. Garza appeared not much older than me. She put her pen down. "There is mention of a third pregnancy in your mother's medical records. . .perhaps it would be a good idea to have a social worker present while we discuss — "

"No." I put my hands up to my face, almost to hold it there, to hold it steady. "It's better that I know. Please."

"All right. Our information is from June 1994, when your mother was admitted following a suicide attempt."

I remembered Papi staying with us, my inability to sleep, tiptoeing past his sleeping form on the couch late at night. Wondering where she'd gone.

"She. . .I was thirteen. My last day of school, I got home, and she had already left."

"She committed herself voluntarily at the recommendation of her psychiatrist. It also says here that she completed an outpatient twelve-week group therapy treatment for depression."

Weekly outpatient groups.

Or, it occurred to me, book club.

"Because of her pregnancy?" I asked.

Dr. Garza glanced through the papers again. "It appears the pregnancy was much earlier, in August 1988. She was hospitalized, overnight, on August 9th, for a D&C."

My voice came out flat. "She had an abortion."

"It was a medically necessary D&C, for a late-term miscarriage — eighteen weeks."

I mentally calculated; eighteen weeks in August 1988 would

have made her about four months pregnant just before Carly's first birthday, making her due sometime in late January. If it had survived, Carly and the baby would have been only seventeen months apart. I tried to remember my mother being gone overnight that summer, but nothing came to mind.

"That's around when — " I realized it as I said it. "That's when my father left."

& In the last few weeks before Patrick and I broke up, he spent most of his time in the law library researching and writing a case study for his Family Law class due in class on the Friday; that night he came home, walked right past me, and slept twelve hours straight. I wondered if he'd taken anything, and if so, what; he hadn't slept for more than a couple hours at a time in almost a month and seemed immune to sleeping pills. Law school made his naturally thin frame even more pronounced. He said he didn't have time to eat. I continued to make Patrick's lunch, hoping that it might help, but the cellophane-wrapped sandwiches and carrot sticks stayed untouched in our fridge. Once or twice, I brought them to work for Conor.

Usually a restless sleeper who would wake if I came into the room or moved too much in bed, Patrick slept steadily even when I came and lay with my face right beside his, listening for breath, waiting for a twitch or a snore. His chest rose and fell in small, shuddery gasps.

He finally emerged from our bedroom, the sheet wrapped around his torso like a chrysalis, its edges dragging on the floor, and stood in the doorway to the kitchen where I sat at the kitchen table, grading math tests.

"Are you okay?" I asked.

He shuddered a little. His hair appeared smashed all to one

side, and his skin washed yellow under the hallway lights. "I failed my paper."

"That's. . .I'm sorry."

He just stared.

"Can you do a make-up?" I asked.

Nothing.

"Patrick, seriously, it sucks, but it's not the end of the world. Why don't you let me — "

"Look," he said, and I realized he had the paper in his hands, all tangled up there with the sheets. He'd slept with it in bed with him. "We had to do the, the. . ." He coughed. "We had to argue the evidence for a case. This guy. . .on trial for. . .abuse, child abuse."

"That's awful."

"I wrote that the guy didn't do it. There wasn't enough evidence."

"And?"

"Our prof came in today and said, I want to tell you guys the real outcome of the case, in case you're curious." Patrick's voice wavered. "It actually happened. The dad — this guy was acquitted and then, a year later, the police got called to the house again — he shook his other kid. His baby. His four-month-old freakin' baby. Have you heard of shaken baby syndrome? This kid's brain sloshed around inside her skull until she hemorrhaged. She was dead when the. . .when the paramedics got there."

"That's *awful!*" I said again. "Did they eventually convict him?"

Patrick shuffled a bit closer, put his paper down on the table, face down.

"If I had been this guy's lawyer. . ." he turned his face away from me. "I would have argued to set the bastard free. Free so he could go home and murder his little girl."

"Okay," I said, "yeah, but, so did his actual lawyer. That's what the evidence said, right? You can't feel responsible for. . ."

"This kid *died* of a *brain hemorrhage!* So what about the fucking evidence?!"

"Patrick!" I exclaimed. "You can't know what you would have done as the actual lawyer. It was just a case study. A baby didn't die because of you! You're scaring me."

He turned away, walked back towards our bedroom.

I took his paper and turned it over.

Good arguing of the relevant points, Patrick. Your detailing of the evidence was well organized. Occasional mechanical errors detracted from the overall quality of the piece. B+

 I stepped outside the hospital and debated calling Aubrey. But what the fuck would I say? I could see my breath in the dark. At 4:30 AM, even faithful morning runner Aubrey would still be asleep.

I walked the loop around the hospital driveway where the cars pulled in and out. When I'd come in, patients lined the doorway, puffing on cigarettes out front, some wearing only housecoats despite the wind. I'd had to pass through a circle of smoke to get through the front door. But, so many hours later, even the smokers had retreated inside. I wondered which ones had gone back inside to heal and which ones had gone back inside to die. I didn't remember where in the hospital I'd left my jacket. I opened my wallet to see if I had enough change for a coffee, and realized I still had the scrap of paper on which Conor had written Joel's phone number. I'd slipped it in beside two folded-up five-dollar bills.

I dialled, expecting to get his voicemail, too. But then, he answered, his voice deep and husky with sleep. "Hello?"

"Um. . .hey," I said. "It's Darcy. I was just um, calling to say that I can't come to your party tomorrow. Or, today, I guess. Because it's technically tomorrow already, and um, I'm in Toronto."

"Hold on a second," he said, and I could hear him getting up, getting out of bed. "Darcy? What's wrong?"

"I'm okay," I said. But talking aloud was like unclogging a drain, all the gnarled hair and spit and toothpaste and grime yanked up from the depths.

"Hey," he said. "Hey, I can't hear you through all that crying. Take a deep breath. What's going on?"

"My. . .my mother tried to kill herself."

I heard him let all his air out. "Oh, god. Is she okay? Who's there with you?"

"She's — she's not dead. I don't know, I haven't seen her. They asked me all these questions — "

"You talked to her doctor?"

"Yeah. The doctor, she um, she said — " It swelled up in me again, and crashed. I smeared the tears across my face with the back of my hand.

"Okay," he said, "It's okay. One thing at a time. Who's there with you?"

"Um. . .no, just me, I — my stepdad bailed, apparently, so — so it's just me, here. I just talked to the doctor, so — I guess I have to go find a hotel, or something, now. I probably have to talk to, to come back in um, tomorrow — or, today, I guess. It's morning now."

"Okay, Darcy. Listen to me. I'm going to hang up for a minute and call the Holiday Inn on Bloor, the one right off Huron. I've stayed there before. I'm going to get you a room. I want you to go outside, and see if you can get in a cab, and just ask them to take you there. I'll take care of the reservation. Is there someone I can call to come be with you? A friend maybe?"

I thought of Aubrey, somewhere, probably in bed, asleep, her arm draped casually over the naked back of her fiancé, a man I'd never met.

"No," I said. "I don't want anyone to know."

"You should have someone there with you."

"No, no, I can't."

"When life gets this stressful, you deserve to have someone take care of you. Everybody needs — "

"No, no one can know. Maybe I should just — "

"Okay," he said, "let's just take this one step at a time, okay? I'm going to call the hotel right now. You just get in a cab. I'll call you back as soon as I have the reservation."

"Okay," I said.

The sheets on the Holiday Inn double bed felt scratchy against my legs. Patrick would have hated them, would have imagined them smeared with body fluid and covered in tiny, imperceptible flakes of human skin. Then I realized that the new Patrick was supposedly fixed, didn't obsess about germs or law school or rules anymore. A Patrick I didn't know, would likely never know. I would never talk to him again. Could never talk to him again.

The room phone started ringing. I grabbed at it with sweaty, clumsy hands. "Hello?"

"Hey, Darcy, it's Joel."

I'd fallen asleep in my clothes. The suitcase I'd packed the previous night in a hurry contained six shirts, most of them left over from my summer collection and therefore unsuitable for the cold that had descended upon Toronto. To add to that, I'd packed the entire contents of my underwear drawer, but not a single pair of pants other than the jeans I had on. I'd also forgotten to bring a toothbrush or contact solution. My eyes burned. I didn't know what time it was, or how long I'd slept.

"How are you coping this morning?" Joel asked.

"I'm okay, I guess." I ran a hand over my face. "What time is it?"

"It's about nine here, so, about eleven there. Are you going to see your mom's doctor?"

"Yeah."

"We had a case study in grad school about a guy who attempted suicide seven times," Joel said. "Then he found a really good psychologist, found an antidepressant that seemed to help — anyway, now he works at the Distress Centre hotline helping others. So, you know, sometimes really shitty things happen, and the outcome seems totally bleak, but then gets better."

Except when people succeed the first time.

"Thanks, Joel," I said. "Really. I appreciate the hotel and everything. It means a lot."

"No problem! It's what I do."

    I brought coffee to my mother's hospital room, though I didn't know whether such a gesture was within hospital policy. She slept semi-reclined in bed, the way one might sit in a lounge chair on a beach at an all-inclusive resort. Maybe this was the closest she would get to a vacation. When I was thirteen, Papi had glazed over the story to make it less horrific. He could not sugarcoat the idea that she had shirked her duties, tried to abandon us. But he had kept me from knowing just how much she had tried. How had he become involved, I wondered? Had she changed her mind, at the last minute, drowsy with medication, slipping from reality, and phoned him to come rescue her? Had she seen him, the way I did, as a saviour, a stable force in our broken little family?

Or had he walked in, twisted his key in the lock, and discovered her, unresponsive, or, perhaps, in a bathtub, swirled with blood from slashed radial arteries? Had he discovered our mother, attempting to die — had he simply wandered in, as he always did, to babysit — he had probably not been alone. Papi did not come over randomly. He came over after picking Carly up from school. She would have walked in with him. She would have seen —

My mother looked puffy and swollen, eyes closed, eyelids yellowed and veiny. Her hair lay snarled and matted against the pillow and it had grown out, longer than I remembered. How long had it been since I'd looked at her — *really* looked at her? I'd spent most of my childhood avoiding looking at her; sad, beseeching, naked and motionless in the bathtub, or screaming to some customer service agent over the phone, or sucking coffee just to stay awake. She had a needle threaded into the delicate skin on the back of her palm, feeding into an IV.

The heat from the coffee cup I had brought for her burned against my hands. I set it down on the window ledge. I could tell my mother had cried herself to sleep. Either that, or cried as she was being drugged to sleep. Dr. Garza had said my mother had cried so hard they couldn't understand her, saying she missed her daughter. Carly? The baby she'd lost? Or had she meant me?

I left the coffee on the ledge, unwilling to wake her. At the nurse's hub, I asked them to page Dr. Garza. When she arrived, I asked her how long my mother could stay. "I want you to keep her here. I want you to keep her from doing this again."

& Sitting there with Patrick's B-plus paper on the table beside me, I didn't know what else to do but phone Aubrey. I took the phone into the bathroom and turned the fan on so that Patrick wouldn't hear.

"What's with the echo?" Aubrey asked.

"I'm in the bathroom. Patrick just flipped out. I don't know what to do."

"Are you guys fighting again? You know, relationships shouldn't cause this much stress."

"No, we're not fighting, he just. . ." I hesitated, unsure whether or not to tell her, feeling disloyal to Patrick. "He just. . .I dunno, he's super stressed. He flipped out over a paper he wrote. He came home and slept basically the whole day. He's super upset."

I heard her turn the ignition off in her car. "I just got home. Listen, grad school makes you crazy. It's a lot of pressure. He probably just had a few too many nights without sleep and got bummed out over a grade. One time, I got a 42 percent on a test and ate three bags of Oreos. He'll get over it."

When I went back into our room, he'd fallen asleep again. I wanted to crawl in beside him, but I had a stack of unmarked multiplication tests still on the kitchen table. Red ink had stained my fingers. I waited at the door for a moment to see if he would wake up, or sense me there. He slept on.

& On the third day of my mother's hospitalization, I tracked down my stepfather by calling the construction company where he worked.

"She can just fuck herself," he shouted, when I told him where she was.

"She tried to kill herself," I reiterated. "She's your wife, and she tried to kill herself."

"Crazy bitch. You fix it. You both can fuck yourselves."

I didn't pass along the message.

I thought of the house. Could she go back? Dickhead paid the rent; I doubted my unemployed mother had enough money to even scrounge up a month's worth. I thought of Carly's vacant childhood bedroom, the now-faded pink and purple butterflies. The doorframe at the bottom of the basement stairs, naked except for the faint pencil scratches of our heights, the gap between them smaller and smaller each year as Carly aged from child to adolescent and I hit adult and stopped growing. In the end, she'd grown taller than me, just by an inch or so. I wondered who lived in our old apartment, the apartment where, for a period of time, it had just been me and my mother and Carly. One of the last times I'd met Papi for coffee, we'd exited the building at the same time as a young woman in her mid-twenties with choppy black hair streaked bright red skirted past us. She juggled an armful of groceries, and as she tried to readjust, two Granny Smith apples spilled from one of the bags. Papi bent to retrieve them with surprising ease given his age, helping others so instinctive.

"Thanks, Elliot," the girl said, and beamed at him.

"She lives in your old apartment," he explained, once we'd exited the building.

I tried to imagine what kind of furniture she would have but remembered instead my parents' old four-poster bed, the '70s quilt my father had given my mother for their wedding, the blue velvet patches. I remembered sleeping in that bed, the three of us, Mom drooling all over the pillow, and Carly, who always sucked her thumb. Her mouth went up and down, sucking in her sleep, with her raccoon curled up in her fist. Both thumb and raccoon (tail or ear). After our grandmother died, our mother slept a lot. Sleeping away our problems seemed to be a Nolan girls thing. Facing our pillows instead of actually facing problems.

Once, while my mother and Carly slept, I took out my sketch pad and got my crayons from the little drawer in the kitchen underneath where we kept the forks and spoons. On the blank paper, I drew two little girls like my father's Diane Arbus photograph, except instead of twins, I drew Carly and me. Carly I drew in round shapes, with a little yellow fuzz on top for hair. Our father had a picture of someone else's kids instead of his own. My own hair I drew in dark brown, in wiggly S shapes. Then I took the crayon called hot magenta and gave both Carly and me BIG smiles.

My picture looked small compared to father's photograph, and compared to the clean white square of wall left behind. I looked down at my drawing, crayon Darcy and crayon Carly, thinking when Mom woke up I would give it to her to see if she would feel better and come play with me. It looked pretty good, I thought. Even if the smiles were a little too big.

&T In the hospital, I brought my mother another coffee in a paper cup from the cafeteria. I pulled the sleeves of my sweater long so that I could hold it without burning myself. My mother appeared both calmer than I remembered her, and puffier, a combination of sedated and resigned.

"You know exactly what I need," she said.

"What's that?" I asked, but she reached with outstretched hands for the coffee, as though it were that simple.

&T I informed my principal of my resignation and began the process of shedding my Calgary skin in three weeks, selling or giving away my few items of furniture, purging the various crafts and cards I'd received over the years from students. In the time I'd lived in Calgary, I'd moved in with and then broken up with my first love, begun and ended my first career. Carly had been dead for almost a full year. Soon it would be Christmas again, my first without her. Eventually, there would be more Christmases without Carly than there had been with her.

Patrick was scheduled to leave January 2nd, but I purposely did not contact him to say goodbye before he flew to London. I did not have it in me. He never called, either.

Conor and Joel appeared to take my decision identically hard. I told them each, separately, and watched their faces contort into the same expression: slightly raised eyebrows, lips parted, eyes widened and then wilted.

Joel tried unconvincingly to be supportive, exercising years of psychological training, saying he understood how unimaginable my stress must be and why it must feel like I needed to go back. "It's probably not a decision you want to make right away. Remember that you have a lot of emotional support here. Me, Conor, your friends. . .Take your time and think about it."

As though I hadn't already made my decision.

I'd had a dream about him at the Holiday Inn, during an intermittent middle-of-the-afternoon nap. In it, he'd flown out to Toronto to surprise me, and he and Papi stood outside my hotel door, knocking, telling me they didn't want me to be alone. But it was just hotel maintenance interrupting my sleep to change the sheets and empty the garbage. It took me a few minutes to wake, and when I did, the housekeeper had already unlocked the door.

"Sorry! Sorry, Ma'am!" She tripped over herself, yanking her cumbersome cart back out the door.

I didn't tell Joel about the dream, even though he continued to call while I was in Toronto during my mother's hospital stay to check up on me, and to try to explain the barrage of doctorspeak I had to decipher about my mother. "It sounds like she's had depression for a long time. Parenting two young children, being pregnant again, having her husband leave, having a miscarriage, losing her mother. . ." He trailed off. After a moment, he said, "It must have been hard, having a mother who was so severely depressed. I'm sorry you had to go through that."

I didn't deserve his concern.

Conor tried a different tactic to get me to stay. He directed me to two chairs near a fireplace in the corner of the coffee shop where I'd decided to break the news. "Quitting in the middle of a year will look bad on your teaching record. This time, you can't say that your sister died. I don't think a principal will cut you a break again; there aren't that many jobs available anymore. Can't you just wait until Christmas break and then decide? You're such a good teacher — I don't want the board to think you're flaky or irresponsible."

"I'm a terrible teacher," I countered. "I don't have it in me anymore. I look at my students, and I just think of Carly. So many of these kids have learning disabilities, AD/HD, shitty parents, crappy life situations. . . I can't save them. If I can't even help my own family, how am I supposed to help all these kids?" I took the lid off my coffee to add sugar, and some of it sloshed over the side.

Conor reached for a napkin.

"I'll get it," I said.

&J I dreamed of squares.

The floor of a shopping mall, a checker pattern.

One blue, one white, one blue, one white.

I hop from blue to blue.

White ones are bad luck.

Mom pushes her shopping cart. She says we need stuff for the baby.

Can't the baby just use my old stuff?

Like my ABC blocks, and my dinosaur puzzle, and my zebra puppet.

I outgrowed all that stuff.

Blue, blue, blue.

"Where's your mom?" says a mom-sized lady, in a flower dress. She squats down beside me.

Where *is* my mom?

I'm looking for her — I see grown-ups and shopping bags and stores.

I'm standing on a blue. I can't move.

The lady puts her hands on my shoulders. "Where'd your mom go, Sweetheart?"

Mom!

I'm crying, and my nose starts running.

She left me here, when I wasn't looking.

"What's your mom's name, Sweetheart? We can go to the desk and get security to call her over the loud speaker."

I can't tell her my mom's name. I wipe my nose on my sleeve. I'll be good, I promise.

Then Mom comes up right beside me. "Why are you crying?" To the lady, she says, "This is my daughter." Then, to me, "Darcy, stop! Be quiet! You're fine."

We go outside, onto the busy street and stand in the snow. I don't like the wind. My jacket isn't zipped up. People keep pushing by.

"You better never wander off like that again!" Mom says. "You stay beside me or you're going to get lost, and something bad is going to happen to you. You have to be good, always."

    I didn't think Dickhead would answer a phone call from me again. Sure enough, I got his automated voicemail.

"I'm bringing my mother home from the hospital tomorrow," I said. "It's her house, too." I paused. Did I have anything else to say? "And I'm moving in with her. So, if you want to keep living there, fine. But you're going to have to live with us both. Your choice."

    The Calgary Stampede, a ten-day-long cowboy-themed festival in July, consumed the whole city, forcing everyone to participate — even Patrick. When the office where he had a summer job threw a pancake breakfast, he'd caved to the Stampede spirit only by wearing jeans, and pushed the sloppy beans and bacon around on the paper plate in front of him. His fellow student colleagues wore bolo ties and cowboy boots, guzzled beer despite the fact that it wasn't even noon yet, and called me "Lassie," as in "Git yer pardner to loosen up and have a drink, Lassie!"

"I read that the rates of hospital admissions skyrocket during Stampede," Patrick commented, one morning, fumbling in the dark with the buttons of his dress shirt. The sun had yet to come up. Way too early for going to work, especially for summer. Patrick insisted on going into work early during Stampede, saying that he hated the crowds that rode the c-train to and from the Stampede Grounds, clogging up his usual commute. I'd tried to convince him that waking up at five was excessive; he'd argued that he'd finish work and come home sooner. We both knew, though, that summer students did not have the option of finishing early; while he was there, associates always found something for him to do.

I tried to go back to bed after Patrick left, but found myself lying awake. The summer before moving to Calgary, he and Aubrey had run a 10k for prostate cancer wearing boxer briefs instead of gym shorts. Louis, who was Aubrey's boy-toy at the time, and I, had waited at the finish line with Gatorade. Patrick crossed the finish line; gave me a sweaty hug that lifted me off my feet.

In bed, unable to sleep after Patrick left, I rolled over and looked out the window. The sun rose through the windows Patrick had cleaned the night before.

& I went to the house before bringing my mother home. Opened the garage. No car. Didn't mean he wouldn't come back, though. The sink lay full of dishes. In their room, drawers hung open, empty. Her ratty clothes took up less than half the space. The basement room — first mine, then Carly's — felt stale, unused, the sheets pulled up and smoothed tight, the way it had never looked when occupied by my sister.

Back in the kitchen, I pulled a chair up to the counter and opened the cabinet above the fridge.

When my father left, I knew because of the absence of his framed photograph.

When my mother's husband left, I knew because of the absence of his booze.

& Back in Toronto, I was reminded of a different kind of cold, a wet cold that licked at my bones. Kipling sniffed around the basement room before settling onto the windowsill. She wanted to be up high, but even on the window, she only reached ground level. I'd moved from basement to basement to basement. So much for moving up. Kipling hung her head over the side. Doleful, black marble eyes.

& The doctors put my mother on a new medication that made her talkative, fidgety. She took up knitting to keep her fingers still, but kept making mistakes, tying knots on top of knots. Her fingers trembled while she tried to undo them. Her stories distracted her, but I wanted her to keep talking.

She learned two lessons the hard way, she told me: that breast-feeding was not a very effective form of birth control, and that my father was an asshole.

They conceived me before getting married, the little push (or maybe the big shove) that led to the quickie courthouse wedding with only two witnesses, and not even their parents. My mother went on the pill right after I was born, but Carly still somehow managed to make an appearance, six years later, right as my father started his master's in Business. He'd finished his undergraduate degree during my toddlerhood, and then worked for a few years to pay back their debt.

"Your father kept taking out student loans," she informed me.

"I told him, you know we have to pay those back, right? He told me I should go back to work. Before you were born, I worked at the Shoppers Drug Mart."

My mother went into labour with Carly on the first day of my father's second year of his MBA. My mother took a taxi to the hospital, left me with my grandmother, and laboured alone for eight hours while my father finished the two classes he had for that day. He still made it to the hospital in time; my mother's labour with Carly took a total of thirty-one hours, which culminated in a c-section.

Nine months later, my mother discovered she was pregnant again; eight weeks along. She'd mistaken her absent periods for normal fluctuation while breastfeeding, thinking it was too early to go back on the pill. She began vomiting as soon as she woke up, so it occurred to her to take a pregnancy test. She told me the stick turned pink right away, before the time limit; outside the bathroom, Carly sat and screamed and pounded her little fists on the door.

She told my father on her birthday, June 1st. He left on June 2nd, before I got home from school. My mother said she went into her bedroom and lay on her bed on top of all the laundry she hadn't yet folded. When she got up, she found Carly in the bathroom, having pulled herself up to the edge of the toilet, dangling her fingers in the basin, splashing the cold water everywhere. "That," she told me, "was Carly's first spanking." She laughed. "First of many, hey?" My mother didn't tell us that my father had left, assuming he would come back in a couple of days.

Sitting on the couch in front of me, she fumbled with a ball of yarn; it rolled away from her, dangling by a single string.

I picked it up, rolled the string around my hand. "Where did he go?"

"First to his dad's. His parents never really liked me; they wanted him to marry someone educated. And they said you girls weren't well behaved. His mom died shortly after Carly was born, and his father was an alcoholic."

"Does he know that you lost the baby?"

"I never told him. He paid child support for you and Carly — it came right off his paycheque, until your eighteenth birthdays. But obviously, he never paid anything for the baby, so. . .bastard probably thought I got an abortion. That's what he wanted me to do." She picked at a tangle in her scarf. "The doctors said if you miscarry it usually happens earlier on. . .They did the ultrasound and told me she was a girl, and then two days later I was standing in the shower and I started bleeding. They had to. . .they had to cut her out of me. I picked the name Vanessa — something really girly. Your father picked your name, and Carly's. This baby was going to be mine. Screw him if he didn't want anything to do with her." She paused, reached to take the string I'd collected. "There was. . .there was so much blood. It was all over the towel. I tried to clean it up so it wouldn't scare you girls."

"He paid child support?"

"Not much; he was still in school, he didn't have a job. I had enough money to keep Carly in daycare for a while, pay the bills. I worked, too — cleaning houses, you remember — and then I waitressed. When he finally got a job, the money got a bit better."

"Did he ever ask to come see us?"

She looked up from the mess in her lap. "I need some coffee. You want some?"

"Sure."

It tasted too strong.

"People say waitressing is good cash, but the other waitresses were younger than me, pretty, with bigger tits. Big tits, big tips."

When she tired of knitting, my mother would bake. She'd burned the underside of a loaf of banana bread that morning.

She didn't seem to notice the blackened bottom, or the fact that it barely tasted of banana. She'd used yellow ones, fresh from the produce aisle, instead of the ripe ones that the recipe called for. I bit into a slice.

"Does he know Carly died?"

She talked with her mouth full. "Do you want more? I'm going to have more. My meds make me so hungry."

"I'm okay."

She'd gone back in the kitchen to cut another slab. I asked again. "Does he know Carly died?"

"I don't know. Maybe."

"You didn't tell him?"

"I haven't talked to him since he walked out on you girls."

And you, I thought.

She swallowed. "I thought I saw him at the funeral, at the very back. It kind of looked like him. He always had that scratchy beard. I couldn't tell. He was too far away."

    & At the temp agency, I passed the typing test and the computer literacy test.

"We have a sales position available," the staffer informed me. He looked like he hadn't slept. "It's for a, uh, cable company."

"What kind of sales?"

"You know, calling people, asking if they want more channels, that kind of thing."

"So, telemarketing."

"Basically. You interested?"

They gave me a six-month contract, a maternity leave. I needed the money. Outside, I waited for the bus, standing underneath the building overhang. I hadn't anticipated the layer of frost outside when I'd dressed; my legs shivered bare without nylons.

There was an old lady who swallowed a goat
Just opened her throat and swallowed a goat!
She swallowed the goat to catch the dog.
She swallowed the dog to catch the cat.
She swallowed the cat to catch the bird.
She swallowed the bird to catch the spider
That wiggled and jiggled and tickled inside her.
She swallowed the spider to catch the fly.
I don't know why she swallowed a fly
Perhaps she'll die.

& When Carly had too much energy to burn, I would lie with her on our backs on opposite ends of the couch and put the soles of my feet against hers. She still had baby soft feet with round toes. Then I would pedal my legs, the motion carrying through to Carly's legs, so that we pedaled in tandem, opposite leg forward and opposite leg back.

"We're a cassette tape, Car," I told her, showing her how the wheels turned around when she put her Raffi tape in the cassette player. "If you keep turning, you'll hear the music."

She would pedal and pedal, and I would sing to her, her favourite songs.

Alouette, gentille Alouette
Alouette, je te plumerai

Je te plumerai la tête
Je te plumerai la tête
Et la tête
Et la tête
Alouette
Alouette
Oh–oh–oh–oh
Alouette, gentille Alouette
Alouette, je te plumerai

"What does it mean?" She stopped her feet mid pedal.

"What does what mean?"

"The song."

"It's French, I don't know what it means."

Curious, that Monday, I asked my teacher if she knew what the lyrics meant in English. She told me she'd write them out for me while we worked in our small groups. After class, she slipped me a piece of paper with her neat little scroll.

Little bird, lovely little bird
Little bird, I will pluck your feathers off
I'll pluck the feathers off your head
I'll pluck the feathers off your head
Off your head, off your head
Little bird, lovely little bird
Little bird, I will pluck your feathers off

& In Toronto, I wore headphones to the grocery store and avoided the pleasant chatter of the cashier, stocked my cart with peanut butter chips and cocoa powder so that I could bake with my mother. The first batch of cookies we made went runny in the oven and formed a giant super cookie with edges like the petals of a flower. Carly had been particularly bad at baking — too impulsive to follow recipes, too eager to lick spoons and improvise by adding ingredients. Often, she confused baking soda and baking powder, or sugar and salt, and on more than one occasion, she'd left confections in the oven, forgot to set the timer, and moved on to other tasks, until the kitchen oven breathed furious fog from its mouth and the fire alarm let out an anxious shriek.

In the evenings, I went running, surprised that my body remembered how to run from the days when I'd run away from lonely nights without Patrick. Running made me high. Adrenaline rushed through my veins and arteries and my body ached — a reminder that I was still alive. I pushed myself, frantic to run farther and faster each night. It became habitual, literally putting one foot in front of the other. I showered the sweat and grimy Toronto air off my body each night later and later, into the early morning hours, fed Kipling and collapsed into bed, sore at the points where bone met muscle met bone. I slept late in the mornings until I could no longer ignore the sun's insistence.

My mother ate everything we baked.

"Good thing I got my appetite back!" she sang. I could see the bits of soft baked pretzel in her mouth. I politely spat mine into a napkin, swallowed to try to rid my mouth of the overwhelming taste of garlic salt. By February, she'd gained twenty pounds, and I'd lost thirteen. Carly had been dead for three hundred and fifty-two days.

&⏀ Had my mother succeeded the first time she tried to kill herself, Carly and I would have, effectively, been parentless. Would we have gone back to our father? Stayed with Papi? Gone into foster care?

"Did you have a will?" I asked Mom, from the kitchen table, while she dumped a cup full of flour into batter without sifting it.

"I don't need a will. Don't have any money. Don't have any

kids to take care of. If I die, you just cremate me and put me in a cardboard box. I won't care. I'll be dead." She turned the beaters on, and noise and flour spouted up from the bowl, into the room.

"When we were kids, I mean," I yelled over the noise, getting up and coming closer to her. "Did you have a will when Carly and I were little?"

She flicked the switch, squelching the sound.

"Didn't have any money back then, either. Get me some vanilla."

& I thought I'd go out for a bit, pick up some ingredients for breakfast. I wandered to the corner store and bought a loaf of basic, whole wheat bread and a litre of 1 percent milk. When I got back home, the bowl was still on the table, beaters leaned against it. Crusty batter glazed the silver blades.

"Mom?" I put the milk down. "Mom?"

Her bedroom door hung ajar. I pushed my way in.

She lay on her stomach, her face sideways. I could see her back moving, a regular pattern. Inhale. Exhale. I tried to do the same.

Back in the kitchen, my cell phone blinked at me: one missed call from Joel. Joel called just to talk, a trait Aubrey had disdained when her previous boyfriends did it, calling it "clingy" and "needy." Three days earlier, Joel had called to say he'd met Conor's new boyfriend, Michael.

"He made risotto — I had seconds."

I fluffed up the pillows behind my head. "Sounds better than what I've been eating."

"He seems like a nice guy. But the motorcycle and leather jacket thing. . .I dunno, don't you think it's a tad cliché?"

Cliché. He sounded like Patrick.

Each time he phoned, Joel asked how long I planned on staying in Toronto, and when I planned on coming "home."

I covered the bowl with Saran Wrap and called him back.

"Hi," he said. "How's your mom?"

"She's okay. Fine. Except when I came home and she wasn't in the kitchen, and I flipped out."

"You flipped out?"

"She'd fallen asleep. I just thought. . .you know."

I'd taken my mother out to breakfast that morning at a diner at Yonge and Eglinton. Our table reflected in the mirror behind her head. There echoed the two of us, wearing lifeless sweaters, huddling around our coffee mugs, just trying to stay warm.

"And you?" Joel asked.

"And me what?"

"What have you been up to?"

"Doing my mom's laundry, making sure she takes her medication on time. Making sure she goes to her therapist every week."

He coughed. "How's work?"

"Okay. The pay is pretty shitty, but it's enough, anyway."

"Are you full-time yet?"

"No, just three days. I can't really be out of the house any more than that. I mean, the meds are helping, but I'm still. . ."

"You can't work from home?"

"No, there's a probation period; I have to be in the call centre, for now, anyway."

During my last shift, a potential customer had blown a whistle loudly into the phone and yelled, "Take me off your list, asshole!"

"Do you miss teaching?" Joel asked.

Did I? "I guess."

"Both my parents were teachers, did Conor ever tell you that? Runs in the family."

"Yeah."

"Yesterday, my mom suddenly announced she's ready for grandkids."

"Mm hmm."

"Conor thinks it's funny. I don't see his boyfriend hopping on that bandwagon. And I see enough kids at work, you know? Have you talked to Conor lately?"

"Uh. . .I think a week ago?" I'd rounded down. When I started counting, I realized I actually hadn't talked to Conor in over two weeks.

"Did he tell you he showed a video in Health class about first aid, and one of the kids fainted because it showed blood?"

I smiled. "I could probably guess what kid he's talking about."

I could hear my mother upstairs in the kitchen, the slam and then whir of the dishwasher closing and starting. Check.

"One time, when we were kids, Conor wiped out pretty bad on his bike, you know, skinned knee, bloody nose. We were playing in the ravine — a good half hour from the house — so I tried to patch him up, but by the time we made it home, we were both so covered in blood my mom said she couldn't tell which of us was actually injured."

"Carly used to get hurt a lot," I said.

"Yeah?"

"Yeah." I picked at some grime under one of my fingernails. Batter? Dirt? "Anyway, Joel, I should probably go, I have to work tomorrow." My shift didn't start until noon, but whatever.

"Oh, okay. Yeah, it's getting late there. Sorry, I always forget about the time difference."

"It's okay."

"By the way — "

"What?"

"Happy Valentine's Day."

Happy. That was one word for it.

&⊤ As though he'd been *my* ex-lover, and not my sister's, I kept tabs on Ryan. After the funeral, I'd phoned daily for a week. I needed to know. Had he had any idea? No. Had she left any other messages? No. Had they had any contact?

"No," he said. My phone battery chirped its forthcoming demise. "You told me not to talk to her," he reminded me, as though I needed reminding. "She called a lot. But I didn't answer. I didn't crack."

He carried the other half of my secret the way Aubrey and I had each worn half of a BEST FRIENDS heart on a necklace for a week in middle school before she declared it cheesy and stopped wearing hers.

After moving out of the apartment he'd shared with Carly, Ryan put school on hold, moved from part-time to full-time at the restaurant, and rented a small, two-bedroom basement suite. Two bedrooms, I imagined, so he would have a room for Autumn. I couldn't tell whether he was not, as Carly had feared, in a relationship with Autumn's mother. I didn't feel comfortable asking him outright.

His answers to my questions didn't change.

Initially, he picked up after one or two rings. Then, my calls started rolling to voicemail.

Hi, you've reached Ryan. Leave me a message.

As simple as that.

I searched his name online, but didn't find anything. When I searched Jessa's name, I couldn't tell which profile belonged to her. One Jessa Ryce had a user photo of a little girl in pigtails and sunglasses. Ryan had told Carly Autumn looked just like him — but I couldn't see the child's face from behind her shades. The rest of the photos were blocked.

For all I knew, Jessa could have moved in with Ryan — Jessa and Autumn both. I pictured the three of them, a little family,

Mommy, Daddy, child. The family neither Carly nor Ryan had ever had.

Sometimes I detoured on my way home and walked past The Upstairs Basement where I was pretty sure Ryan still worked. I'd gone a few times to visit Carly during a shift, sitting at the bar and dipping warm pita into their specialty dips: red pepper hummus, roasted garlic and spinach, and Brie fondue. The smell walking by reminded me of my sister, but I could not go inside.

One evening, a few weeks after I'd settled back in Toronto, I walked past an elementary school, my arms straining to carry heavy grocery bags. About a hundred feet away from me I spotted a dad and his young daughter. I stopped, still holding my groceries. They wore bulky winter coats; the little girl had matching pink mittens and boots. The father pushed his daughter on the swing. She rose away from me, then swung back. Away, and then back. I could hear the trill of her laughter, like a bird oblivious to the cold.

I moved a few steps closer, put my groceries down on the sidewalk. Ryan? I couldn't see his hair, tucked underneath a dark grey toque. The swing slowed down, and he scooped the girl up under her armpits and placed her back down on her feet.

"Catch me, Daddy!" she challenged him, beginning to run away from the play structure. He waited a few seconds before starting after her. I put my hands up on the chain link fence surrounding the school, a bit shocked by the coldness of the metal.

Just as she came closer to me, the girl slipped on an icy patch of snow and stumbled chest first into the ground. She paused upon impact. Her father caught up to her a few moments later, at which point, she began to cry.

When he scooped her up, I saw his face.

Not Ryan, after all.

&Joel received a subpoena to go to court to testify about the parenting skills of a client of his, having worked with both the mother and her four-year-old son. At eighteen, he told me, she'd had a brief relationship with a bartender at the nightclub where she worked as a waitress. The relationship didn't last very long, and when she missed her period, she went to her doctor and had him run a pregnancy test, which came back negative. A month later, when her period still didn't come, she went back to her doctor and had him re-run the blood work. Again the test came back negative. Two months later, she experienced spotting and abdominal pain, and went to the ER, where a nurse ran an ultrasound and discovered that the woman had been pregnant the entire time. She was, by that point, almost halfway through her pregnancy. But, reassured repeatedly that she was not pregnant, she'd continued waitressing at the nightclub and indulging in her lifestyle, frequently drinking on the job and with her friends. Her son arrived six weeks premature, with symptoms of fetal alcohol syndrome and a seizure disorder. The young mother became embroiled in a legal battle against her ex-boyfriend's parents, who wanted to terminate her parental rights and adopt the boy themselves. Joel had been asked to give his opinion on her fitness as a parent, or whether her lifestyle had endangered her son's life.

"I always knew I might have to go to court someday," he admitted, over the phone. "I know a lot of people who've been practicing for years and have never had to go. I hoped to be in that group. Sounds naïve, but I'm kind of freaking out. I've always hated public speaking."

"Make Conor go in your place," I suggested. "He loves public speaking."

"Yeah, somehow I don't see that working very well." Joel laughed. "Hold on, I'm going to go grab some juice. My throat's getting dry just talking about having to testify."

When he came back to the phone, I said, "Did I ever tell you my father was a twin?"

"Really?"

"Well, kinda. The other twin didn't live. Stillborn."

"That's really sad," Joel said.

"Not as sad as growing up together and having his brother die later. At least this way, he never knew."

"True. But psychological repercussions can happen from loss at any stage."

I had a blister from running on the back of my heel. I pressed hard against it until it popped. It hurt more than I expected. "So what are you going to say?" I asked.

"About what?"

"At court."

"Well, I don't feel the blame should be put on my client — she got a test as soon as she missed her period, medical professionals told her the tests came back negative; she did what lots of eighteen-year-olds do. She's taking care of the baby now, she comes to counselling regularly, she stopped drinking as soon as the pregnancy was confirmed. She's trying her best. . .plus, she feels horrible. The last thing the court should do is take away her kid. She's going to already have to live with her guilt for the rest of her life. If only she'd known earlier. Sorry, you probably don't want to hear all this."

"It's fine," I said. "When's the court date?"

"Thursday. It could get pushed back, though. Depends what happens with the other witnesses, I guess. I'm hoping it's just over and done with on Thursday. I don't want to have to cancel any more of my client sessions. Plus, there's this other thing I wanted to talk to you about."

"What?"

"There's a conference on childhood trauma in Toronto — second week of May."

"That's just after my birthday," I told him.

"Right! Well, I thought if uh. . .maybe if I came out, if you might want to have dinner or something. I've heard great things about the food in Little Italy."

Eating out meant more time away from my mother. At home, I could make food and make sure she didn't kill herself at the same time. I could craft actual meals now, meals that tasted half decent; a meat, a carb, a vegetable. Dinners that would have made Patrick proud. "Yeah, Little Italy's good."

"Yeah? That's what I heard, so. . ."

"Yeah."

I wandered out of my room and up the stairs, peered into my mother's room. Still sleeping. Check.

"So. . .okay, so, what do you think?" Then, "Oh, great, I just spilled juice all over the carpet."

My eyes felt itchy; I'd left my contacts in too long. "What kind of juice?"

"Um. . .sorry, it's just everywhere. What?"

"If it's apple, it probably won't stain that bad."

He laughed. "Apparently being nervous makes me a klutz. If we have dinner, I promise I won't spill anything on you."

 On days off, and when my mother slept or knit or baked, I wandered up and down Bloor and its side streets, Carly's cherubic ghost traipsing after me like a dawdling child, compelled by the battered Tim Hortons cups of homeless people collecting change, distracted by the soulful tunes of street buskers. I smelled the smouldering flesh of sausages pressed into a grill and heard Carly begging me for a toonie and two quarters so that she could buy some "street meat." She used to joke that the way to tell when it was spring in Toronto was when the hot dog vendors appeared. Spring. Already spring? Soon, summer would creep up on me, too. Summer, fall, winter, spring. More and more days without Carly.

I'd forgotten how, in Toronto, you saw rain before you felt it, in the light drops ahead of you on the pavement, and in the haze of the sky. You'd touch your hair and realize it was damp, with the sky so warm and humid. And then it would start to pour, fat tears sobbing from the sky. One rainy afternoon, I waved down a cab and had the driver take me to Carly's cemetery.

Her rectangular stone looked small compared to the others: a lacklustre greypink granite, with her name carved simply into the stone. I ran my fingers over the letters.

I lay down with my head at the base of the stone, my body parallel with hers. My ears buzzed. I imagined her, five years old, standing on the sidelines of our apartment pool, knees bent, her arms wrapped around her torso. She wore bright orange water wings, a blue one-piece with a puppy appliqué. A hand-me-down from her big sister. The water came up to my chin. I bobbed up and down on my tippy toes. I stretched my arms out to her. The sign on the wall read: *Children under 13 must be supervised.* Nobody ever came up to the pool anyway, and Mom had fallen into one of her deep sleeps, where even Carly, poking at her, squirming into the bed beside her, fluttering at her with cold little feet couldn't wake her up.

Carly, in her blue bathing suit, stood in front of me on the dock. "I don't wanna."

"You need to learn how to swim," I told her. "Big girls know how to swim. I promise, I'll catch you."

"What if you don't?"

"I cross my heart."

"I'm scared."

"There's nothing to be scared about. Come on."

"I'm scaaaaared."

I lifted my toes up off the bottom of the pool and dogpaddled for a moment, watching her. That morning, I'd put a French braid in her hair. She'd been so excited she couldn't stop touching it. Now, it was a frizzy mess, strands loose and falling in front of her eyes.

"Jump, Carly."

She paced back a few steps, unsure, then pointed one foot hesitantly forward. Set it back down.

"Jump, Carly," I insisted. "Just do it. Jump!"

She fixed her wide blue eyes on me. Then, in a split second, she leapt into the air, falling down towards the water. Waiting for me to catch her.

    & I slept in on Sunday, and when I woke up, my mother was not in her bedroom. Not in the kitchen.

She'd wake randomly, not on a schedule. She made two dozen red velvet cupcakes one morning as the sun came up, made a full pancake breakfast one evening just as I shuffled off to bed.

At work, I phoned her after every ten client calls.

"Good afternoon, Ma'am. Are you interested in upgrading your Internet to high speed?"

I wondered what she did while I swivelled in my desk chair and twiddled with my pen. I broke a series of pens with my fiddling; snapped off the backs and burst the ink.

"Hi, Mom. Just calling to say hi."

"To see if I'm alive," she'd say. "I'm not stupid."

I rid the house of razor blades, started waxing my legs and armpits instead, which burned. I flushed all the over-the-counter meds I could find, but I couldn't get rid of her prescriptions. I started carrying them with me, leaving only those she needed for that day in a small bowl on the kitchen table.

After a week of this, I came home and found a triple-layer

fudge cake that she'd sculpted in my absence. She'd left the oven on, and the room felt hot. She'd cut me a piece and left it in the bowl with a Post-it note that read simply, *I'm not a child*. I turned the oven off. The cake tasted too sweet, the icing slippery. I scraped the contents of the bowl into the trash.

Then, Sunday morning, I couldn't find her.

"Mom?" I checked the bathrooms, then the closets. I stood at the top of the stairs, my body tingling.

She'd gone to jump.

Why use pills or razors? They'd never worked for her in the past.

But throwing herself in front of the subway — it'd worked for Carly.

Together again, mother and daughter.

And I would —

Keys in the lock. The front door opened.

"Mom!" I cried. "What the *fuck?*"

Her hair sagged, damp from the rain. She unwound a purple scarf from her neck, shed her faded jacket. "What?"

"Where the fuck were you?"

She dropped her keys onto the side table. "You look like a skeleton. I bake all this food, you never eat it."

I sunk to sitting. "Where were you? You scared the hell out of me."

She sighed. "I went to church. For fuck's sake. I just went to goddamned Mass!"

&ꓕ When the rain let up enough to go for a walk, I wandered past The Upstairs Basement and caught the scent of warm, oven-baked bread, mingled with the wet scent of spring. I stopped to inhale a memory of Carly in mud-spackled rain boots. A dull ache squeezed my breastbone.

Ryan exited, with his back to me, and turned around to wave at someone still in the building, calling, "Thanks! I'll see you tomorrow!"

When he turned, I saw that he'd put on weight and had grown out his beard. He exhaled; his breath smelled brightly of beer.

"Darcy."

"Hi," I said, looked down. Mud lined the sides of my sneakers.

"What are you doing here?"

In fact, all of him smelled like beer. He ran his hand over his face, as though trying to smooth out his expression.

"I. . ." I felt stupid saying it. "I just sometimes take this route home. It uh. . .it reminds me of Carly."

"You live here now?"

"Yeah," I said. "I moved back a while ago."

A pigeon stumbled between us, pecking at the ground, shimmery shades of pink and green under the bland grey and white of its neck feathers. Ryan and I had never been big talkers; Carly had always engulfed all the possible space and silence.

"Okay then," I said, and turned away. "Well, I'm going to go."

"Wait." He put his hand on my arm, stopping me. "I just got off. Do you want to go for a drink?"

We found a small hole-in-the-wall, cash-only Indian restaurant with gloomy, barely-there lighting. I ordered a chai and some naan, wondering whether I should splurge and pick up food to take home to my mother. Would she notice I was taking longer than usual?

Ryan ordered a Newcastle but no food, and when his drink came, he took a large gulp of the dark ale. There was foam in the hair on his upper lip. His skin was sallow, and there were rings under his eyes.

"How's work?" I asked.

"Oh," he said, "you know. I do okay, with tips and stuff. I got moved up to bartender, finally. Maybe in a couple years I'll apply for a management position." His words lacked enthusiasm.

"Did you ever go back to school?" He'd had only one semester of college completed when he found out about Autumn.

He swallowed some more beer. "Can't afford it. Especially not now, you know? Child support."

Child support. So, he probably didn't live with Jessa. Probably didn't love her. *Possibly* didn't love her. Still, I didn't want to ask.

"How is she — uh, your daughter?"

"She's great. She's amazing. She's the only thing that keeps me going, really, when some days I just want to. . ." Another sip. "She's so damn smart. She's about to finish kindergarten. The other night, we were at Swiss Chalet, and she said, *Daddy, I want one of these,* and pointed to the menu, so I said, *Do you know what that says?* And she said, *Chocolate milkshake.* There wasn't even a picture. Those are long words, too."

I pictured them, sitting beside each other in a vinyl booth, Ryan and Autumn, her hair in pigtails, holding the giant plastic menu. Her calling him Daddy.

"You see a lot of her?" I asked.

He took the last gulp of his drink. "Not as much as I want. Jessa's parents. . .I don't get to see Autumn much. Apparently I'm a shitty, irresponsible high school kid who got their daughter pregnant."

"Hey," I said, tearing off a piece of the buttery naan. "You're there, aren't you? You want to talk about shitty fathers? My dad bailed on us when Carly was still a baby."

"I know. My parents bailed, too. I didn't want Autumn to go through what Carly went through."

"What do you mean?"

"You know, never having a dad, always feeling like it was her fault, like she did something wrong. I don't want Autumn growing up thinking I don't love her."

"Carly talked to you about our father?"

"A bit. Especially after I found out I had a kid. It killed her — she said how come I didn't even know my daughter and I wanted to be a dad, when her dad left because of her?"

"Because of her?"

"I guess she felt the timing of it — like, when he left — he stayed around for you, she said, then after she came along. . .she thought. . .plus she said your stepdad always told her she was a brat, too hard to handle. Makes me want to punch that guy. I've thought about it."

I'd shredded the naan into mulch. "Carly thought our dad left because of her?"

"She never told you that?"

"Never. I didn't think. . .she didn't even remember him."

He shrugged, put his glass to his lips even though there was no liquid left, then set it back down.

"Maybe on some level all kids blame themselves for deadbeat parents. My grandma told me my mom got sick because of drugs. But maybe that's an excuse. She could have stopped, I think."

Did all kids whose parents left feel responsible? Had I felt that way, on some level, when my father walked out? I'd felt the absence of my father's framed photograph more palpably than the absence of him. Guiltily, I recalled being a teenager, thinking that our mother had checked out because of Carly. However abusive it had been for our stepfather to constantly harass Carly for being a challenging kid, there was truth to it. I would have never said it to her face, or left her because of it. But sometimes, I'd wanted to. Sometimes, she'd been *so*. . .

In the dark, I wanted to drown myself in alcohol. Poison myself with it.

"I miss her," Ryan said. "I miss her so fucking much. You told me not to call her."

I wondered if anyone had heard, despite the noise of the dark restaurant. I wiped my greasy palms on my jeans. "Do you hate me because of it?" Of course he did.

"No, I just wanted. . .I didn't want her to hurt anymore. I didn't know it would — "

"I know," I said. "I didn't either."

He reached in his back pocket and slid out his wallet, pulled out a limp twenty-dollar bill. "I'm going to take off," he said, and stood.

I nodded, fished in my purse for some change.

"She always thought it was funny that the two of you looked nothing alike," he added. "I guess it's a good thing, now — sometimes, it hurts to be reminded."

& I took another cab to the cemetery, listening to the static of the dispatcher giving directions over the radio. The driver tried to chat with me a few times, but gave up after several one-word answers. A hole in the back of the seat revealed the gaping guts of yellow foam. I picked at the spot, making it worse.

The driver changed into the left lane and ran over the decomposing corpse of a dead bird; a crow, its body crushed and stiff against the pavement. I turned around to look, as car after car rushed over it. Flattened, flightless, lifeless.

At Carly's grave, I sat with my back against the headstone. The shadows of the trees shifted under the vigilant eye of the sun, marking the dawdling time. Half an hour felt like a whole afternoon. Time without Carly had slowed to a standstill, dug its heels into the dirt, refused to pick up the pace. I would drag it by the wrist for the rest of my life.

I called a cab to take me back home. When we passed over the same spot where the crow was, I watched for it, out the smeary window. There — I could see it. Repeatedly crushed each passing second. As though anything could possibly flatten it more.

&J In May, Joel flew to Toronto for the conference on child abuse offered through the Hospital for Sick Children. The seminar so happened to fall the week after my twenty-seventh birthday. That morning, waking up in the bed I'd abandoned as soon as I'd graduated high school, I wondered whether Patrick would phone. But he couldn't. He didn't know I lived in Toronto again. I'd changed my cell phone, my address. My life.

A recent cold turned into an ear infection. I went to Dr. Martin, who wrote me a prescription for antibiotics. At the drugstore, I paid for my amoxicillin and my mother's latest stash of antidepressants and mood stabilizers. Happy birthday to me.

My mother asked me what I wanted for my birthday.

"Nothing," I said.

She wore one of Dick's old sweatshirts, the frayed cuffs pushed up around her elbows. "I'm going to bake a cake," she said. "Black Forest. We had Black Forest once for your birthday. Remember?"

I remembered a Black Forest cake from one of Carly's birthdays. She plucked the fake, saccharine cherries from the top of the cake, put them in her mouth, and plucked off the stems. Her lips turned red.

One week and three days after I turned twenty-seven, Joel took a cab to the airport and I went to work, where the company offered to make my temporary contract permanent. I needed health care benefits; it made the monotony worth it. That same day, as I walked home, a man started walking in my general direction, screaming obscenities. "Fucking whore! Fucking cunt! Fucking cocktease!" Was he angry at someone in particular? Or just at the world? I crossed to the other side of the street.

What I didn't know at the time, but would discover three weeks later at work, having suspiciously and violently thrown up the half can of pineapple I'd consumed that morning for breakfast, was that at some point during the few days prior, I'd conceived my first child.

As its mother-to-be walked home, attempting to ignore the hatred spewing from the passerby, my baby remained completely oblivious. It had yet to develop ears, or a heart, or a brain. Maybe being oblivious was safer.

 Patrick had insisted we use as many forms of birth control as possible. I took the pill each night at exactly the same time *and* we used condoms. I kept my mouth shut about several of Patrick's rules — such as hand-scrubbing between the grooves of the mosaic bathroom tiles, which were each only approximately an inch square — but I agreed with him about pregnancy prevention. Though I enjoyed other people's children, and my stomach swooned when one of my co-workers on maternity leave brought her six-week-old son to work and I touched the velvet curve of his bare foot, I had little desire for my own child. At three-thirty, I could say goodbye to my students, close myself in the expanse of my empty classroom with a cup of coffee and sit in silence. The idea of my own child growing older, having something inevitably awful happen to it — dropping out of school, contracting an STI, being arrested for driving drunk, or, perhaps, even, being killed by a drunk driver — that idea always crawled cold up my spine and made me grateful for Patrick's fastidiousness.

So it did not surprise me that, despite almost three years of potentially procreative episodes with Patrick, I never became pregnant.

With Joel, it only took four times.

By the time Joel came along, I'd stopped trying so hard. He wanted me. So, why not? I thought. Things were going to happen in my life. Things were going to just keep happening. Time was just going to keep going. It didn't matter.

   I'd forgotten the heat of Toronto summers, forgotten how the haze of smog gives the misleading impression of a cloudy, overcast sky. I'd forgotten about the dark berries that hung, ripe and pregnant from trees, only to fall and become stamped on the sidewalks like tar.

When we finished eighth grade, Aubrey's mother took Aubrey and me to get pedicures as a graduation gift, and got one herself, telling us that well-manicured feet were a necessity when wearing sandals. We met her at the floral boutique where she worked, and she pinned daisies behind our ears.

"Come on, girls," she said, an oversized pair of dark sunglasses masking her face. "Let's go get spoiled."

When I got home, my flower hung hot and wilted, and my shoulders glistened pink with the beginnings of a sunburn. My mother watched as I took my sandals off in the doorway, noticed the polished scarlet of my nails. Aubrey's mom had said red was "classic and timeless."

My mother wore a grimy sweatshirt, even though it was over thirty degrees with the humidex. She looked like she had spent all day cleaning.

"Well, don't you look hoochy," she said, as I came into the living room.

"What are you talking about?" I leaned up against the door-frame. My feet felt sweaty. "Aubrey's mom took us for pedicures. So what?"

My mother scratched the nape of her neck, where an elastic twisted her hair into a ragged loop. "Be all fancy and fake. Get all the attention you want. Suit yourself."

"You're crazy," I said. "You're not making any sense."

She turned away from me, took out a bottle of all-purpose cleaner. "You should worry about your personality instead of your looks."

I clenched my toes into the carpet. *"You* should worry about *your* personality! God!"

She spritzed the cleaner repeatedly onto the counter. Started wiping forceful circles. "If you're going to be a snarky little bitch, go do it somewhere else."

 I think Kipling knew about the baby before I did. When I rescued her, Papi's neighbours told me that Papi's nurse had found Kipling curled up on Papi's feet as he lay there, dead. She was a bait-and-switch kind of cat, the kind who would approach me and butt her head against my leg for attention or crawl up onto my chest while I slept to knead at my chest, only to skitter away when I reached down to pet her or pick her up. Sometimes she hid under the bed for no reason. Typically, she slept on the desk chair on the opposite corner of the room from my bed, watching me through the slats.

The basement room trapped all the cold in the house, even in the summer, and I woke up shivering. I rolled over onto my stomach and bunched the blankets around me for warmth. Kipling crouched on my back. I didn't want to move. I felt her shift a little, tuck her paws underneath herself, then lower her chin down onto the space between my shoulder blades.

 My first kiss with Patrick was something we talked about, something I saw coming well in advance. The stitches in my lip following our car accident prevented us from being able to kiss for days. Patrick confessed that he'd intended to kiss me that night, had planned it all out. When I saw Carly the morning after my first kiss with Patrick, she lay back on my bed, her yellow hair fanning out behind her, and bemoaned her own lack of a boyfriend, of romance.

"You're fourteen, Car," I pointed out.

"Some day, I want to be loved like Papi loved his wife. *So* romantic."

"Papi's love story wasn't romantic; it was tragic," I said. "His wife died when she was twenty-five. They never got to have kids. He ended up a lonely widower for the rest of his life. He never had love again."

"Yeah." Her hair stood out, bright against the grey backdrop of my duvet cover. "I know. It's, like, *Romeo and Juliet* love. Beyond-the-grave love."

I'd told her to get up and stop mooning around. "You always make me late."

"I have to pee first," she said, and sat up. "Whoa, head rush."

Carly took her time in the bathroom, then emerged wearing my lipstick. "If I had someone who wanted to kiss me, I would let him kiss me all the time."

My first kiss with Joel happened during his visit to Toronto, in a small restaurant we'd stopped in when it started to rain, thwarting my ability to show him the city. His breath tasted like chicken soup. He pulled back. "I'm having a good trip so far," he said.

"Okay," I said.

Conor called a couple days after Joel's trip ended.

"So," he said, "how was it?"

"Good," I said. "It was a good trip."

"Yeah, okay. But I meant you sleeping with my brother. How was it? Was it good?"

"Conor!"

"What? I'm teasing."

"He told you?"

"Even my holier-than-thou brother isn't above spilling *these* beans. Plus, I beat it out of him. He really likes you. He's not-so-secretly hoping you'll move back."

"I can't right now. My mom's a basket case."

"Yeah, I know. But we'd both like you to move back eventually. A best buddy and a knight in shining armour. What more could a girl ask for?"

   A memory — a nightmare, darkness, heartbeat, light feet, pushing open her bedroom door, crawling up into the bed, my shivering body, her sweaty sprawl, open-mouth stinky breath, unaware of her daughter wriggling in beside her.

Did it actually happen?

I pulled the hotel sheets up around me, tucked them up under my shoulders, adjusted them around my naked breasts. Pulled my fingers away from where they intertwined with Joel's as he slept. Joel sighed, shifted.

Maybe it wasn't me who ran to my mother after a nightmare.

Maybe it was Carly.

It *had* to be Carly.

Carly — afraid of everything. Of Papi's dolls, of bumblebees, of E.T., of the homeless guy on the corner with one arm.

I'd told my mother that I'd had to go to Hamilton for a two-day work training session, and that I'd be back in a couple days. Not ten minutes away, at Joel's hotel, while he visited Toronto for his conference, for my birthday.

I got up out of the bed, slid my underwear on, pulled my T-shirt over my head.

I shouldn't have left her. Calling didn't cut it. She could be —

I sat back down on the foot of the bed. Would Joel understand if I wrote a note explaining that I needed to go back home to make sure my mother was okay? If I slipped out, called him in the morning? I could check on her and still make it back for breakfast.

I pulled my jeans on, zipped the fly. Reached for my jacket. Scrawled a quick note on the hotel stationery, words I could barely see in the dark. Joel slept.

Wait, I thought, then. Carly would not have run into my mother's room for comfort from a bad dream. She always climbed the ladder from her bed to mine, pushed up against me with bony knees and elbows. "Darcy! I dreamed that I was trapped in a cabin and a millionbillion bumblebees were chasing me, so I climbed out the window, but then. . ."

I closed the heavy hotel room door lightly behind me.

    I knew I had to keep the baby. Walking down Bloor Street one afternoon, before I even told Joel, I passed one of my favourite sushi restaurants, and a young man outside held out a tray, debuting a new roll with thick, glossy slabs of salmon on top.

"New red scorpion roll!" He announced. It had teeth fashioned out of cucumber, stripes on its back squirted in mayonnaise. I'd spent that morning lying on the couch with a cold towel over my eyes after having vomited as soon as I'd woken up. I'd stayed on the couch, in the only position bearable, until I felt brave enough to see whether the morning sickness had passed. When I felt stable enough to venture off the couch, I showered and dressed. I'd lost weight after Carly died, either turned off by the taste of food or impassive to it. I'd forgotten what food tasted like. Sometimes, I'd forgotten to eat. I'd lost even more weight when I'd taken up running again after returning to Toronto. I looked gaunt, my collarbone protruding. I couldn't tell if my breasts were larger or not. They felt sore when I slipped into my bra.

"Darcy!" My mother hollered from upstairs. "I'm not feeling well. Can you do the dishes?" The bowls and measuring cups she'd used to bake an apple rhubarb pie filled the sink.

I hadn't eaten that morning; had vomited the contents of a stomach mostly empty aside from the remnants of the bland crackers I'd chewed on the night before, having read that eating carbs before bed might offset early morning sickness. It hadn't worked. The sushi looked fresh and fatty in the outdoor light. The man smiled at me, thinking I would take some.

"Sorry," I said, "I can't, I'm pregnant."

I'd said it aloud.

The baby was supposed to happen, was here for a reason. Maybe it was why Joel and I had somehow ended up together, without me even realizing how it'd happened. I could not conceive of being responsible for the loss of another life. I wanted the baby to be inside someone else, where it would be safe. Each morning, I climbed wearily out of bed, lifted the sweaty hair off the back of my neck, sunk to my bare knees on the cold bathroom floor, and vomited. Penance that I deserved.

Morning sickness persisted, following me around much like Kipling still did, perching on the edge of the bathtub, a shadowy smudge behind the opaque shower curtain. I called in sick from work two shifts in a row. I lined up a row of crackers and a glass of water on my bedside table. I wondered what it would be like to have a boyfriend or husband with me to hold my hair back, to scrub vomit circles out of the inside of the toilet. I held off telling Joel. Perfect Joel, now tethered to me for life.

Joel sometimes called later than he said he would, always apologetic, noting that he'd accidentally let a session run too long or got caught up in a call with a client's parent. He ordered more textbooks on child development than he could possibly read. He was too good a listener, often pausing as if to mull over my comments before selecting his words. He overused semicolons in emails, even in texts. He sometimes dictated pro/con lists out loud while trying to make a decision.

Even his dating flaw — being drawn to damsels in distress — didn't really feel like a flaw. He just wanted to take care of others.

I did not deserve his support.

& One evening, when the queasiness persisted past dinner-time and my mother had gone to bed early, I found myself restlessly flicking between channels, finally settling on an evening news station broadcasting the story of a mother who, in her haste to get to work on time, had accidentally backed out of the driveway and crushed her six-year-old daughter, who was pedalling unsteadily on her new bike, a birthday gift she'd begged to try out that morning. The child's father saw the whole thing from the front window. I imagined what it would have been like for that mother; the sound of her daughter's body and twisted metal being compressed under the massive wheels of her SUV. The thump of the car upon impact and then the horrific silence of the engine stopping, one lone bicycle wheel spinning, training wheels still attached. The mild fluttering of purple tassels in the autumn wind. Their daughter's picture stayed on the screen a little too long.

When I thought I couldn't stand looking at her face anymore, the story transitioned to a seventeen-year-old girl with hair halfway down her back and a pink cardigan buttoned all the way up to the neckline, who'd been out driving just a few weeks after getting her license, her boyfriend in the passenger seat. She'd hit a patch of black ice and overcompensated, sending the car spinning forward across the median line and into a tree. Her boyfriend hit his head on the top on the car ceiling and snapped his neck. The girl driving the car came away from the wreckage uninjured. The police deemed it an accident, but noted that the girl's inexperience had likely led to the crash. She had not had any alcohol, hadn't made any phone calls, hadn't fiddled with the radio. The girl's tears streamed down her face. Her mother, whose hand rested firmly on her daughters' knee, held out an 8 × 10 photo of the deceased boy. Her daughter's first love. The girl reported that, since the accident, she had to start homeschooling, because her boyfriend's friends had written MURDERER on her locker in permanent marker.

What was the point of trotting out these people and their guilt for everyone to gawk at them? I wanted to turn it off, but I couldn't move. I felt a buzzing from the centre of my breastbone out. My stomach rose and boiled over. I leaned over the edge of the couch and vomited onto the shiny laminate floor.

& It rained and rained and rained and rained. I remembered a day without Papi, a day when Carly mourned by the window while it rained the long, steady, never-ending rain of a song stuck on repeat. The next morning, when the sun glazed the windows, Carly slipped on her red ladybug rubber boots, a hand-me-down from Aubrey, and went outside. Mom had "asked" me to babysit. I took the novel I'd chosen to read for English class downstairs and sat on a bench out front of the apartment. I could always tell where Carly was by the noise she made; she hummed and stomped and sang and cried and yelled and cheered. After a while, though, I noticed that I hadn't heard her for some time.

"Carly!" I yelled. "Carly!" Had she wandered off? Distracted by a red-breasted robin or the neighbours' newly installed trampoline? Stefany Beale ran through my mind, her red ponytail bouncing behind her. "Carly!" I ran alongside of the house to the gate. "Carly!"

When I reached the back of the apartment, still screaming for her, she looked up from where she squatted beside the sidewalk.

"Carly!" I barked, breathlessly. "Why didn't you answer me?"

"I'm collecting earthworms!" She held out her hands. Slick, fat, and struggling, some dangled in pieces, a severed head or body segment writhing in her palm. I couldn't tell which was which.

"Listen," I said. "You're supposed to play where I can see you. I call you, you come. Okay?"

"Do you know what's cool about earthworms?" she said. "If you kill them, they can just come back to life again. They can get cut in half, even, and then they just. . .grow another head or something. They can never die."

I'd forgotten to bring an umbrella to work, and by the time I made it home, my clothes clung to my body. I peeled them off and stepped into a steaming shower. Outwardly, you couldn't tell I was pregnant yet.

Joel and Conor had actually been born on separate days; Joel just before midnight on August 11th, Conor just after midnight on August 12th. I'd mailed Conor a CD and a card the previous week, but hadn't figured out what to send Joel. He wanted me to fly back out to Calgary.

"What does your mother's therapist say? Maybe she'd be stable enough for you to come and visit."

"I don't talk to her therapist," I said. "I take her there, I pick her up. That's it." He wanted me to visit in September. I was due February 10th, but my obstetrician had told me that first babies were often late, commenting, "Maybe you'll have a Valentine's baby."

In my recurring nightmares, my abdomen bulged with twins. Joel, my father — it ran in the family. I dreamed that two little girls came into my room, identical Carlys in corduroy jumpers. One happy, one angry.

They were both equally bad scenarios: finding out via telephone, or not being told for three months.

I got out of the shower and plucked my wet jeans, sweater, and underwear up off the bathroom floor and dropped them in the washing machine. Dark spots along the carpet traced my path in wet footprints. I climbed into bed still wearing my towel. Kipling, asleep on the foot of the bed, stood up, arched her back, and stretched, paced in a circle a few times, then coiled into a ball.

I dialled Joel's number.

&J "Wait. . .what? You're. . .I came out there in. . .May! Which is like — "

"Three months." Could my mother hear me upstairs, like I'd heard her all those times, through the floorboards?

"You said you were on the pill."

"I was. But I also took antibiotics for an ear infection. I'd just finished taking them when you came out, I thought — " I could imagine Aubrey telling me I was so ignorant about sex. "I thought they only affected the pill while you were actually taking them."

"Well, great. So. . .you're. . .so you didn't tell me. Why?"

"I wanted time. To think."

"You wanted to think? Are you sure it's mine?"

"Yes," I said. "It's yours. I'm not seeing anybody else."

"Christ!" he muttered. "And now it's too late."

"To late to what?"

"To have an abortion."

"You would have wanted me to have an abortion?"

"Well?" He paused. "Wouldn't you? Do you know how irresponsible it is to have a child when you're not prepared for one, when you weren't planning on one? What did you think we were going to do, Darcy?"

"I never wanted an abortion."

Kipling's ears were perked, listening. Unable to hear him, only able to hear my side of the conversation. Words. Words could be anything, to her. Just sounds. Just noise. "Well, good thing you decided for me then," Joel snapped.

"Joel — you *love* kids!"

"I do love kids. Doesn't mean I want one. The kids I work with have so many issues — I'm with that all day, I don't want to come home to that, you know? I told you I didn't want kids."

"Not outright. Not like, I never want to have kids, ever."

"But you knew. I told you I saw enough kids at work."

"Yeah, well, I didn't want one, either. But — "

"But you've got one now, I guess." I heard him get up, start going down a flight of stairs. Or — up a flight of stairs? Where was he going? Where was all of this going?

"You're Catholic," I pointed out. "You're not supposed to believe in abortion."

"*Conor's* Catholic. I live in the real world. There are lots of studies that show that embryos — it's not even about that. Do you know how messed up kids can get, even when the parents try their best?"

"I worked with kids, too."

"Okay, well, then you should know! And, really, do you think you're in a good place to raise a kid right now? You're in a co-dependent relationship with your mom, you can't even take care of yourself — "

"Hey." I sat up, clutching the towel to my chest. It was too early to feel the baby move, but maybe deep inside me, I could feel it fighting. "Isn't that why you wanted to be with me in the first place? Because I'm damaged? So you could swoop in and be the saviour?"

"That's ridiculous."

"This isn't a game, Joel. This is real life, now."

He took a long time to respond. "Look. If you want to do this, that's your choice."

& "What do you think about coming with me to therapy?" My mother's open mouth revealed chewed spaghetti. *Pisgetti,* Carly had called it. When I'd tried to make meatballs in the frying pan, they'd crumbled, refused to hold their shape.

"Did you use enough raw egg?" my mother had asked, hovering. Her baking had actually improved. That morning, she'd left a plate of oatmeal raisin muffins on the counter. Comfort foods. I'd eaten one on the way to work. It actually tasted good.

I'd taken her to the therapist every week, sat in the waiting room reading magazines for fifty minutes, and then taken her back home. The first few months I'd read through six issues of *Reader's Digest*. But in the last month, I'd started reading parenting magazines: practical articles on diaper rash, schmaltzy articles on mother's intuition.

Mother's intuition. Everyone has it, you just have to find it.
Right.

Now she wanted me to come in with her?

"Why?" I twirled my fork around my noodles.

"Because I think it would be helpful." My mother chewed her last mangled meatball. "I'd like to talk to you."

"So talk," I said. "I'm sitting right in front of you."

She got up, went to the fridge. Poured herself a glass of milk. Then came back, and sat down. "Did you know that, when I was pregnant with you — that winter before you were born — your father went to work in Burlington and he lived with one of his relatives for a couple of months. I was so tired and lonely and it was so cold out. . .we lived across the street from a little gas station with a convenient store in it. Sometimes your father didn't phone for two or three days at a time. I was too pregnant to work — we had a little TV that got only two channels. I got so big with you that I couldn't do up my winter coat anymore. I used to hold my coat shut and waddle across the street to the store and get Oreos and Orange Crush every day, and then sit real close to the TV until my eyes got sore and I fell asleep. I couldn't wait for you to come. So I'd have someone else to talk to. Someone else to do something with."

"Okay," I said. Was this supposed to have a point?

She leaned back in her chair. "You can't just replace people."

"I don't get it."

"You can't just replace people. Having you didn't fix things with your father. You having this baby isn't going to replace your sister. And, whoever the father is. . .it doesn't work that way."

I tensed. Pulled in my abdominal muscles. *Suck it in!* Carly used to say, right before a photo was taken. *I want to look back years later and think I was skinny!* "I don't know what you're talking about," I told her.

Milk lined my mother's upper lip. She wiped it off. "You look exactly like I did when I first got pregnant. I can see it in your face. Except you're so skinny, so the fact that you're preggo is more obvious."

How long was I planning on hiding it from her? A couple more months and baggy shirts wouldn't hide it anymore. "I'm not trying to replace Carly," I said. "I didn't plan this."

"Exactly."

"Well — "

"You plan everything. You don't make mistakes. Miss High and Mighty. Always judging me. And Richard. And your sister."

"That's not true!"

"You and whoever this guy is. . .you're just going to go off together, have this baby, move out. . ."

My insides squeezed; a fist closing. "There is no guy. It's me, on my own. I fuck up too, you know. I make mistakes! I'm human!" I clenched my hands, my nails digging into my palm.

She rocked back in her chair the way Carly used to. At the dinner table, growing up, I'd hooked my foot around the leg beam of Carly's chair to prevent her from rocking, to prevent Dick from having something more to yell at her about, to prevent her from falling backwards and cracking her head open.

Nobody likes a pussy.

My mother rocked forward. The chair landed on its front legs. Skidded a little bit. "So what do you plan to do then?"

"I don't know."

Again, she rocked back, tilting the chair on its back legs. It balanced there, unsteadily. "Well, I guess now you know how it feels."

"How what feels?"

"How I feel." She scratched her scalp. "How I felt, all those years. When your asshole father left, the two of you girls, needing me, always *needing* me — and then Richard. . ." She got up, put her plate in the sink. It clattered against the other dirty dishes. "I'm going to bed."

& My mother began to bring me a series of small gifts, purchased with money I didn't know she had. First, a set of days of the week underwear she said she thought were funny. As kids, Carly and I each had a set, each day with a different colour; I wore mine in sequence, while Carly insisted on wearing Tuesday over and over because she liked pink the best.

First underwear, then white-chocolate-covered pretzels, a notepad and pen bearing a Realtor's logo and slogan, and finally, a tube of hemorrhoid cream.

"When I was pregnant with you, I got hemorrhoids so bad it hurt to shit," she said. "Figured you could use some."

Neither my mother nor Richard had officially filed for divorce. The lease for the house remained in Dickhead's name, which meant he was legally obligated to pay it, but he closed his account and their joint account. I knew when he called; if I saw his number on call display, I picked up and hung up before my mother got a chance to answer. But I had to delete the call display feature from our phone plan to try to save money. I made enough to pay for rent, and put groceries on my credit card, paid only the balance.

Sometimes, when she answered, I would pick up and listen and try to breathe as quietly as possible.

"I have a pregnant daughter to take care of," she barked. As though *she* were taking care of *me*.

"Well, don't expect my money to pay for anymore of your brats!" Richard barked.

I kept expecting him to come and kick us out. Or, maybe, take my mother back and just kick *me* out. In the night, I awoke to noises, imagining Dick shuffling around in the kitchen, as he had done years before. My mother, who hadn't worked the last few years, should have claimed alimony.

"Don't you think you should file to make your divorce legal?" I asked, while my mother pulled honey oat muffins out of the oven. The smell wafted over the smell of cleaning products; earlier, she'd had a burst of energy and had scrubbed out the fridge, thrown out all our expired eggs and mouldy bagels.

She closed the oven door with a slam, held the hot muffin tin in one gloved hand. "Seriously, *lay off!*"

I wanted to make it permanent.

  Carly loved the Disney movie *Peter Pan,* which she made me watch with her ad nauseam, until the soundtrack echoed in my head all day: "You can fly! You can fly! You can fly! You can fly! You can fly!"

"This movie is racist, you know," I said.

Carly wore one of her nightgowns and, like Wendy, read to her menagerie of Beanie Babies. When I came home in a grumpy mood once, when a boy I had a crush on started dating one of my classmates, she wiggled her fingers over my head and told me she was sprinkling pixie dust on me, and that I should think happy thoughts. I'd shoved her away, told her to get lost.

Lost.

Maybe she saw herself like Wendy, but now, I saw her as one of the little Lost Boys. In the first edition of *Peter Pan*, the Lost Boys were infants who'd fallen out of their strollers and, when seven days passed and no one returned to claim them, their souls flew off to Neverland.

Carly would never grow up. Would never have a career, own a car, make babies. My beautiful sister, her body crushed and compacted under the wheels of a train.

Stefany Beale, disappeared late one September afternoon, obviously dead, her body lost, too, buried or stashed somewhere, decomposing in secret, becoming less and less. Disappearing altogether.

And then, the last of the Lost Girls, my sister-who-would-never-be, not-even-born. At eighteen weeks, she would have weighed half a pound, measured about five inches long. Eighteen-week-old fetuses go through the motions of crying but, without air, don't make a sound. I wondered if she cried as she slid away, as blood began to trickle down my mother's legs and slip down the shower drain.

Eighteen weeks pregnant, I lay on the ultrasound table as my obstetrician slid the monitor across my abdomen, still small enough that I could hide the baby behind baggy shirts; play pretend.

What the fuck was I going to do? I had a temporary job, lived in my mother's basement, had an invalid adult to take care of, and my child's father wanted nothing to do with me or his baby. A child's father who wanted nothing to do with it. Where had I heard that before?

Joel agreed to pay child support. Of course he did. "I'm not going to avoid my legal obligations," he said. "You can let me know when it's born, and my lawyer will draw something up." So clean.

"Congratulations," my doctor said, and pressed down with the monitor on the space just below my belly button. "You're having a girl."

"Just one?" I asked.

My doctor smiled. "Just one."

There was an old lady who swallowed a cow.
I don't know how she swallowed a cow!
She swallowed the cow to catch the goat.
She swallowed the goat to catch the dog.
She swallowed the dog to catch the cat.
She swallowed the cat to catch the bird.
She swallowed the bird to catch the spider
That wiggled and jiggled and tickled inside her.
She swallowed the spider to catch the fly.
I don't know why she swallowed a fly
Perhaps she'll die.

&T Patrick emails me a few days into January 2009, another year Carly will never see. I can't imagine her any older than nineteen. She keeps popping into my memory as a seven-year-old, her hair and skin streaked with multicoloured magic marker ink, twirling on the spot, frenzied in anticipation of a Halloween sugar rush.

"Darcy! Darcy! I'm a rainbow!"

I'm going to be in T.O. for a few days. Would love to see you.
Andrew told me you were back at your mom's. I have some time
in the evening of the 5th. Not sure what your schedule is like but
hope you can make it. Café Piazza @ 6:30?

I stride west towards Ossington. The baby inside me kicks, hiccups, then kicks again. For the last week, she's pressed herself

259

against the front of me so that I can make out the different parts of her, like pieces in a puzzle. Foot, elbow, bum. But as I gain momentum, she quiets, introspective, huddling inside me to keep warm.

I arrive too early, and my wandering takes me in circles, past the old brick houses, past the skeleton of a snow angel. Carly could never get her snow angels right. Every time she struggled to get up, she'd leave footprints behind, marring the angel's wings. Stomping out the angel's heart.

I sit down on a frozen bus bench to rest, put my hands on the underside of my belly, where my daughter hides. The mottled grey sky hints at snow. Exhausted, not used to walking such lengths, I surrender my head into my hands, elbows on my thighs. My body is not just mine anymore. I am already hers. She dictates the choices I make, already. I shape myself around her, as I will continue to do, after she exits. A role I know well.

The physical exertion places two thumbs on either side of my temples and pushes. My head aches. I put my elbows on my knees and rest my head in my hands for a moment, breathing in and out. I have not felt sick since the early months. The only pregnant belly I ever felt was my mother's. This time, I feel things from the inside out.

I stand up, feeling the pressure of the baby pushing up against my ribs. I inhale.

Then, looking up, I see it: pink curtains, and behind them, the partially obscured, stoic face of the Virgin Mary.

I call Patrick.

He answers after just two rings and his voice sounds familiar and unfamiliar at the same time, slightly higher in pitch. Is he wondering whether I'm calling to cancel? The call happens so fast neither one of us acknowledges the strangeness of suddenly hearing the other's voice again after so long. I tell him the address.

He knows the area well but says he's never actually seen the place. Pink curtains and the Virgin Mary don't ring any bells.

"I'll find it," he assures me. "I'm probably only five or ten minutes away."

I hang up and cross the street, open the door on the main floor of the little walk-up. One flight of rickety steps leads to the second floor. I ascend them slowly, my centre of gravity off-kilter, my joints sore from all the walking. I rub the small of my back, massage a stitch that has formed there.

A small, elderly woman greets me at the top. A man I assume is her husband buzzes by with a plate of steaming, dark green vegetables. Two other couples already sit, consuming meals. This tiny, nondescript restaurant is perhaps not so unknown after all. From the back, the old man looks kind of like Papi, lithe and gangly.

"Table for two?" The woman says, and I nod.

"Yes, thanks."

Then Patrick comes up the stairs, two at a time. "Sorry, I was just parking," he calls ahead of himself. Then he reaches the top of the stairs and his eyes register confusion. His short hair has grown out a bit, like how he styled it when we first met. His hair falls in his eyes, and he makes a motion to push the strands away. He looks more relaxed. I smile, maybe a little too widely.

"Come, come! Table for two!" The little woman gestures for us, puts her hand on my back, ushering us forward. "Sit, you must be so tired and hungry!" She pulls a chair out at a little table with a vinyl tablecloth the colour of split pea soup.

"Did you order already?" Patrick asks, when she leaves. He keeps looking at my big belly.

"Long story." I rest my hands on top of the table, and he copies the action, puts his hands out to touch mine. I wonder if he is checking for a ring. I put my hands down in my lap. "How was London?"

"Great. Loved it. Super rainy, though, and humid. Kind of reminded me of Toronto that way, but even worse. I still catch myself saying some things the way they do in Britain. Like how I still ask for a lemonade sometimes when I go to a pub. In London that means a Sprite or a 7UP. Sometimes I forget and then they bring me actual lemonade. And I lived in this great little flat on campus, a tiny bedroom with just a bed and a little single stove and bathroom, totally claustrophobic, so I used to go wander around a lot, just to get fresh air. Anyway, one day I found this little church. I went in just to check it out and sat in there for like, an hour, and nobody else came in. You couldn't hear a thing. I just sat in there, doing nothing, but it was nice, very spiritual. On my way out I said a prayer for your sister."

"Thank you," I say.

"So what about you? When did you move back to Toronto?"

"Um, right after. Right after you left. Pretty much."

He looks a little stricken. "Was it because of — "

"No. Just — I had my reasons."

"Living with your mom?"

"Yeah," I say. "She and Richard are getting a divorce. We moved out of the house a couple months ago. We have a little apartment in the Annex."

"Do you see a lot of Aubrey now that you're back?"

"No."

"How come?"

"It's complicated," I say. "She's getting married, though. Or — I guess she already is married."

"Aubrey? Really? Huh. Well, I guess everybody changes, eventually."

We sit in silence. Patrick takes the pink Sweet'N Lows from the sugar container on the table and separates them from the white sucrose packages, makes them all face the same way. Then our food arrives. It feels fast but maybe we have sat here awkwardly longer than I've realized.

The old lady has brought me roast beef, three slabs of it, steaming on a plate beside a swirl of mashed potatoes, all of it soaked in gravy. I'd never been a huge fan of roast beef; our stepfather's rendition always came out of the oven chewy, over-cooked.

"Healthy protein for the baby!" the old woman announces. She has a plate of pasta for Patrick, tiny ravioli pillows smothered in something green — pesto, maybe. She smiles at us. "You two are a very nice couple. You will be very, very happy together."

Patrick smirks, just slightly. If she sees his grin, the old woman doesn't let on. She puts her wizened hands on my round belly. "Hmm, little girl, I think. Not too much longer." She pauses. "And I think. . .red hair. Yes, definitely, she will have red hair. Very fiery, this one."

The baby stays motionless under her hands. "Thank you," I say.

"Enjoy your meal," she instructs.

We sit back in our chairs. I spread my napkin out in my lap, trying to figure out how to drape it with the baby in the way.

"In high school I had this terrible crush on a girl with red hair. What was her name? Kristen something. I once had to go over to her house to do a science project, but she had the world's most annoying little sister who kept butting in. Between Kristen's red hair and her irritating little sister, I could barely think straight. I think I bombed the project. Which, of course, I hated, because I couldn't stand getting anything lower than an A." He smiles, remembering. "Beale. Yeah. Kristen Beale."

I stop fiddling with the napkin. "What?"

"Kristen Beale."

"What was the little sister's name?"

"Mmm. . .I dunno, Darce, it was a long time ago." He sticks

his fork into the pasta, swirls it around a bit. It releases another whorl of steam.

"Was it Stefany?"

He cocks his head. "Yeah, that sounds right. Did you know them, too?"

"No," I say, "I just. . .when I was in Grade Six, this girl in my neighbourhood went missing. I obsessed over it for years. Her name was Stefany Beale, she had red hair, and she had a sister named Kristen. I'm sure of it." It all comes out fast. "And now you're telling me she somehow returned from the dead to bug her older sister years later? Not possible."

Patrick puts his fork down. "Really? Weird. Well, I don't know what to tell you, but she was alive. Alive and obnoxious. Trust me."

My heart has quickened. I force my lips to smile.

"Hey," he says, and pushes his plate forward a little bit. "Want to switch?"

"All right." I take a bite of the meal intended for Patrick. The pesto burns my tongue.

It cannot possibly be another Stefany Beale — can it? I try to remember, but Patrick has started talking again, and I don't really hear what he's saying. Stefany. Stefany alive, maybe. And Carly, here, in this restaurant. Here and breathing and eating chocolate cake with a pudding centre, gooey-eyed across from the boy who would later leave her. I wonder what the old woman told her would happen to her in the future. I know she believed it.

&T In a small, covert restaurant, behind pink panelled curtains and under the solemn gaze of the Mother Mary, it is not my own future revealed to me, but rather the future of a girl whose death I once dreamed, whose body I left buried under the anonymous earth.

As soon as I get home, it takes only a few minutes of digging around on the Internet in the online newspaper archives, a few dollars on my credit card. Words that have existed all along, any time I'd wanted to look.

Missing girl found after three years; Case of parental abduction

[Ontario Edition]
Toronto Star — Toronto, Ont.
Author: A. Sperling
Date: June 16, 1995
Start Page: A.25
Section: NEWS
Text Word Count: 485

For almost three years, Angela Vergara (nee Beale) did not know what happened to her daughter, Stefany Beale, after the nine-year-old disappeared while playing outside one afternoon. That is, until she got a call from the police department in Lethbridge, Alberta, this past Wednesday.

Police located Beale when the now almost twelve-year-old admitted her true identity to a classmate. Beale, who was raised in Toronto by a single mother, and who has an older half-sister, Kristen, was abducted in September, 1992, by her biological father, James Allen Kramer. Police had originally ruled out Kramer as a suspect because Mrs. Vergara reported that Kramer, with whom she had a brief relationship, had never known about her pregnancy. Additionally, at the time of the abduction, Mrs. Vergara did not have any current contact information for Kramer, and police were unable to locate him. Following his apprehension, Kramer admitted to police that he had been tipped off by a friend who worked at Stefany's school. Kramer took Stefany to Lethbridge, where his deceased grandmother owned property, to avoid detection. At the time of the abduction, police turned their attention away from Kramer, reporting that the case was likely an incidence of stranger abduction.

In 1992, Mrs. Vergara appealed to Stefany's captor to bring her daughter back unharmed. Several searches of downtown Toronto and surrounding areas were conducted, but Stefany was never recovered. Mrs. Vergara reported that, initially, police considered her and her then boyfriend, Adrian Vergara, suspects in her daughter's disappearance. Mr. and Mrs. Vergara, who police cleared of any involvement, were married six months ago.

Mrs. Vergara's brother, Gregory Beale, acting as the family's spokesperson, read the following statement to the press on Mrs. Vergara's behalf: "It is unfathomable, as a parent, to experience the kind of hurt and suffering of not knowing where your child is or if they are even alive. I was robbed of three years of Stefany's life. Not only did I have to endure the thought that my daughter had been raped and murdered, but I had to endure suspicion of the police and my community thinking that I or my husband may have caused harm to my precious daughter. I am thrilled beyond belief that my daughter was returned to me safe and sound. I hope that James gets the punishment that he deserves for what he did to me, my daughter, Kristen, and first and foremost, to my beautiful and innocent daughter, Stefany. After being followed by the media for so long after Stefany went missing, I now hope that we will be granted our privacy so that we can reconnect and heal as a family."

Stefany was returned to her mother on Thursday afternoon. Mr. Kramer will await trial and sentencing. Police also intend to re-examine early case files to determine whether any mistakes were made that resulted in the dismissal of Kramer as a suspect so early on.

Stefany. Alive. I get up — I need to get up. A grey layer of dust and Kipling's hair lines the baseboards. I want it gone.

I haul the vacuum out of the closet, but drop it once before finally getting it upright. Kipling wanders sleepily from wherever she's been hiding, woken by the vacuum crashing onto the floor. I plug the vacuum in and hit the power button with my foot.

Kipling darts away. Mom sleeps through anything, the medications take care of that.

The dust won't suck. I push the vacuum into the wall once, and then, again, harder. The force dislodges the canister, making it tip forward and dump a pile of grit and powder onto the carpet. I kneel down on the floor, and then try to secure the canister back into place. It refuses to lock in. I struggle for a few minutes, then give it one hard whack. I whack it again, and then again, until I hear the snap.

&   Mail slides through the slot of the front door and falls to the floor. It takes a while for me to bend down and get it. I have to sink down to my knees to retrieve it. Two bills and then a manila envelope forwarded from Calgary, with Andrew's illegible scrawl on the front. I'd asked him to forward any mail that came to me, but after so long, the bills and letters have stopped trickling in.

I hoist myself up by bracing myself on the side table. I'm in pain from the hours of walking, and I'm having mild cramping that began in the early morning hours, spilling into my dreams but not fully waking me. Patrick drove me home in his rental car after dinner. Curious about where I lived? Wanting to know whether I had a partner? Or just trying to be a gentleman, in the self-effacing way he had inserted himself as a pillar in my life after my sister died. My dinner sat heavy in my abdomen — I'd eaten too fast. I tried to find a comfortable way to sit in the car and took deeper breaths. When the cab pulled up at my apartment, Patrick stalled, telling me that he would call me the next time he travelled to Toronto. He'd moved back to Calgary to start a Ph.D. Patrick and Joel — maybe I had a type. I hadn't noticed it before.

"If you ever move back, we should keep in touch," he suggested. I nodded, trying to ignore the pain.

Holding the envelope, I try to remember instructions I've read about alleviating Braxton Hicks. Lie down on your left side. Empty your bladder.

I tear the large envelope open along its side, revealing much smaller contents: a square, royal blue envelope with my name and address, handwriting I can't place. The return address tells me this letter has made its way from Toronto, to Calgary, and back to Toronto again, kind of the way I have.

Your presence is requested at the reception
for the grand opening of
PAARC
The Papiczaw Abraham Animal Rescue Clinic

on Saturday, April 18, 2009
at 2:30 p.m.
at the Toronto Park Hyatt Hotel
4 Avenue Road
Toronto, Ontario
M5R 2E8

in honor of Elliot Papiczaw (1919–2003)
employee at the Toronto Feline Rescue Foundation for over 30 years
&
Dr. Laura Abraham (1938–2008)
head veterinarian at the Mississauga Wildlife Veterinary Clinic
for 27 years
PAARC is a state-of-the-art hybrid Animal Rescue Foundation
and Veterinary Clinic

It will serve the dual functions of rescuing and housing
homeless, rejected, and feral animals
and attending to and treating animals' medical needs on site
using state-of-the-art veterinary equipment

Please RSVP to
Dr. Isabel Abraham
(416)-555-0283

I feel my body soften, heavy and tired. Something about the invitation reads like a wedding announcement. I remember Laura's round, happy moon face. Had she and Papi been more than friends? Some part of me hopes he hadn't simply pined over Tati for the rest of his life. Maybe he'd felt that happiness again. Maybe.

I put the invitation in my purse and carry it with me to my prenatal appointment.

My doctor squirts gel onto my belly, slides the monitor along the right side, where stretch marks have mottled my skin. "How long have you been experiencing the cramping?" she asks.

"Just since this morning."

She slides the monitor to my other side, and the whomp whomp of the baby's heartbeat echoes in the room. "Might be Braxton Hicks. They're not uncommon at this stage." After a moment, she adds, "Okay. Let's check your cervix."

I shimmy down to the edge of the exam table. Her cold fingers slide into me. My doctor pulls her hand back and slips her blue rubber glove off, turning it inside out, and flicking it into a nearby garbage can.

When I sit up, her lips pinch tight, serious.

"Darcy, you've started to dilate. Only one centimetre, but since we're a little on the early side, you need to spend the remainder of the pregnancy off your feet. We'll have you come in again tomorrow afternoon to see whether things are progressing and we have to slow them down, or whether baby's going to hold her own." She smiles again, a big dentist's smile. "At this point, it's just a precaution, but I think this little girl needs a bit more time. I don't think she's quite ready."

   A parent at St. Sebastian ran into Conor in the restaurant that sits at the top of the Calgary Tower. The restaurant revolves, so that patrons can get the entire view of the city. I'd gone with Patrick, back when we first moved to Calgary. We'd gone together to the revolving restaurant at the top of the CN Tower, too. Both times I'd sat at a window and watched our perspective of the city seemingly change around me. But it was really me who was changing, me who was rotating. Outside, things were staying exactly the same.

Conor had gone to celebrate his boyfriend's thirtieth birthday. Near the end of the evening, Conor had indulged in a few glasses of wine, rose from the table to pay the cheque, and ran his hand along the side of his boyfriend's stubbled chin.

When he arrived at St. Sebastian the next morning, the principal called him into his office.

"You should get a lawyer," I tell Conor, over the phone, while he does dishes, rants over the noise and the clatter.

"I knew working at a Catholic school was a risk. It's my reputation I'm pissed about. I mean, Jack's mom actually questioned my whole reason for being a teacher. Just because I'm gay and I work with kids doesn't mean I'm molesting them in the change room."

"She said that?"

"Pretty much."

"You should get a lawyer. Patrick was a summer student at Cooper and Lau, maybe try them."

"The PTA is going to lose it. I'm just going to quit." Dishes crash.

"You haven't even tried to fight it yet," I say. "I don't think all the parents will be as extreme as Jack's mom."

"I bet enough of them are homophobes that working there from this point on would be unbearable. Even if firing me is against my human rights."

"What does Michael think?" I still haven't met Conor's boyfriend.

"He's pretty mad. It's just ridiculous, I mean, Andrew sleeps with everybody. He fucked a woman who had cancer! She lived in his basement before you did — he brags about it to me all the time. Never in front of admin, of course. That doesn't fit with Catholic values either, but nobody's going to question him. No one's going to accuse him of being a pedophile."

"I hate this for you. Your personal life should be your business."

I hear the dishwasher start. "I showed your sonogram to my brother," Conor says.

At thirty-seven weeks, my baby is the size of a honeydew. "Why?" I ask.

"Because he's being an idiot. Because she's my niece. I want to come out there — for when she's born. Maybe he doesn't want anything to do with her, but I do."

"Is that what he said?"

"What?"

"When you showed him the sonogram, he didn't want anything to do with her?"

"The whole thing's fucked up. He did the same thing when Caroline — when his ex, the one with anorexia — went into inpatient treatment, for her eating disorder. That's when he broke up with her. He wants to be the hero, I told you before you guys even started all of this. Do you know what I mean?"

"Not really." I pull skin away from my cuticle. It stings.

"He likes to be in control, you know? He likes to feel like the saviour."

My head hurts. "You pushed me to date him."

"He really liked you. I thought, she's just sitting around her apartment, depressed. . .he's my brother, I gave him the benefit of the doubt. Maybe I shouldn't have."

"I thought he liked me, too."

The dishwasher gurgles. "He did. He does. I don't know what

he's going to do. He's not an asshole. Maybe I'm stupid for believing in him. Having a kid. . .he never planned for that. He needs time to process it, to figure out what he's going to do. Maybe he doesn't deserve to be in the baby's life, I don't know."

Blood wells at the place where I've torn the skin away from my finger. I press down hard with the thumb and forefinger of my other hand. Cut off the flow.

"I'm going to be there no matter what," Conor adds.

&   When we finally moved out of Dick's house, my mother spent a day in the basement storage area. She refused to let me help, saying lifting boxes would make me go into labour on the spot.

"You think the family moving in is going to like it if your water breaks and they have a giant puddle in their basement? Do you know what it smells like when your water breaks? I am *not* going to be in the hospital room when they wrench that kid out of you, just so you know."

With me on bed rest, she ventures out of the house more. The YMCA near our apartment offers free swimming the last hour each Wednesday; she goes at the request of her therapist, but comes back annoyed by all the teenagers who swam at the same time. "Those prostitots, lounging around in itty bitty bikinis. Who lets their thirteen-year-old girls go out dressed like that? Those mothers better watch out, or those little sluts are going to get knocked up out of wedlock." She laughs, deep and throaty, and pats my swollen belly.

Between meds, Mass, and baking, my mother has formed some semblance of a life. I can't imagine a day when she might hold down a job again, let alone help others with mental illness like the seven-suicide-attempts guy Joel told me about. But maybe now she won't get to seven attempts, either. Two. Two's enough.

She never legally filed for divorce, but Dick eventually beat her to it. She signed the paperwork, then baked two dozen cupcakes that spelled out FUCK OFF ASSOLE, one letter per chocolate mound. The remaining cupcakes had little hearts doodled in icing. She forgot the H.

With me on bed rest, my mother has vowed to fatten me up. She herself weighs probably forty pounds more than when I grew up. I try to sneak out of bed to fold the laundry or to do some dishes, but she yells at me, "Don't be a shitty mom before your kid even pops out."

I keep shifting in the bed. My lower back aches, my knee itches. I shift the pillows around, prop myself up into different angles. I want to get out of bed and move. Take care of something. Fix something. I can't just lie here anymore.

My mother comes in with a small white book, perches in what little room remains on the foot of my bed. I scoot my feet up and she wriggles in. "I found some old photos in the basement when we moved."

She flips the album open to the first page and hands it to me. She wears a pale green T-shirt that reads, "Kiss Me, I'm Irish!" and leans up against a tall tree. Her hair looks noticeably lighter, piled on top of her head in a loose bun.

"How old were you here?" I ask.

"Eighteen, nineteen."

I flip the pages. Here's my mother in a bikini at the Harbour-front, her abs toned, showing off her perky breasts, sticking her tongue out.

And here, wearing a winter toque with a pompom and posing with some girlfriends. Her cheeks glow pink from the cold. I don't recognize any of the women with her. I don't recall her ever really having girlfriends, either.

"These don't even look like you," I comment.

She leans in so she can see the pictures too. "My parents called me Ratty. Short for Rat's Nest. Because of my hair. Your hair's like that, too." Pregnancy has made my hair thicker, shinier.

I flip to another photo. Mom with her arms wrapped around the chest of a man at least a foot taller than her, with dark hair almost black and a white polo shirt. "My first boyfriend," she says. "Scott Perry. He rocked my world."

"You never showed this to me before," I point out.

"Your dad didn't like that I kept pictures of me and Scott."

I scoot over a bit, so she can come closer. "What happened?"

"I kept them anyway. I just put them at the back of the closet. Forgot I even had this album."

"What happened with Scott?" I ask.

"You know, we were young. He went away to college, I met your father. . ."

"Right," I say.

The remaining pages, a good two thirds of the album, are blank.

"I just want you to know," she says, "that I *was* happy. Back then. I wasn't always such a miserable rodent."

& On bed rest, the baby grows, and I shrink. My belly-button becomes the highest point, the apex. I surf baby name websites on my laptop out of boredom. I have already picked her name, but I have nothing better to do. Conor arrived three days ago, pledging to stay until his niece is born. I find my own name, "Darcy — Gaelic *dark*," and Conor's, "Gaelic *hound-lover*."

When I tell him this, he says, "Sounds like a personal ad. *Must love dogs.* Any other good ones?"

Patrick's name and my mother's name mean the same thing: *Noble.*

"What about Carly?" Conor asks.

I'd looked up "Carly" the week previous, getting a slew of different meanings. *Little. Womanly. Peasant. Diminutive of Carla (Latin). Diminutive of Carol (English). Diminutive of Charlotte (French). Feminine form of Karl (German).* I settle on the meaning I'd liked best, and tell him — "Free."

It is freedom, in a sense, I want for my daughter. To not be tied to others the way I've always been — with knots I tied myself and can't undo. I want her to have wings, not strings.

Ava — Latin *bird*. Ciel — French *sky; heaven*.

  Pregnant with me, my mom gained forty pounds, and closer to fifty when pregnant with Carly. Conor sets up a crib in the tiny corner of my bedroom. "I may assemble this completely backwards," he tells me, turning the instructions sideways and examining them from another angle. "I failed shop class, you know."

When Carly grew big enough to sleep in a bed, mom finally dismantled her crib, swearing and straining and breaking one of the bars. Mom's room became bigger without Carly, who moved into my room, closing me in.

"Carly was a big chubber," Mom says. "You were six pounds, two ounces. Carly was nine pounds, eight ounces. She had a face like a little bulldog — big cheeks." My mother always looked more like me, but when she puts her hands on my belly and feels the baby move, a flicker in her smile reminds me of Carly.

As my due date approaches, I get permission to be more active, but I'm suddenly hesitant instead of restless, not wanting anything to happen to Ava before she has a chance to even *be* Ava. My doctor reassures me that women deliver a couple weeks before their due dates all the time and their babies are completely healthy. But my baby is safer inside than out. Last week I got my hair

275

cut. Without all the extra weight, my curls spin tighter, and I feel lighter and heavier at the same time.

Then, getting up in the middle of the night to get a glass of water, I feel fluid trickling down my leg. I stand still in the kitchen. The microwave lights blink 2:35 AM.

I picture my mother, standing in the bathroom, blood between her legs, blood on a white towel, blood on her fingers. I picture her two girls playing outside the door. Carly singing. No — she'd been a baby, too little to sing. It's me singing, me singing to Carly.

Twinkle, twinkle,

Little star

How I wonder —

Today is February 5th.

Seven hundred and twenty-one days.

 The epidural numbs me, and I'm alone.

My mother says she needs to go for a walk, to get some fresh air.

"It's the smell," she tells me, and I don't know what she means, and then I do — the smell of hospitals.

After the anesthesiologist put my epidural in, Conor fell asleep. The sky has blossomed pink with morning, Carly's favourite colour. When he woke, Conor went to see if he could find some semi-decent cafeteria food. I think of having Italian wedding soup with his brother. Waking up, they look exactly the same.

I sleep. Carly and I walk together in the sun. One long shadow, one little shadow. I don't know how long I sleep for. Maybe only minutes.

A faint line runs along the side of my hip, about an inch long. It's the scar from when I was a child, when I tried to wrangle one of Papi's still feral cats. But when my body started to change, and my skin started to shift, the scar opened up and stretched out. It's no longer the only scar on my body. There's the slight discolouration on my lip left from my first date with Patrick, and now the dappled stretch marks of pregnancy.

When Conor returns, I say, "I want to show you something."

"Everything okay?" he says.

"Yeah. But look, do you see this line?" I lean to the right, shifting my weight, hospital gown bunched around my middle, blanket pulled up to my waist.

He rubs his eyes. "I shouldn't sleep with my contacts in. Everything's kind of a blur."

I swallow. "What?"

"I said *everything's a blur.*"

It's cold in here; I can feel the air slip under the gaps in my gown to the bare skin underneath, run up the back of my neck.

Conor says, "What? Everything okay?"

"Yeah," I say, "you just reminded me — the morning Carly died, she sent me this text message. I didn't get it because I wasn't awake yet. I never figured out what it meant."

"What did it say?"

"*Always blur.*"

"That doesn't make much sense."

"I know. I never figured it out. It kills me." The monitors spike, the rumblings of a contraction I can't feel. I'm getting closer, now. She's getting closer.

Conor sits down on the chair beside the bed.

"Always blur?"

"Yeah. It makes no sense." The monitor spikes, indicating pain and contraction I can't feel.

"Maybe that's not what she meant to type."

My mouth feels dry. "What do you mean?"

"I never send text messages, because when I try to, I always type the wrong thing. I either spell something wrong or my phone corrects me. One time I typed an email on my BlackBerry to a parent, and I typed the word hat, except the phone picked it up and changed it to 'gay.' Same keystrokes, apparently." He slips his phone out of his back pocket, fiddles with the keys. "Okay, the word *always* is probably right, but *blur* doesn't make sense to me, so let's see what else she meant." He types for a few seconds, muttering to himself. "Blue? Always blue? No, that doesn't make sense either."

I stiffen. "Oh my god."

"What?"

"Always blue. . .that's — she used to say that, sometimes. It was her way of asking if — it was like saying, *do you love me?* The answer was, I always love you, just like the sky is always blue." I'm crying and trying to sit up, trying to get out of here.

"Hey, hey — just breathe," Conor says. "Just breathe, just relax."

"She wanted to know if I still loved her," I say. "And she died because of me, it's my fault." My hands form fists. I try to breathe. "She jumped — she jumped because Ryan didn't call her back, she thought for sure he would call back on Valentine's Day, but I told him not to, I told him he had to stop calling her — "

"Who's Ryan?"

"Her boyfriend, her ex-boyfriend. He broke up with her! She couldn't stop crying, she got so depressed, I didn't think she would ever get over him, ever move forward. I told him. . .I told him to stop calling her, and he did. And then she killed herself. She died. Because of me, because of. . .because of what I did!"

"Darcy!" Conor puts his face close to mine, puts his hands on my shoulders. "Calm down. Listen to me, okay? You told Ryan to stop calling her because you wanted her to feel better. Right?"

"Yeah."

"You didn't know. You couldn't have predicted what would

happen. When my college boyfriend broke up with me, Joel told me I was an idiot for staying in touch with him — he said it was like picking a scab open."

"But you're not Carly!" I can't explain.

"People don't jump in front of a subway because of one thing. People who commit suicide. . .usually there's a history of other issues, like depression. Your mom attempted suicide, too — that kind of thing, that kind of depression runs in families."

"I didn't know what else I could do. I went out there, I stayed with her, I tried to cheer her up, I tried to — but she just — she wouldn't. . ." The monitor surges. She's too close. Too close.

"You need to calm down," Conor says. "You're getting too worked up, this is going to put stress on the baby." He climbs into the bed beside me, on the very edge, puts one arm around my shoulders. Squeezes. "Did you ever tell you anyone what you just told me?"

I shake my head.

"I know it feels like it's your fault, but there are so many factors. Maybe what you said or did had something to do with it, or maybe it didn't. Probably she would have tried to hurt herself anyway. Maybe something else happened in-between when you told Ryan not to call her and when she actually did what she did. But you were trying to help her. You know how much you loved her."

I turn my face away from him. We lie there, breathing together. Inside me, Ava shifts, breaking the stillness. She's too big now; there's nowhere for her to move. Each contraction pushes her down more and more. The only way is out.

"Hey," Conor says, after a moment. "How do you know she was asking if you still loved her? Maybe. . .maybe she was trying to say she would always love *you*."

There was an old lady who swallowed a horse—
She's dead, of course.

& When the dishwasher buzzes, I leave Ava on her back on the living room floor, spread out on one of the towels I haven't had a chance to fold yet. Three generations of laundry; Ava's, mine, and my mother's. Someday, Ava and I will get our own place. Someday.

Ava stares straight at the ceiling, beyond me. Kipling trots in and butts her furry head up against my daughter's downy one. Still, Ava gazes up at the ceiling, her O of a mouth hanging open.

Above us, a fly strikes against the spherical overhead light, then dizzily spins away, only to turn and slant back towards the light, crashing into it again, and then again.

Once, during a cleaning frenzy, my mother unscrewed the light fixture in the bathroom of the apartment she and Carly and I shared. She'd held out the frosted glass dome for us to inspect. Inside huddled half a dozen fly carcasses, their legs and arms gnarled into the fetal position; their still wings surprisingly intricate.

"How'd they get in there?" Carly asked. I wanted to know, too.

Mom shook the dead flies into the trashcan. "They're stupid."

The fly above my head buzzes instinctively towards the brightness, slamming up against it once more, unaware of its repeated mortal mistake. Just trying to navigate.

Ava turns her head. Kipling steps delicately through my piles of folded clothes.

I get up and flick the light switch off. Give the fly a little peace.

& It's overcast the morning of the celebration for the Papiczaw Abraham Animal Rescue Clinic. I'm running late, and I've forgotten to call a cab. We bought a car after Ava arrived — a real junkjob — but Mom took it to book club, having decided to join one for real.

"It's my week to bring dessert," she insisted. "I'm bringing Sex in a Pan."

This is my first formal outing with my daughter. My first formal outing since Carly died, really. By the front door, I strap Ava into her car seat, her pale hair swirled damp and sweaty on top of her head. Ava resembles Joel in colouring: eggshell skin, flaxen hair, navy blue eyes that have yet to darken into brown, like mine, like my mother's. I hope her eyes stay blue like Carly's.

She falls asleep with all her fingers in her mouth, not just her thumb. Sometimes she cocks her head a little, asking me questions I don't know the answers to. At birth, she had a pale red birthmark on her forehead — a stork-bite, the doctor called it. It's faded over the last couple of months. But when she's thinking something, deep and intense, it flares up a little, all strawberry pink.

Right after birth, she had some trouble controlling her suck/swallow reflex. I tried to breastfeed, but it didn't work. Her pediatrician said even though breast is best, bottle-fed babies turn out just fine. My mother begs to feed her all the time.

"Soy formula?" she chirps at my daughter, rocking her in the crook of one arm and making me nervous. "You're going to grow up to be a hoity-toity snob, are you?" She tickles the round dome of Ava's belly. Ava beams. "That's a real smile," Mom tells me. "Not just gas. Carly smiled on day one. She came out smiling."

I slept through one six AM feeding, and when I woke up at seven, panicked, found my mother in the rocking chair in the living room, Ava's bottle empty, sleeping in my mother's arms, her little fontanel moving up and down with each breath. At the hospital, the nurses demonstrated how to properly swaddle her, telling me that the enclosed feeling of a good swaddle would make my newborn feel safe. "That looks like a straitjacket," my mother said. "I never tied you or your sister up like prisoners." Across my mother's lap, my three-week-old daughter lay draped and peaceful, her arms and legs free, one foot exposed. In her sleep, her fingers stretched, then closed into a lazy fist.

Sometimes, when I'm holding my daughter, alone in the mornings, her skin on my skin, and her microscopic little heart beating double-time to mine, I think of Ryan, and the first time he would have seen his daughter. He missed out on this time, Autumn's first months and years. Sometimes I want to call him, but I don't. When go for walks with Ava in her stroller, I still look for them, their little family.

Blankets, burping cloth, extra diapers. . .I rummage in the diaper bag for a soother. The one I recover looks a bit shifty. I turn the tap on hot to sterilize it and the water scalds my fingers.

Kipling sleeps in my laundry basket, curled up peacefully amongst our dirty clothes.

I hoist the car seat into the crook of my elbow and carry Ava down the hallway to the elevator, lean against the elevator wall for support as we make our way down. Out the front door. The street rests, absent of cabs. It's hard to balance everything — my daughter, my belongings. I walk to the corner. No cabs. I put Ava's car seat on the sidewalk and squat down beside her. Garbage — food wrappers and cigarettes tossed from a car — is crushed into the curb. My cell phone blinks, the battery dying. Maybe I can find a cab if I cross the street. I hobble across the bare intersection. I haven't worn heels in so long.

I don't have a choice. There is no other way to make it on time, and I want to do this for Papi. I want to see the people who cared about him, not just the people he cared about.

I cross back to the other side, to the gaping mouth that leads underground into the subway tunnels.

I take the steps one at a time, getting farther and farther in, deep into the subversive belly of Toronto. My centre of gravity is off, with the diaper bag thrown over one shoulder and the handle of Ava's car seat gripped in my other fist. At the bottom, I put my baby girl down on one of the benches, the farthest from the yellow line that splits platform from track. She has all her fingers in her mouth.

The subway is coming — there's that familiar rumbling, the scream of metal on metal. I'm breathing, I'm breathing.

And then, we're on. I take a seat at the back, and rest Ava's car seat in the empty space to my right. We're pulled away, sucked down the tunnel. We've done it now. No turning back.

Acknowledgements

I wish to express my deep appreciation and gratitude to everyone who helped this novel grow from idea to story (in no particular order):

My editor, Nicole Markotić, for circling many "excellent" examples of the verb "to be," for pointing me in the true direction of my story, for making me rewrite the ending (thanks!) and buying me coffee to soften the blow.

My mother, Carol Adair, for teaching me to read by giving me butterscotch chips for correctly identifying the sounds letters made (S is for Swallow!); and for reading and critiquing early drafts of this novel, my previous novel, and lots of my childhood chicken scratch.

My father, Francis Bischoff, for passing down a musician's soul and an artist's imagination; though you probably would have preferred I became a violinist, I managed to use the family creativity genes somehow.

Those who brought Toronto, the setting of this book, to life for me during the years we shared together there: Ashley Sperling, Alyssa Adair, Nicole Petrowski, Maddy Cooper, Jennifer Lau, Sera De Rubeis, Katie Lok, Melody Ashworth, Heidi Kiefer, Ravi Thiruchselvam, Topher MacFarlane, Devita Singh, Amelia Hsu, and Aarti Kumar.

My writing instructors, Nicole Markotić, Suzette Mayr, and Helen Humphreys, and the students in my creative writing classes, who provided invaluable critique and shaped me as a writer; and those in my current writing community, especially Naomi Lewis, Meghan Doraty, Kari Strutt, Robin van Eck, Samantha Warwick, Sarah Ivany, and the many students I've had the privilege of teaching.

Those who may have had nothing directly to do with the writing of *Swallow*, but nevertheless infused my life with colour and support and love (sometimes of the tough variety), especially David Gishler, Eisha Alemao, Alyssa Adair, the Taylor family, Jennifer King, John Siddons, Kim Dunlop, Cherinne Kilroe, Nicole Blaszczak, Nicole Ko, Joan Peskin, Sandy Fleming, Perry McScott, and the members of my immediate and extended family who supported me during this time.

Katie Hyde, for years of shared adolescent — and then young adult — and still, often, current-adult angst, and for sharing your talent via the wonderful photograph that graces the back of this book and my amazing website.

And finally, the talented crew at NeWest Press, especially Paul Matwychuk, Andrew Wilmot, and Natalie Olsen.

Quite simply — thank you all.

Theanna Bischoff is a novelist and creative writing instructor in Calgary, Alberta. Her first novel, *Cleavage*, was shortlisted for both the 2009 Commonwealth Writers' Prize for Best First Book (Canada/the Caribbean), and the 2009 Re-Lit Awards. Theanna holds a Concentration in Creative Writing from the University of Calgary (2006) and a Master's Degree in Educational Psychology (2007).